STRUGGLE & STRIFE

STRUGGLE & STRIFE

MYTHVERSE BOOK 4

KATE KARYUS QUINN   DEMITRIA LUNETTA
MARLEY LYNN

Little Fish Publishing

CONTENTS

Visit MarleyLynn.com to sign up for the Mythverse Newsletter and you'll receive **FREE** SHORT STORIES—all set in the Mythverse!

PART I

EDIE

1

I have visited actual, literal hell. Wisconsin is way worse.

It's not completely Wisconsin's fault, I guess. Maybe it was nicer before the end of the world. And the earthquakes. And the floods. I guess Boston fell into the ocean, and California is now an island. Also, it's all happening because of me. I made a huge mistake that kind-of-sort-of ushered in the apocalypse.

And now I've got to fix it.

Apparently, the way I do that is by finding a girl by the name of Brandee Jean. I've been scouring the Midwest, flying the not-so-friendly skies in my dragon form, trying to find this girl. At first, people took shots at me. One super serious guy in Indiana must've been some sort of prepper, because he spotted me in the sky and came back out into his yard with a rocket launcher.

That's when I decided Brandee Jean probably wasn't in Indiana.

Luckily, my sister Mavis has a shifter form that's a little more acceptable to humans. She's a housecat, and she recently followed the gossip coming out of a fae biker gang—

yes, all the supernaturals have come out to play in the human world (also kind of my fault).

It's my mess to clean up, after all. Finding her is the first step. And luckily, it doesn't look like it's going to be very difficult. I mean, Brandee Jean kind of stands out, even from the air. Having that many Swarovski crystals on a ball gown will do that. Also, wearing a ballgown in the middle of the end of the world while on a grocery run.

I maintain my soaring altitude, keeping an eye on Brandee Jean's old beat-to-crap pickup truck. I guess she must spend all of her money on dresses, not transportation. A few minutes later I see her cart a load of Quik-Powder out to the truck. It's an all-purpose protein powder that the government started pumping out as soon as the food supply collapsed.

Brandee tosses her baseball bat—apparently her weapon of choice—into the back of her truck to load up groceries, and that's when I descend, shifting into my human form as soon as my feet hit the ground. I approach her cautiously and quietly. I've seen what she can do, and I know that the ballgown only makes her look delicate. There's insane strength in that award-winning body.

"Brandee Jean?" I ask.

She spins, bat back in her hands, raised and ready to strike, her eyes narrowed in suspicion. "What do you want?"

I put my hands up in the air, studying her face. She really is beautiful, with the kind of cheekbones people pay for, and perfectly formed eyebrows. The crystals on her dress hug her slim waist, and accentuate her bust, which is most definitely not slim.

"My name is Edie," I tell her. "And I'm here to take you to Amazon Academy."

"Ha!" She barks out a laugh, and tosses the bat into the passenger seat. "Is that what they're calling it now? An *academy?"* She puts air quotes around the last word, her pouty lips twisted into a sneer. "Girl, they already tried to get me into porn a long ass time ago, and I told them these titties might be made for television, but you'll never see them there."

"Porn? What?" I'm so confused, then I see her eyes roving over my outfit. I'm still wearing my Mount Olympus Academy uniform, and I guess I can understand where she made the jump to Catholic school-girl porn.

"No, wait. Listen," I try again. "It's not like that. I just don't have any other clothes right now."

"Oh, tell me!" Brandee suddenly becomes animated, like we're buddies talking shop. "This here getup cost me an arm and a leg. That's kinda a joke, but also kinda *not*. Last week, I totally saw Miss Teen Dairy Queen on the side of the road. She was missing her left leg and had bled out. I tried real hard to *not* think about how that might've happened. You know she had those long legs insured for something like a hundred grand a piece? Seems unfair the insurance won't be paying out on them suckers."

I can't keep up, my head is spinning, and my arms have dropped to my sides as I stare, open-mouthed at this girl who has no idea the enormity of the power she has inherited.

"I guess a lotta things ain't fair these days," she goes on, her mouth slipping into a frown again. "But that doesn't mean I'm interested in making any sex tapes. So you tell your boss, or your brother, or your momma or whoever sent you out here, that I'm not interested, and to stop asking."

"Wait a minute," I say, but Brandee Jean is on a roll and she keeps talking right over me.

"You're becoming a real pain in my ass. And it's an award-winning ass. Do you know Carl?"

"Wait, what?" I ask, lost again.

"Carl," she thumbs over her shoulder back at the Piggly

Wiggly. "Works in there. Bandits killed his dad a few months back. He's got a machine gun right there by the register and I will load you up with lead if I see you again, kay? You're a real pretty girl, you know that?"

"I..." I don't know what to say. We've gone from death threats to compliments in the same breath.

"Maybe you could've done the pageant circuit, if you wanted," she goes on, her gaze sweeping me top to bottom. "We'd need to take care of those split ends, maybe put a little more in your bra. You know I saw a dragon last week?"

"A dragon?" I repeat. At least I know she pays enough attention to have spotted me before.

"Yep," she confirms. "The world is a messed-up place now. Six months ago, I would've thought I was taking too many diet pills. Or that I just needed a Lunesta and a good long nap. Now, though, a dragon doesn't even count as the weirdest thing I've seen lately. Before the news went out, there were reports that vampires are real. And I swear, last month I saw a girl change into a cat and run off."

I could tell her that vampires are definitely real. I've got one for a boyfriend, and that housecat was probably Mavis, keeping tabs on Brandee Jean. I'm about to tell her that, but she swings up into the truck, and revs the engine, letting blue exhaust belch into my face.

"Get out of your line of work, girl," she yells at me, then peels out, leaving two black ribbons of burnt rubber behind her.

That did not go down the way it was supposed to. I have battled gods and been in full-fledged battles with monsters, but I have never, ever been as flummoxed as that human made me. Okay, I guess it's time to pull out the big guns. I shift into my dragon form, and fly low, tailing Brandee's truck to her home on Colby Court. I'm so low I can see her reflection in the rearview mirror, and I don't get any mixed messages from the double bird she flips me, either.

Brandee parks and starts unloading her groceries. I land and shift, approaching her on foot once again.

"Brandee, wait," I call, and she turns, shading her eyes against the dying sun.

"Seriously? What did I tell you? And how did you get here so fast?"

"I flew," I tell her. "And you really didn't need to flip me off."

"What in the seven pageant hells are you talking about?" she asks. "And think hard about your answer because circle two is the swimsuit competition."

I shift partially, allowing purple wings to sprout out of my back.

"Shit!" She jumps backward, the crystals on her dress scratching the paint of her truck. "*You're* the dragon?"

"Are you ready to listen now?"

"Sure," Brandee Jean agrees, after considering it for a second. "But only if you help me get the groceries inside. My mama taught me that whatever else is going on, keep your priorities on track. Right now my priorities are moving this Quik Powder into the house before anyone spots us."

"And no shoes in the house," she calls over her shoulder. I shoulder a hefty box of Quick Powder, and stagger a little under the weight, making note of how easily Brandee Jean glides even carrying three. We go inside and she makes us both a glass of it, which I can't really wave aside without being rude. I'd rather eat a whole hog raw, but that might offend my host.

"Drink up," she tells me. "That stuff's precious."

I take a hesitant sip as she eyeballs me over the rim of her own glass. "So," she says, "What do you want with me?"

"Well, here's the thing—god is dead."

"Oh no, are you one of those end-of-the-worlders?" She shakes her head. "I'm not joining your dragon cult and sacrificing myself to the flames, or whatever it is you weirdos do. Sorry, but I already got plans to join this 'we keep girls in cages' group next time they come through town recruiting."

I frown. "You want to join a group that plans to put you in a cage?"

"Long story, I'd rather not get into it right now. So if your group is looking for some sucker to feed one of their organs to a warlock who promises to roll back time, well sorry, but I'm not voluntarily giving any of them up. Mostly because one year, Miss North County Bee Hive Queen donated a kidney, faked appendicitis, and had her uterus removed, all in an effort to lose a few pounds. Her scars totally showed during the bikini competition though." Brandee Jean shakes her head. "Not worth it."

"There are no warlocks who can turn back time," I explain patiently. Then amend the statement in case I'm lying. "Probably. Not that I know of, anyway. We've gotten off course. Let me start again. *A* god is dead. Zeus, to be exact."

"The lightning bolt guy?"

"Yes. Exactly." It's a relief that she knows who Mr. Zee is, or *was*. "That's one less thing I have to explain."

"No…I think you still got a lot to explain," Brandee Jean says, wiping away her Quick Powder mustache. "But let's start with Zeus. You're telling me he's real and also that he's now dead. And I'm…what? His long-lost daughter set to inherit everything he left behind?"

"Actually…" I hesitate and I see laughter in BJ's eyes. This girl is messing with me. "*I'm* his long-lost daughter. After Zeus died, things went to Hades overnight. A bunch of the minor gods went haywire without anybody in charge. There were crazy storms. Earthquakes. Hurricanes. Tornadoes."

"I noticed," BJ says. "Here in Wisconsin we had a blizzard in August. Also, you know, vampires." She takes another gulp of her drink and then side-eyes me. "And I *did* see a girl turn into a housecat."

"That was my sister, Mavis," I explain. "With all the chaos in the world, many of us supernatural creatures have been doing what we can to restore the balance. Mavis has been keeping an eye on you for a while."

Her side eye still stands. *"Because?"*

"We're pretty sure some of Zeus's powers went to you when he died. Notice anything weird lately?"

"Oh, I don't know, like maybe that time I got struck by lightning and it didn't kill me?"

I lean back in my chair, drink forgotten. "Can you walk me through exactly what happened?"

"I was out looking for Bethany Ully—she's Miss All-Midwest Body Butter. I had a bone to pick with her, on account of I found out she'd been using body wraps to shed some pounds."

"Is that illegal in a pageant?" I ask, and she shakes her head.

"No, but we'd all made a pact that we were playing it straight for the summer. Strictly self-starving. But I spotted Bethany's name on the sign-in sheet at the Skinned and Tanned—that's a local business that used to do real well around here. The husband is a taxidermist and the wife is a cosmetologist."

"So they're both into preservation," I say, with a wry smile.

"Anyway," she says, waving her hand, "I went in for my bi-weekly tanning bed bake and that's when I saw her big loopy handwriting three slots above mine. She'd been in for a wrap appointment earlier that day." She shakes her head, still peeved about it. "Beth didn't even bother covering her tracks.

You can be shady or you can be sloppy, but not both. At least that's what my mama taught me. As a friend, I decided to deliver that message to her in person."

"Just a friendly chat?" I ask, raising my eyebrows and remembering her threat to machine gun me in the Piggly Wiggly parking lot.

"Not hardly. I was gonna rip out every single one of her new extensions. I stopped home before paying her a visit. I wanted to wear my crown from the Miss Street & Sanitation competition, just to remind her what's what. I was cutting across the high school soccer fields when the first storm whipped up."

"Let me guess," I interrupt. "The sky went from bright blue to darkest black in an instant?" This moment is familiar to me. It's when I killed Zee. Or maybe a few minutes after. I got a few minutes to savor my victory at least before I realized the fresh hell I'd accidentally unleashed.

"Out. Of. Nowhere," she confirms. "I made a run for it, but I might as well have had a lightning rod on my head. Took all of three steps before—*WHAM*! Just like that I was on my ass, smelling like a Pop Tart that's been in the toaster too long."

"And…?" I prompt her. "Did you notice anything after the lightning strike? Anything unusual?"

"Like the fact that I can deadlift three hundred times my own body weight?" She asks, chugging down what's left of Quik Powder. "It took me a few weeks to figure that out. At first I was just happy to have survived that lightning strike. Then all the social fabric busted wide open—kinda like when Jenny May Malone dropped her baton at the third annual Miss Midwest Pure Pork Princess and the seams on her dress couldn't continue hiding her five months along baby belly. It wasn't pretty."

"Uh-huh." I've learned to just let Brandee keep going. And she does, with zero prompting.

"I can't remember much of the dark days right after that. Mama was real low and I didn't see the point of pulling her out of it. But then one night she woke me at 3 a.m., all hopped up on something that made the smile on her face look all painful and stretched out. Mama said she'd had a vision that mani-pedis would help pull us through the apocalypse. By the time I pulled on the dress Mama insisted I wear, she was passed out cold. But I figured I'd go and get the nail polishes Mama wanted anyway. Figured it might keep Mama from sinking back down in the darkness…and taking me with her.

"I was picking my way across Main Street when an abandoned car rolled onto my evening gown hem. That's when I noticed the not-so-nice guy eyeing me from the alley. Instead of ripping my dress…" she pauses for the first time, thinking hard. "It was my pink one, Dolce & Gabbana, secondhand, $4,500. I tried to lift the car instead…and succeeded.

"I thought it was just the adrenaline, you know, like when a woman goes all mama bear because her baby is in danger? But then when I got back home I did an experiment and flipped the neighbor's RV. So…"

"That's not normal," I say, grinning, relieved to know that I've definitely got the right girl.

BJ shrugs. "So fine, if you say I got a bit of Zeus's power or whatever, I believe you."

"Good!" I sit back, honestly relieved. "You're way ahead of where I was when I started."

This is actually the understatement of the century. I grew up thinking I was a sickly girl with asthma and back problems. Then my adopted father was killed by a monster and a god arrived to show me the wings that had been hidden in my back for my entire life.

"You still haven't said what you want with me," she says.

I take a second to gear up. I'll to have to put on my showmanship skills if I'm going to impress this girl.

"If you want to keep your new power, you have to come with me to Amazon Academy. Once you're there, they'll find out if you can fill the void that was created when Zeus died. A bunch of different people got different pieces of him. We need all of you to compete. One winner will end up with all of Zeus's powers, and he or she can then restore order to the world."

Brandee Jean eyes me critically, and I know if this was a pass / fail, that I just got the big F. "Okay and what about the losers?" she says.

"Oh, um," I clear my throat. "If you lose, you lose your powers."

"But you just said I gotta go to this Amazon Academy if I want to *keep* my power!" The words explode out of her, and I realize she's probably been relying on this newfound gift to keep her going in the post-apocalyptic hellscape that I'm responsible for.

I hold my hands out in a calming gesture. "Okay, look. Anyone who doesn't arrive at Amazon Academy by the evening of the opening ceremony will lose their powers. And that's tomorrow."

"Tomorrow!" She takes a deep breath, clearly fighting back panic. "So let me get this straight. If I want to stay super strong, I gotta follow you to this Wonder Woman Academy, Hunger Games it out with a bunch of other suddenly supers, and eventually rise to the top?"

"Don't freak out, but"—I reach across the table and take her hand—"the other contestants aren't all *people*. Some are vampires or shifters, like me, and yes, some are humans like you. And there are quite a few royals in the mix."

A sharp laugh escapes her. "Like another pageant queen?"

"Well…no. Royalty by blood," I admit.

"So you got stuck with recruiting me, a beauty queen? Are they punishing you?"

"No, actually. I chose you."

I don't add that my best friend is a seer and I asked her for a little help. She narrowed the list of ten down to five who she felt good about—and from there I landed on Brandee Jean.

She barks out a laugh. "You had the option of picking an actual princess or queen or whatever, and you chose me? Aren't I a longshot? What's wrong with you? Mama always said you gotta back a winner, even if you like the loser."

"I'm not going to lie to you," I tell her. "The general consensus is that you're the underdog. But I was once like you. I thought I was normal and then discovered I had incredible power. With my help, I think you can do this. You can be crowned the new Zeus."

She's still thinking, a little crease forming between her perfectly manicured brows. I bet she doesn't know she's doing that, because it will leave a wrinkle eventually.

"I'm not explaining this very well, am I?" I ask.

"Nah, you're doing just fine," she says. "It's pretty basic, right? You want me to compete for a crown. If I win, I'll be in charge of the gods. I mean, I've spent my whole life competing."

She gestures around the house. It's clear that her Mama wasn't much into decorating, but the walls are covered with pageant pictures. From a young age to the present, Brandee is there on the wall, competing for sashes and scepters.

"Usually winning meant a crown, a sash, and a cash prize,"

Brandee tells me. "Most of the money would go to paying for my dresses, the dance choreographer, and dental work. Shiny chompers don't come cheap. Any money left over, Mama would hide in a Ziploc at the back of the freezer. Her not believing in banking institutions is why I still got any money at all.

"Some of the bigger pageants cost so much up front that —even though Mama never said it aloud—losing wasn't an option. I always at least placed, and Mama always said, 'You're a diamond, Brandee Jean. You shine brightest when you're pressed the hardest.'"

She looks at me and I try to dig deep and find a convincing smile. "Your Mama sounds... lovely."

Brandee laughs. "Mama also said, only losers worry about what happens when they lose."

She pushes her chair back with a screech. "Girl, I understand perfectly what's about to go down. Let me grab my tiara, then we'll go show them what a real queen looks like."

2

____

BJ is not happy about the flight arrangements.

"You're flipping kidding me?" she'd screamed at me when I first told her we were flying in a regular plane to get to Amazon Academy. "You've got free wings and I gotta pay my way?"

She had a full-on pout session when I explained to her that those are the rules. Every contestant must get to the island under their own power. Of course she was then irritated that we were flying coach, and I have to admit that her best ball gown is a little at odds with the cramped, business like cabin. When I gave her outfit choice the side-eye, BJ said the competition might not have started yet, but she wants to make an impression. The kind that she said makes the other girls step back about two feet…hopefully off a cliff.

Even though I wasn't sure about her tactics, I was happy that she was at least already thinking competitively.

Now, I squirm in my seat, highly uncomfortable. Our wind speed velocity has not been stable and we've hit more than a few thermal pockets. We've been bouncing around for the past thirty minutes as a storm tossed our plane like a leaf in autumn. I tell Brandee Jean that, leaning over and deciding to make conversation to calm my nerves.

"A leaf in autumn?" she repeats. "We didn't get an autumn this year. Wisconsin went straight from summer into winter and the trees were so confused some of them decided to die rather than figure it out.

"Mama made the same choice, downing the rest of a bottle of Valium and telling me to make sure I kept using the whitening toothpaste, because by god, the world would rise again, and so would the beauty pageant circuit."

I press back into my seat, horrified. "BJ, I'm so sorry. I had no idea... I didn't know your mother had passed away." And never thought to ask, I reprimand myself. I was so intent on getting BJ out of Wisconsin that nothing else mattered. "Were you close?"

"Mama gave birth to me at sixteen," Brandee says. "She hid the pregnancy up until the day she gave birth, rushed to the hospital from chemistry class. When she got home, her parents locked the doors against her. Though they said they'd take me. She showed 'em her two middle fingers and left. Never saw them again. I don't even know where they live."

"I understand," I say, nodding. "My own family life is—"

"I dug a big deep hole for Mama in the backyard," BJ interrupts, as usual just allowing her thoughts to take the path to her mouth. "Didn't take long with my new strength. But in the end, I couldn't put her in it. I didn't want to be sitting outside, talking to a patch of grass. It was wrong. I wanted to see her face. Hold her hand. And I didn't want to be living in Mama's house without Mama."

"Yes," I say. "I can see why—"

"So I preserved her the best way I knew how. I sure hope no one goes poking around our house. If they do, they're gonna get a big surprise when they open the freezer chest in the basement. Once I get Zeus's powers, I'll come back for her. Maybe I'll make friends with a vampire and they can turn her after the fact. I'm pretty sure stranger things have happened."

"Well," I try again. "My boyfriend is—"

"But I can't think about Mama right now," BJ sighs. "I've got a shot at being the next Zeus. So how did Zeus die, anyway?"

"Uh…" I glance around at the other passengers, but most are asleep, and not that many seats are full, anyway. Not a lot of people can afford vacations during the apocalypse. The only passengers even close to us are another pair of teenage girls; a black-haired beauty and… oh shit. Are you kidding me? How did we end up on the same plane?

BJ follows my gaze and locks eyes with one of them, who stares daggers back.

"What's her problem?" BJ mutters.

"Just ignore Tina."

"Wait…you know her?"

"Yeah," I say, settling into my seat and trying to resist the urge to slide down. I swear I can feel her gaze on the back of my skull "She's my old roommate. She's mentoring the vampire princess."

"That girl with cheekbones is my competition?"

"Technically, we all have cheekbones," I tell her. "Tina is trying to get back into the good graces of the vampires. It's a long story."

"Girl, as my guide in all this, you need to tell me when an opponent is sitting five feet away. And when she's a freaking vampire. Give me the deets. Now. Mama always said, know your enemy. Well, she actually said, 'Google your enemy,' but the internet's spotty these days."

I sigh. "Look, I don't know much. Sophia is vampire royalty. She's been training her whole life to be a leader, and now she inherited something extra from Zeus as well. She's going to be hard to beat."

BJ nods in agreement. "Especially since I don't know what I actually have to beat her at. Tell me what you do know, then." She adjusts her bodice and peeks back over the seat. "Sorry," she says. "Tina's glare made me wonder if my other set of eyeballs was peeking out at the world."

I shake my head to get rid of the visual, and try to explain. "Amazon Academy isn't the only school for the supernatural and super-gifted. There's also Underworld Academy—a school for the dead—and Mount Olympus Academy—that's where I'm from."

"Uh-huh." She leans forward, resting her chin in her hand, then yelps when she notices what she's doing. "Sorry! Mama always said that'll make me break out."

"So," I continue, "Mount Olympus Academy was founded by the gods in order to draw in students like me—shifters. But also vampires, witches, and seers as well. Anyone they thought would make a good soldier in the war against the monsters."

"Monsters?" She asks. "Like nightmares in my closet kind of stuff?"

"No," I shake my head. "Like monsters from Greek myths —minotaurs and harpies, creatures like that."

"That's way worse than what I had in mind," BJ says. "The nightmare in my closet is a knock-off pageant dress Mama ordered from China that definitely did not look like the picture. So, you fought monsters?"

"At first," I say, lowering my voice and glancing around to make sure no one is listening in. I glance at the competition.

Both Tina and Sophia have their eyes closed and are sharing a pair of earbuds. I bet they're listening to Vampire Weekend.

"But then I realized the monsters were actually the good guys. The gods treated them like crap for centuries. They were only fighting for their freedom, while the gods were using the Mount Olympus students as human shields to protect their own skins."

"Like really good moisturizer?" BJ asks.

"No, not like that," I say.

"It's kind of the same thing," BJ argues. "This one time, when I was in the tri-county circuit, there was this girl— Candy Messmer—her mom ran a lot of the behind the scenes stuff and one of her jobs was recruiting new blood to come into the pageant life. But what she did was find girls with like, overbites and really bad skin."

I just stare at her.

"That way she had no real competition," she explains.

"Yeah, I get that," I say slowly. "But I don't see what it has to do with Mount Olympus Academy."

"Well," BJ says, her voice getting louder as she breaks it down for me. "Your gods didn't want to fight their own battles, right? And Candy's mom saw the writing on the wall. Her daughter was pretty and all, but on stage she was like a bag of cold French fries. Except it turned out that this one girl cleaned up pretty good, and ooh could she sing too. Candy and her mom had to resort to some low tricks to win that one."

"I can't believe I'm asking this," I say, "But what were the tricks?"

"They rubbed all that girl's razor blades in a poison ivy patch day before the swimsuit competition," BJ tells me. "Her bikini line looked like a war zone."

"Oh my gods," I say. "That's terrible. Okay, so maybe there are some things in common with Mount Olympus, then. We definitely had people operating behind the scenes. Spies and traitors."

"You were one of them?" BJ guesses.

"Yep," I nod, and she grins back at me.

"There's a little bit of a spark in your eye. I've seen something like that before. Like when Miss All State Full Fat Milk purposely loosened the heels of the Two Percent girl right before the runway walk. Miss Two Percent broke a hip in that fall, and nobody ever crossed Full Fat again. Sometimes it's the quiet ones you've got to look out for."

"Right," I say after leaving a moment of silence to see if there was anymore to that story. "With Zeus dead, Mount Olympus Academy has folded. The war with the monsters is over. Themis, who was Zeus' second in command, has been sending former students out into the world to fix the mess that Zeus's death caused. She's not powerful enough on her own to keep all the other gods in check. Not like Zeus. Getting rid of him seemed so right at the time. I didn't know it would cause so much trouble in the world."

"Wait…did *you* kill Zeus?" BJ asks me, her expression changing from interest to anger. "You did, didn't you?"

Clearly pissed, she puts her tray table back in the locked position and gathers the rest of her stuff from under the seat. Standing, she lurches out into the aisle, bumping the seats around us and knocking Sophia's earbud out. She stares at BJ in disgust.

"Wait," I say, trying to keep it quiet. "You don't understand."

"Screw you, dragon-breath," BJ says, not bothering to keep her voice low. "Because of you, I don't have a mom anymore, or the Real Housewives, or…cheese. Okay, I totally still have cheese. Everyone in Wisconsin has cheese. But I said it because it seems like a very crappy thing to say to someone, accusing them of being responsible for a world without cheese."

Tina is smirking at us. "I told you yours was going to be a dud," she says. "The only thing she's the queen of is Dairy Queen."

"Hey," BJ yells down the aisle, her face getting flushed. "I woulda worn the Dairy Queen crown with pride. And by the way, the one streak of color in your hair thing is so five seasons ago. You go full head of green or you don't go there at all."

Tina stands. There's murder in her eyes and her fangs have erupted.

"Leave Brandee Jean alone." I warn, stepping between them before the passengers can get a better look at Tina's pointy teeth.

"Wait, her middle name starts with a J…and her first name starts with a B?" Tina asks, glee lighting up her face.

"Yeah, those are my initials," BJ seethes. "And look at how fast you figured it out. Now what were the two words you were gonna connect it with? Butterscotch jellybeans? Ben and Jerry's? Baby Jesus? Or were you leaning towards what's sometimes known as a hummer, lollipop love, peenie polish, or most commonly, a blowjob?"

Sophia's lip curls. "You are disgusting."

"Suck it. Blow it. Beat it. Bitch." BJ snaps the words at Sophia along with her fingers on each syllable for accent.

Sophia turns to Tina. "That peasant insulted me!"

"Oh, screw this!" BJ says, her eyes meeting mine. "What was I thinking? Running away with a dragon lady who couldn't even pay for my airfare? This is bullshit. I'm going back home."

"You're on a plane," I remind her. "You can't go anywhere except the bathroom."

"And that dress is not going to fit," Tina says with a sniff.

"I don't want to be here anymore!" Brandee Jean wails, throwing her arms up in the air. "I'd rather be second runner up in the Miss Potato Plow contest. I'd rather break a heel during the swimsuit competition. I'd rather do a weigh-in right after going to an all you can eat pizza buffet. I'd rather die!"

That's when an engine goes out.

3

The plane jumps and for a moment we're all floating. The sparkles in BJ's dress glittering as they enjoy zero gravity. Then we come crashing down. I hit the hard floor at the same time that air masks fall from the ceiling above the seats. They dangle down in a way that almost looks festive. Like party streamers.

Why did I ignore the flight attendants when they were telling us what to do if the cabin lost pressure? I mean, no one ever pays attention to them, and now everyone is scrambling, fighting over masks, and praying to a variety of different deities. BJ is just kind of stunned, and trying to get her bosoms back inside her dress after enjoying their own moments of weightlessness.

There's a tug on my elbow, and I turn to find Tina.

"It could be one of the wind gods; I never did trust Zephyr," she says.

I shake my head. "But all the gods agreed to this competition. Any god who interferes would face Athena's wrath and from what I've heard Zeus was the only one who ever went toe to toe with her. I also can't see how eliminating Brandee Jean and Sophia helps Zephyr."

"Edie," Tina says, cupping my chin. "Sweet naive Edie. Did you learn nothing at MOA? The gods are assholes and backstabbers. We could stand here all day guessing at their motives, or we can do the smart thing and exit this airplane before it falls out of the sky."

I think about it. "You're right. If a god is behind this, we need to get off. We can't risk the lives of the other passengers."

Tina rolls her eyes. "Right, I was thinking more about our lives. But sure, let's also think of these strangers we'll never see again."

I grab BJ by the elbow and haul her up off the floor. "Okay, let's go."

"Go?! Go where?" she shouts. "We're in a freaking airplane."

Tina unconcernedly flips her hair. "Um, you realize that Edie *is* a freaking airplane, right?"

BJ looks at me. "Please tell me we get to leave *her* here."

"Go ahead," Tina smirks. "I don't need Edie's scaly dragon ass; my contestant can fly."

"That's right," I say. "I knew she got something good off Zeus, but couldn't quite remember what it was."

"Something good?" BJ's gaze goes back and forth between the two of us at the two of us. "Flying is just *good*?"

"Well, all vampires can already levitate, so—" I say.

"And that's different how?" BJ asks.

"It's like, floating a little," Tina says. "Because vampires are awesome and we are born to win."

Brandee Jean folds her arms over her chest. "Oh yeah? So far floating a little and sometimes looking like you need to have your teeth filed doesn't sound so winning to me."

Tina's eyes narrow to slits. "Come closer and I'll show

you."

Sophia yawns. "Stop playing with the milkmaid. We need to go."

I prod BJ up the aisle as I explain, "Vampires are also super strong and very fast. Don't underestimate them. And maybe stop trying to piss off Tina. She's part nymph and gods know what else. That means she has extra powers, and could mess you up in ways even I don't know about. And I roomed with her for almost two years."

"Wait," Sophia puts her hand out. "Part nymph? Are you saying my mentor is a *Moggy*?" She says the word like it hurts her mouth and then shoots Tina a look that could curdle milk.

"Thanks a lot, dragon-ass," Tina hisses at me.

"What's a Moggy?" BJ asks.

"It's a mixed blood," Sophia spits the words out.

As Sophia and Tina bend their heads together to argue in low voices, I leave them to it. BJ is trying to grab her carry-on from the overhead compartment.

"Leave it," I tell her. "We've got to go."

"My entire life is in this bag," she argues. "Not to mention my crown. Also all my makeup. I'm not walking into a competition *au naturel* with no change of clothes."

A flight attendant struggles down the aisle toward us, evading the grasping hands and shouted questions of passengers. "Please, return to your seats," she says, her polite words delivered in a tone edged with panic.

Tina holds up a hand that demands silence…and gets it. At least six of the freaking out passengers just fall into a type of stupor.

"You'd better buckle in and make an announcement that the cabin pressure is about to drop," Tina tells the flight attendant. "Because when the wind gods decide they don't like you, they aren't just blowing hot air."

The flight attendant opens her mouth, then closes it. To emphasize Tina's point, I pop out my wings. The stewardess must have seen enough paranormals in her lifetime already, because she heads back to her seat and gets on the speaker.

"If you want to live, buckle up," she grimly informs the passengers. Then straps herself in.

BJ follows me to the door, still hauling her bag. "How are you even gonna get this door open? The pressure from outside—"

But she doesn't get to finish her sentence, because Tina sticks her hand out again—this time literally over BJ's mouth.

"Seriously, Edie?" she asks. "You backed this wreck? She doesn't even know her own power. OUCH!"

Tina yanks her hand away from BJ's teeth.

"The hell I don't," BJ says. "Mama always said half the competition is in your teeth, and your hand just learned that."

Then she wrenches the door open, the strength of Zeus running through her foxy toned arms. She's sucked out instantly, her dress billowing around her.

"Eeeeeedieeee," she screams, still clutching desperately to her suitcase.

"Oh gods," I say, and then pitch myself out the door. My wings catch the draft and I shift, sliding underneath the easy-to-spot fabric balloon that is my mentee. She thumps onto my back.

"Edie, oh my god," she grabs onto me frantically. "You just saved my life, but you have the skin texture of a crocodile. I will never get mad at you again. I don't care how many gods you killed, or how many bottles of Lubriderm I'm gonna have to give you from my own limited supply."

I can't speak in dragon form, but it's not like Brandee needs me to answer her anyway. We pass through a cloud, and she has something to say about it.

"This is dampening my dress, and totally ruining my hair. I've always been better at the controlled look; windblown just doesn't work for me."

We break the cloud cover and under us is blue, endless ocean. Well, nearly endless. Way in the distance is a speck of land. I veer sharply lower... and buck BJ off. Seconds before BJ falls into the water, I land gently on the soft sand of the beach.

"Screw y—" she tries to yell, but doesn't get the last word out because she's eating ocean. She splashes the last few feet to shore, dragging her suitcase behind her.

"Forget that whole 'never being mad at Edie again' bullshit. You're gonna get the wrath of Brandee Jean. And nobody likes an angry BJ!"

I shift back into a girl and remind her of the rules. "You have to find your own way to the island. Even if it's just the last few feet. We don't want to get you disqualified."

"And where are those vampires?"

"Sophia and Tina were both sucked out the door along with you, but they managed to close it from the outside so the airplane could get back on course. As soon as we were off the flight, the storm evaporated. Tina was totally right about that being a god."

"But why would they do that?" BJ asks, as she wrings out a hunk of hair.

Should I be honest? I feel like I've already thrown a lot of BJ and she's taken it like a champ. And it's not like things are going to get any easier for her in the near future. Once this competition starts, she's gonna be tested like she's never been tested before.

I decide to be a straight shooter with her, no sugar coating.

"Well, it seems like one of the gods wants you or Sophia dead."

4

———

B J sits down in the sand, not caring anymore that she's wet. I join her in the sand, the warmth of it pressing through my clothes.

"These waves," BJ says, sniffing. "They roll in endlessly, one after another. Big then small then big again. It reminds me of my problems. One after another crashing on top of me. And here comes another: some god maybe wants to kill me. That seems like the type of wave big enough to carry me away for good."

I take her hand. "Brandee Jean, it's overwhelming. I know."

"You don't know anything."

"My adopted father was killed by a rogue wave the size of a five-story building," I tell her. "It was actually a monster, I later found out. That was the beginning of it. When my life went from normal to... not normal at all."

BJ sniffs and rubs her nose. "I know this is meant to be comforting, but now all I can think about is my mama. And how she died. Did your father jump into the wave because he saw it was hopeless? Did he tell you good luck carrying on without him?"

"No! Gods. He would *never*—" I abruptly stop, realizing I stuck my foot in it.

"Yeah," BJ nods. "My mama killed herself. After I got my powers she kept making all these comments 'bout how I didn't need her no more. Guess I shoulda seen it coming…"

I put my arm around her shoulder. "Brandee Jean, I'm sorry about your mother. My adopted mom left me in a similar way, so I do understand."

She leans into me a little, needing the comfort of another human body. Someone else nearby to make her feel a little bit less alone. I know what it's like.

She sniffs again. "After Mama died I made friends with another girl I met while scavenging. Shauna and I got real close, real fast. Fighting for survival will do that."

"Listen," I say, "Don't let this whole plane incident throw you off your game. It might've just been a spat between the gods or one of them playing a joke. That's why the competition is so important; with no Zeus, there's no order. But I think you could be the person who sets things right."

"Well," she pushes her wet hair away from her face. "I was thinking earlier how it'd be nice having the power to send a bolt of lightning into anyone who wears socks with sandals. Just a little zap, you know? A warning, really, to make 'em treat their feet better."

"I really hope you're joking," I say, even though I'm pretty sure she's serious. I don't think fashion is a joking matter for her. Reaching down, I help her to her feet.

She turns away from the ocean to take a good look at the rest of the island. "Okay, so where is this academy?"

I point above us. On a hill overlooking the ocean is the Academy. There's a building that looks like the White House, all pillars and stone.

"I don't suppose you can fly me up there?" she asks.

I shake my head. "No, but it's a nice hike."

She sighs and opens her suitcase. Amazingly, the clothes inside are mostly dry.

"Lead the way," she says after changing into yoga pants, a tank, and some sneakers. "But set a 'walking and talking' pace, because girl, I've got questions."

As we trudge up the mountain together, she makes sure to get all the questions out.

"Do I have to wear a school uniform? Is that uniform leather? Does anyone on campus struggle with chafing? Can I still wear my tiara?"

"Seriously," I say, pushing sweaty hair out of my face. "You're competing to become the next ruler of the gods and *these* are your questions?"

We come to a full stop on the trail, pebbles rolling out from under my shoes. "Don't underestimate chafing," BJ tells me. "Chafing can be the difference between a crown and a handful of roses that wither in a week."

"Okay, fine," I say, continuing the climb. "At Amazon Academy, yes, there is a uniform. I don't know how strict Athena is with the dress code, but I'm guessing you'll be wearing some form of uniform. You know, the usual plaid skirt, white shirt, and knee socks type deal."

"Porny," she sniffs.

"At least to classes," I say.

She stops again. "Um, what now?"

"Classes." I keep going, not looking back. "Athena offered up Amazon Academy as the proving ground for the next ruler of the gods. But it came under the condition that all of the contestants must also attend Amazon classes. Which really is not a bad idea. The Amazons can be brutal, but they are also loyal and trustworthy. Everyone wants the next ruler of the gods to be fair-minded. Athena can help ensure that's the case by having them train as an Amazon would."

"Uh-huh. So I'm going to be like an honorary Amazon?"

"Kind of," I say hesitantly. "But I definitely wouldn't say that out loud. Amazons are incredibly proud women. The application process to attend Amazon Academy is grueling. Only a very select group makes it in. I'm guessing the students aren't going to be thrilled that the contenders are on campus."

"Right, so it's like I got a free ride to an Ivy League college, but I didn't actually earn it?"

"Pretty much, yeah," I agree.

"Only it's not a bunch of future lawyers and doctors that are pissed at me, it's girls with anger issues?"

"Um…That's not absolutely accurate. You might want to self-filter your thoughts before you say them out loud," I tell her, just as we clear the edge of the cliff. "Or you might end up with highly skilled 'angry girl' enemies."

The campus rolls out in front of us, the white marble pillars of the buildings blinding in the sun.

"Wow, whoever decorated this place was super into statues," BJ says. "There's at least ten in every direction I look. At least there's lots of flowers and ivy climbing up the sides of buildings. The green is comforting, reminds me of home. Well, in the summer at least."

BJ follows my lead as we walk onto campus, her mouth still running a mile a minute.

"Once we went to Vegas for a pageant conference and Mama fell in love with the whole strip. Said it was surely the most beautiful thing she'd ever seen. Then, at the airport on the way home, I heard two ladies talking about how tacky the same hotel we'd stayed at was. The lights. The glitz. The fountain show set to music. Mama and I thought that was high class, but they called it 'culture for the culture-less.' I think Mama heard 'em too, 'cause she started talking real loud about this male stripper show she went to. Sometimes when people made Mama feel like trash, she got determined to show 'em just how trashy she could really be."

"Uh-huh," I say.

"So anyway," BJ goes on, "Which building is—" Then there's a loud crack from above. And something falls from the sky, landing on my mentee. She catches it…er, him in both arms. Or tries to, but he's squirmy.

"Hey! Watch the hands," BJ shouts. "They're going places that Brandee Jean doesn't allow just anyone to touch. Not without a third date, a good dinner, and some flowers, anyway."

"Sorry, sorry, sorry," the boy says in a charming English accent as he jumps off her. His face is bright red and there are sticks in his hair.

"Let me—" He reaches toward where most of her sports bra is showing above her shirt's stretched out neckline. "Worry not, my lady. I am a master clothing adjuster." Despite his hulking size, there's a litheness in his movements. Carefully pinching the seams at her shoulders, he gets her shirt back into position.

"You got a nice 'n gentle touch, that's for sure," Brandee says, her years of whitening toothpaste use on full display.

"Ah, as a master clothing adjuster, I must be an expert in all the ways of touching. For clothing adjustment purposes only, of course." His eyes twinkle and I'm pretty sure there's some chemistry I feel sizzling between them, which is not a great idea if this guy is who I think he is.

The boy steps away, still not breaking eye contact with BJ. "And there we are. Again, my most sincere apologies." He does this courtly sort of bow. Then, grinning, he turns his attention to me. "I haven't quite mastered this teleportation thing yet."

"Tele-pa-wha-wha?" BJ asks.

"Instant travel," I explain to her. "Inherited from Zeus. My guess is there was a big storm and you were struck by lightning?"

"Yes! And then I could teleport!" he says. "It's not easy. I accidentally sent myself into the New York City sewer system yesterday."

"Ugh," BJ wrinkles her nose. "I hope you telepore-tated straight to a bubble bath right after."

"*Teleported*," I correct her, and she repeats it.

"Elocution is very important in the pageant world," she says. Then turns back to the boy.

"With the sticks out of your hair, you're not half bad. In fact, I'd say you're a Wisconsin 10, which translates as a 7 on the east coast. Your cheeky quality could easily bump you up a whole number higher. But I'll stick with seven. It's always been my lucky number. I'm Brandee Jean," she says, holding out her hand. She's got her hips cocked, one shoulder dropped, neck slightly tilted so that her hair is falling just right, fanning slightly in the breeze.

"Alaric," he says, shaking her hand. "My friends call me Rick. It's a pleasure to meet you. Dreadfully sorry about..." His eyes flick down to her cleavage, then back up to her face. "Everything," he finishes cutely.

"Not your fault," she says, resting her hand on his shoulder. "Teleporting sounds really difficult."

"*Brandee Jean*," I say, and grab her hand, pulling her away from Alaric and into the shade of the tree. "You realize he's your competitor, right?"

"Competitor for my heart," she shoots back, glancing over her shoulder as Alaric lifts his T-shirt to wipe sweat from his face. He's got a six-pack. Wait no...my eyes drift downward. Make that an eight-pack.

"Brandee!" I squeeze her wrist, trying to get her attention off him. And honestly, mine too. "How do you think you win at Amazon Academy?"

"By being the best, duh," she says.

"No," I shake my head. "You win by being alive. I don't care how hot Alaric is. He may try to kill you."

"Shut the front door,"she says. "People are gonna get killed? Um, I was joking when I said that Hunger Games thing earlier. I don't even like that movie except for the fashion, which was amazing." She turns on one heel and heads back down the cliff path. "Nope, no, nah ah. Not playing murder games."

As she passes Alaric he looks really confused. "Um, my mentor said that killing was a possibility, not a requirement."

She stops and turns back to me, arms crossed. "Well? How possible is it that getting dead will be a part of this?"

"It's dangerous," I tell her. "People will get hurt and people may die. And I don't like it any more than you do." I eye Alaric. "Can you, you know, leave us alone?"

"Oh. Right. Sure." He gives BJ a wink and then saunters away.

"The fate of the world rests in your hands," I tell BJ.

"I know, but I haven't had a decent manicure in weeks."

"Brandee, this is serious."

She shakes her head. "I'm not a wimp. You can't win a pageant crown and be a wimp. I just don't want to actually kill anyone."

"Yeah, I've been there with the whole not wanting to kill thing, so I get it. Really, I do. But well, sometimes killing is not something you want to do, but something you have to do. If you get to that point…well, just know, whatever you do, I'll be here for you."

"Like, *whatever* I do?" She asks, eyes narrowing. "If I skinned a dog and ate it, you'd be like, totally cool with that?"

I consider for a moment. "Yes, but no cats. My sister would kill me."

"You're too much. I really hope there's no eating weird

things test," she tells me, and I can't help smiling back at her. She stays looking happy right up until the moment when I sprout my wings.

"Um, where you going?" She asks. "Don't we have work to do?"

"*You* have work to do," I say. "I'm your mentor, but I'm only allowed intermittent contact. I'll be in touch throughout the competition, but I can't be by your side constantly."

"And why the hell not?" She asks, grabbing my wrist and jerking me back down to the ground as I try to ascend. "You're my coach. You're supposed to eat, breathe, and sleep the competition. Besides, you're the one that got me into this mess!"

I pop a talon and give her hand a little slice, forcing her to let go. "No," I say as I rise into the air. "Zeus is the one that got you into this mess. And the only way out is to take his place. Or lose."

"Brandee Jean Mason doesn't lose!" She screams up into the sky.

"Good," I shout back. "Then get your ass to the assembly before you're disqualified." I point to a white building with pillars and a dome on top.

"But I'm still wearing my yoga pants! Mama always said that confidence is half the battle. The other half is having a tight ass!"

"Then those pants are perfect!" I yell. I watch from a distance as Brandee unzips her bag and yanks a brush through her hair. Then she tucks it behind her ears before carefully placing a tiara on her head. Instantly, her shoulders go back and her chin rises high.

My heart gives a little squeeze of pride and I realize that Brandee Jean has already grown on me. More than that, though, I'm happy with my choice.

The other mentors wanted to pick a winner. But I wanted

someone who was the opposite of all the Zee was. Selfish. Cold. Hardhearted.

Brandee Jean, on the other hand, is all heart.

Now I just have to hope that BJ and her heart survives whatever the gods decide to throw at her.

PART II

BRANDEE JEAN

5

My heart thumps in my chest as my mentor flies away leaving me on some island way out in the middle of nowhere. Sure this place looks like paradise, which is not something that anyone has ever said of Wisconsin, but right now I'd gladly trade it for the comforts of home.

I pretended for Edie that I was full of sass and confidence. The truth, though, is a little more complicated. And that truth is that I'm not at all sure I've got what it takes to win.

I take a deep breath and make myself repeat my new focus phrase.

I am beauty, I am grace. I will punch you in the face.

This has become my focus mantra since the end of the world. My old mantra was, *Miss Teen Wisconsin or Bust,* but sometimes ya gotta adjust your goals.

I've done a lot of that lately

Six months ago I was just little old Brandee Jean Mason, resident Beauty Queen. Headed for big things and the bright lights...or at least, the state fair circuit. I've toughened up a lot since then. Learned how to survive in a hard world, using the talents I'd developed on the pageant circuit.

Like for instance, I dug an old baseball bat out of the back of my closet, leftover from a "Damn Yankees" dance routine I did years ago. It was spangled and painted bright red. Weaponry is the to-die-for accessory this season, and I do like to stay on trend.

When two guys came at me in the Piggly Wiggly parking lot a few weeks back, I kick ball-changed one of them and used my bat to knock the other one into a dumpster.

Afterward, I went home and shook so hard that my teeth chattered. But when I was done with being scared of what could've happened at the Piggly Wiggly, I started thinking about how easily I'd kicked their butts.

And it felt good.

Mama always said that confidence is half the battle and the other half is having a tight ass. But I think there's a third half that she missed. It's having the ability to be scared out of your mind, and still smile, pick up your bat, and take a swing.

I unzip my bag and then find the padded dust bag hidden at its center. I yank a brush through my hair and tuck it behind my ears before carefully removing my best crown and placing it on my head.

Instantly, my shoulders go back and my chin rises high.

I have no idea what I'm walking into, but they better be ready.

'Cause Brandee Jean has arrived.

You'd think a room full of drop-dead-gorgeous, all out tens would make a girl feel insecure. Not me. I was raised on the pageant circuit, eating Vaseline and putting hairspray on my ass since I was like, five.

But when you add in that some of the girls in the room have bows strung over one shoulder, it does make things a little more tense.

And I don't mean ribbons and bows. I mean like, bow and arrow.

And all the gals touting them look pissed.

"Brandee Jean?" A woman with serious resting bitch face approaches me the second I walk in. The clipboard clutched to her chest nicely complements the wicked-looking crossbow strapped across her back.

Crap. I can't compete with a clipboard *and* a crossbow.

Mama always says one clipboard is worth five crowns in confidence.

Still, I've got at least three inches on this girl, so that's something—and she's wearing heels.

"I'm Brandee, yeah," I say. "You looking for me?"

"Yes." She extends her hand for a shake. "I'm Taylor, Athena's assistant. Amazon Academy Graduate. Mistress of Film Studies and CEO of Craft Shaft."

"Craft Shaft!" I exclaim. "I love that place!"

Seriously. Craft Shaft is *the* destination for sequins and body glitter. The fact that every storefront also looks like the Washington Monument makes them really easy to pick out from the interstate—smart marketing on their part. Craft stores are usually so old lady, but the Shaft makes even cross-stitching seem cool. I practically consider it a home away from home since they're all over. I've had so many busted out seams on road trips that Mama's membership card achieved platinum status before I was in fourth grade.

But why is the CEO of Craft Shaft on a magical Turkish island? She must get that question a lot, because she's already answering it.

"Athena is the goddess of many things," Taylor says. "She

delegates some of her duties to her assistants. I drew arts and crafts."

"Okay," I say. "Well, I'm Brandee... uh," I stammer, searching for words. Taylor followed her name up with a slew of titles. I feel like I've got to throw something out there or I'm gonna lose face, real fast.

"Brandee Jean Mason," I say. "Miss All-State Cottage Cheese Princess three years running. Five times nominee to Miss Teen Wisconsin Anti-Antibiotics Court, and future Miss America."

Okay, the future Miss America thing is a bit of a stretch, since pageants don't exactly exist in the apocalypse and I might die here anyway. but I feel the need to get a little creative as Taylor's smile turns upside down, and she glances at her clipboard.

"Um..." She keeps her eyes on her clipboard, fanning sheets as her confusion grows. "Brandee, I..." She finally looks up, exasperated. "Are you sure you're supposed to be here?"

"Excuse me?" I say, raising an eyebrow so high that it touches the rim of my crown. "I am definitely supposed to be here."

Taylor follows the path of my derisive eyebrow, her own raising in response. "I'm sorry are those..." She reaches up and runs a finger over my crown. "Are those *rhinestones?*"

"All one thousand two hundred and fifty-three of them," I tell her archly. "The Miss Quad County Interstate Princess Board didn't skimp last year."

"The Miss..." Taylor tries to repeat what I said, but seems unable to keep up. It's probably the number of rhinestones that's so shocking.

"Brandee," she says, turning her clipboard around so that I can read the paper. "I think there's been a mistake. You have to understand. The other contestants competing here at Amazon Academy are *actual* royalty."

"Am I not on the list?" I ask, and glance at her clipboard.

There's a list of names—my competition, I assume. The next column has their mentor listed, followed by their titles. Like, real ones. I spot a duke and a princess, plus a czarina.

Taylor whisks the chart away before I can read more, but what I saw was enough to leave me feeling like the country mouse who just got hit by the big city bus.

"You are…*technically*, I guess," Taylor says, resting a hand on my arm. "I just don't think you belong up there."

I follow her gaze to the stage, where eight other teens are sitting. They're all disgustingly beautiful, with the kind of posture you only acquire from premium genetics. Around me and Taylor, the audience of angry girls is still milling around, adjusting their bows and quivers of arrows as they find their seats.

"If you'd like, I can arrange for transportation back to…" She glances at her clipboard again. "Back to Wisconsin."

She says *Wisconsin* like it's got the taste of a day-old tampon. Screw this girl. There was another section of that sheet I saw before she snatched it away from me. Our special powers were marked there. Maybe I need to remind the CEO of the Craft Shaft that Brandee Jean Mason does, in fact, belong up on that stage.

Mama always said, "There are times when actions speak louder than words."

So I reach out and get a good grip on Taylor's hips. She looks confused, so I smile, and then throw her straight up into the sky

6

———

I was never into ball sports, so my stance and follow-through and whatever else they teach about throwing ain't all it could be.

But I guess I'm a natural, because that girl sure flies a good ways up regardless.

She's just a little speck of a person at her highest point.

In gym class they taught us the bit about keeping your eye on the ball, so I watch her steadily, not even blinking, as she starts to descend. I gotta shuffle a few steps over to make the catch—my second of the day, I realize.

Taylor looks a little stunned as she lands in my arms. Behind us her clipboard clatters to the ground and shatters. That's my bad for sure. Forgot to keep my eye on that.

I set Taylor back on her feet. She wobbles a bit as she blinks up at me, stunned.

"Super strength." I point a finger at my chest. "Came about after I got hit with lightning. So it seems like Zeus chose me."

Taylor wrinkles her nose, then leans down to gather the

pieces of her shattered clipboard. When she straightens again she looks disappointed to see me still standing here in front of her. She sighs. "You may go join the other contestants now."

Adjusting my crown, I give Taylor a regal nod, and then turn to climb the stairs up onto the stage where the rest of the competitors sit waiting.

Luckily, stage fright isn't something I've ever experienced. Mama used to say I was a natural exhibitionist. Other girls had a harder time. Mollie McGregor had to keep a puke bag on hand at all times for when her nerves got the best of her.

There are two empty seats; one next to Sophia, my vampire friend from the flight in. She's got her nose so high in the air it looks like she's examining the clouds Taylor punched a hole through. You'd think that sort of active bitch face would get ugly after a while, but there must be some sort of vampire magic at work, because Sophia looks hot as hell.

I guess that explains why the boy on the other side of her has got an erection from hell. Catching sight of it, I do an actual double-take. I could camp under that thing. The poor guy must think he's hiding it by wearing a shirt that's two sizes too big, but he's really not. I can see why he'd want to keep it under wraps, though. In the audience, several of the angry Amazon girls are pointing in his direction. They definitely do not look happy about the impressive display of manhood in their midst. In fact, several of them are making sawing gestures.

Eesh.

I quickly move on, not wanting to get caught in the crossfire.

The only other empty seat is next to a girl who has a mane of red hair that would set fire to the beauty pageant circle. Too bad about the freckles. She'd need a bucket of foundation to cover those bad boys up. I plop down next to her, accidentally knocking into her quiver of arrows.

"Sorry," I say, as she adjusts them without giving me a glance. "You can get those lasered off, you know."

She turns, giving me a sweeping head-to-toe as I cross my legs at the ankle. "What?"

"The freckles," I tell her. "You don't have to walk around looking like that."

"*Excuse me?*" she says, her voice rising a little higher this time.

"Oh damn," I say, after seeing the person to my other side. She looks like a bag of dried skin with wings attached. And I'm only guessing at the pronoun. There's a pair of withered bumps on her chest that I'd cover up if I were her.

"Never mind," I tell the redhead. "You've got this."

"Who in Hades do you think you are?" she asks me.

"I'm Brandee Jean," I say, sticking my hand out. Maybe the frenemy tactic won't work for this competition like it does on the circuit. "What's your name? Ginger?" I give it another shot.

She remains unmoved. "My name is Rada," she says, eyeing my hand. "I'm representing the Amazons. My power is healing."

She takes my hand, and most of it is swallowed up by hers. "I'm representing Wisconsin," I tell her. "My power is kicking ass."

Rada's mouth twitches in response. I won't call it a smile, but at least it's a reaction. Speaking of reactions...

"So, what's up with Captain Horny Toad over there?" I nod toward the poor guy with the pole boner, who is manspreading. Not because he's rude, but because he has to. I figure a little gossip about our fellow contestants might help us bond a little.

Rada flicks a glance in his direction and then back at me. She studies me for a long moment, and I can almost see her struggling to decide whether she should tell me everything she knows or tell me to mind my own damn business.

The urge to gossip wins as Rada leans into me and drops her voice low. "That's Constantine. He's the son of a werewolf queen."

"Oooh, fancy," I say. "And what's with his…" I spin my finger in the air.

"That's the power he inherited from Zeus."

"Duuuuuude," I say, drawing it out. "He's got a super dick? Good thing a girl didn't get that!"

"Virility," the dried-out bag next to me corrects. She sounds like she smokes three packs a day.

I give her some side-eye to let her know this gossip-fest is by invitation only.

Rada whispers, "I hear Constantine's the only person determined to lose the competition. Poor guy's flying at full mast until Zeus's powers are taken away."

I jerk my head toward the audience full of angry girls. "If he can't help it, why do they all seem ready to neuter him? Are all Amazons man-haters and lesbians?"

The warmth goes out of Rada's eyes. "I'm an Amazon."

"Oh." Realizing I've stuck my foot in it, I backtrack. "When you said you were representing the Amazons, I thought it was some sort of sponsorship thing. But you're an actual Amazon, which wow, I've heard you're like the Navy Seals of, um, magic people schools."

Rada fights another almost smile. "We are not all man-haters or lesbians. But every girl who comes here does so because she cannot stand ever having a man rule her."

Confused, I squint at Rada. "It's a dick, not a magic scepter."

The hag next to me laughs at this. Leaning in she jumps

into our conversation once more. "No kidding. He's got such bad blue balls, he'd probably be eternally grateful to anyone who took a moment to jerk him off."

I turn to her, not quite so shocked by the ugliness anymore. "And it would definitely only take a moment."

We cackle together while Rada just shakes her head.

"That's the problem with these cloistered schools," my ugly new friend says with a shake of her head. "These girls think men are good for nothing except target practice." She holds out a talon to me, and after a moment of hesitation, I realize I'm meant to shake it. Gingerly I grasp her ugly claw and give it a firm shake as she says, "I'm Zahara, a harpy Marquessa."

"What power did you get?" I ask.

Rada, apparently over being mad at me, or just sick of sitting by quietly, jumps in. "Zahara is incredibly smart."

"Oh yeah?" I turn back to the harpy. "What's seven times seven?"

"Forty-nine," she says absently.

"Damn. You didn't even have to think about it."

Rada sighs. "You realize that incredibly smart means more so than a fourth grader? Now give her a really hard question."

I gotta take a minute on that one. But finally it comes to me. "How many times has Miss Wisconsin won Miss America?"

Zahara looks utterly bewildered. She leans around me to ask Rada, "Is she serious?"

"Ha!" I'm delighted. "Stumped ya!"

"I can't believe I'm asking this," Zahara says, "But how many times did Miss Wisconsin win?"

I'm able to look straight at her this time without wincing. Sometimes they'd have these inspirational speakers for some of the pageants. It was nearly always 'bout how beauty comes from the inside. Normally it'd be paid for by someone wanting to sell us waxing or teeth whitening.

Mama said pageants and irony didn't go together and I guess that right there is a good example of why.

This harpy girl reminds me a bit of this one speaker who'd been in some terrible fire. She talked about all the surgeries she had done to fix her face, but I thought she probably needed at least a dozen more to get herself back in the realm of acceptable-looking. The big thing she talked about was how ugly can be beautiful. The next week I told Mama I was just gonna let my roots go because of the burned girl. I thought it was a real nice gesture, but Mama threatened to light a real fire under my ass if I didn't get it in the car and make our salon appointment.

Now, looking at Zahara, I remember the Japanese word that speaker used that I really liked. Wabi-sabe. It meant finding beauty in things as they are. I focus in on her eyes and realize they're nice, a bright blue with surprisingly dark thick lashes. But eyes is kinda a cop-out; everyone's got pretty eyes if you look.

I finally answer Zahara's Miss Wisconsin question. "It was two," I tell her. "And also, your wings are just gorgeous. Look at them feathers. Real, I'm guessing? Between them and your legs, you could be a Vegas showgirl. Off the main strip, but still—"

Zahara laughs and the sound is like a rusty old chain saw. "Thank you, human."

I turn back to Rada who is looking at me with an actual real smile. You know, her freckles aren't that bad, really.

"When does this thing get started?" I ask.

"When Athena deems it time," she responds.

Right then, there's a strange high-pitched whine, almost

like mic feedback, and a woman appears on the stage. Everyone is silent.

Athena has arrived.

7

On stage, all nine of us sit straighter as a very tall, nicely muscled blonde takes the podium. While I was chatting with the girls, the audience filled to capacity with even more angry girl Amazon students. Most are in private school girl uniforms but some wear leather skirts and bodices. Almost all carry a bow, a knife, a sword, or some kind of weapon. Overall, they're not what I'd call a super friendly crowd.

"Ladies," Athena says, then pauses, as if pained. "And gentlemen," she adds, that last word sticking in her throat. Her voice carries throughout the hall as if she's on a sound system.

A ripple of unease runs through the crowd, followed by some hisses. Athena raises her arms—which don't have an ounce of wobble—and silence falls.

"My women," she says, her silver eyes scanning the crowd. "I know this is not our way. I know men are not normally permitted on our island."

There's a murmur of agreement, and I shade my eyes against the stage lights, checking out our audience. Quite a few of them have arrows notched on their bows and more than one is aiming at Constantine's crotch.

I nudge Zahara and whisper, "You see that?"

She nods. "What did I tell you? Target practice."

I wait for Athena to tell her students to chill out, but she takes a slightly different tactic.

"I, Athena, daughter of Zeus…I promise you, we would not allow males on our campus without good reason. My father died and another must take his place. Seeing as how my father's inability to control his own masculine urges led to his downfall, I argued that the boys should be stripped of their powers without further ado."

The girls cheer this idea.

Even though it would've been nice to compete against fewer people, nothing about that idea sounds fair.

"However," Athena continues, "the other gods felt strongly that this would go against Zeus's final wishes. With Mount Olympus Academy in ruin, there were few places on earth equipped to host the competition for choosing the next leader of the gods."

Athena pauses. "Amazon Academy," she says, which is followed by a rousing cheer from the crowd. "And Underworld Academy," she finishes, to a series of boos and hisses.

A man in the front row stands up, his own arms raised for silence.

"Underworld Academy is perfectly capable of hosting the competition," he says.

"Hades…" Athena warns from the podium, but the man pulls his toga up past his knees and leaps onto the stage.

"You're on an island entirely full of women!" he yells, grabbing one of the contestants, an extremely good-looking Asian guy. Like insanely good looking. Mouth dropping, lip licking, eye-catchingly attractive. He's a California ten *plus* ten.

"Who is that?" I ask Rada.

"Hades. God of the dead." she whispers to me.

"No, no." As Hades releases the Asian guy, I point directly to him. "The smokin' hot hottie."

Rada glances in the boy's direction and then quickly away again. "That's Sora. I can't look at him."

"Huh?" I ignore Hades, who's still ranting about his school not being chosen. "Why not?"

Zahara leans in. "Because," she cackles, "the last time she did, she drooled all down the front of her shirt."

Rada's face goes bright red. "I'm not the only one drooling. He's got the good looks of a god. It's what Zeus gave him."

Hades stomps across the stage, pulling our attention back to him. "Amazon Academy might sound like heaven," Hades goes on. "But there's a dark side to this haven of hoo-hoo!"

Athena sighs heavily. "Get it out of your system."

"A rotten underbelly!" Hades repeats, yanking a dark-skinned boy out of his chair. The contestant immediately shifts into a lion and takes a swipe at the god of the dead. "You won't leave here with your boy bits—"

"Uncle, I warn you," Athena says in a low cold voice that sends shivers down my spine. "You are well aware we do not practice castration here at Amazon Academy."

At the word *castration* the lion pivots toward Athena, baring his teeth. Constantine, however, seems almost interested. I guess maybe it would at least make his jeans more comfortable.

Hades is still busy avoiding Athena's eyes, as she continues. "Maybe you should tell the contestants what the price of admission to Underworld Academy is?"

"Oh," Hades pulls at his shirt collar. "You just have to die."

There's a sudden crack of thunder, and I'm super impressed by Hade's marketing team, but then I realize even he's confused, looking around for the source.

Rada nudges me and then jerks her chin toward the girl in the sari sitting a few seats down from us.

She seems to be trying to make herself smaller. "Excuse me," she mumbles.

"Was that you, girl?" I ask.

She nods, her color rising. "I inherited Zeus's thunder and I can't quite contr—" There's another crack and the lion spins again, his hair raised in an alarmed ruff down his back. But he has no idea which way to flee.

Hades plants himself in front of us contestants. "Come on. You want Athena's boot on your back for the entirety of this competition, or would you rather come to Underworld Academy where every night is a party and it's always night?" He grins at us in the same way a scary old man asking us to get into his van in exchange for candy would.

And yet, everyone sorta just sits and stares at him, like they're actually thinking about his offer.

I can't believe this is even debatable. Am I the only one who heard the part about having to die?

Mama once signed me up for this Bald is Beautiful pageant. The prize was a trip to Disney World and I'd been wanting to go real bad. It was meant for kids with cancer, so it seemed maybe not nice for a professional like me to even participate. Not to mention that I was healthy as a horse. But Mama said them cancer kids were selfish. They already went to Disney all the time with the Make-a-Wish folks, for them to go again with this pageant prize was dirty double dipping.

In the end, though, I didn't do the pageant. I'd like to say my conscience caught up with me, but the real sticking point was when Mama realized nobody was gonna be fooled by the bald cap she'd bought. She wanted to shave my head for real.

There's some things that aren't worth giving up for a free trip to Disney World.

And even though I wouldn't mind relocating to a co-ed school for this contest, there's no way I'm dying just to have more boys to flirt with.

"I'll stay here with the thunder girl—" I point to her, wanting a name.

"Prisha."

"Yeah, I'll stay here with Prisha, rather than dying, thanks," I say loudly. Hades glares at me.

"Same here," says Rada, and the other contestants nod their heads in agreement. Hades raises his arms in frustration, but leaves the stage, disappearing in a poof of fire.

"As I was saying before the dramatics," Athena continues, looking not a bit ruffled. "The competition to decide who will be the next leader of the gods is being held here at Amazon Academy, regardless of the fact that half the contenders are male. While this violates our custom, it will give Amazons the chance to instill our own way of life, our values, and the high esteem we hold for our own sex into each and every contestant."

"So important," Rada agrees heartily. I guess as an Amazon she's gonna rubberstamp anything Athena says. It also occurs to me that she's totally got hometown advantage.

Beside me, Zahara's a little more skeptical. "You can take the boy out of the toxic masculinity, but can you really take the toxic masculinity out of the boy?" she queries in a quiet undertone.

"Toxic what?" I say, probably not in my quietest whisper. "You telling me these boys are poisonous or something?"

Athena is suddenly standing in front of the three of us. "Ladies, there is a lot of chatter in this section."

Rada immediately goes so red I'm afraid her face might

burn off. "I'm so sorry," she whispers.

Zahara nods. "We'll stop."

I know Athena's right. Stage-side whispering isn't in good taste. Save it for the judge, Mama used to say. She also used to say, "Bury your mistakes in roses, so nobody knows how bad they stink."

"Excuse me, we were discussing this very important topic amongst ourselves."

"You were?" Athena skewers me with a skeptical look. "Please tell me more."

I gulp and smile and then pushing my shoulders back, I stand gracefully. One hand on my hip, the other at my side. Right hip forward. Left foot slightly back. Feet in a pretty feet formation. It's as natural to me as breathing. As is delivering my opinion on tough topics in front of a crowd.

"We all want world peace. That much is obvious. And sure it'd be easier if us girls could just get rid of all the angry boys. But we can't. We need boys to help us make babies. And I'd argue we need them for other things too. Without boys, who will take out the garbage? Who will open the tight pickle jars? And it's not just these little things. Imagine our world without all the tall monuments men build because they're so impressed with their wieners? In conclusion, when given the correct guidance boys can be really good kissers and if we could all remember that, maybe we might someday actually have world peace. Thank you."

I nod to Athena and sit.

There is dead silence. It stretches out to where it becomes a little uncomfortable. Maybe I said the wrong thing? I run back through my answer and it was solid. An intro, at least three specific examples, and a conclusion.

Sophia stands. "That peasant does not speak for me."

"Nor I." Prisha stands with a roll of thunder.

Whoa. Now that I've gotten a good look at her I can tell

she's definitely competition in the looks department. She wears her sari and head scarf with casual grace, and her skin is absolute perfection. I'm officially jealous.

Prisha continues, "Not that she's a pheasant, but I was raised in an all-female coven and we never had any difficulty in taking out our own trash."

The lion dude stands. "I, Malik, am not here to take out trash or open these jars of pickles or make monuments. I have come to claim the powers of Zeus." After a slight pause, he adds, "And I do not take kissing directions." He folds his arms over his chest, looking pleased with himself. It's a decent personal statement. Lacking in detail, but very clear.

"Uh, Sora here." The Asian guy stands.

All eyes are on him. He is just so...I wipe a bit of drool from my mouth. Even the man-haters are looking on in appreciation. I have a weird desire to feed him grapes as he lounges in a toga. What the hell? I shake the thought from my head.

Next to me Rada whispers, "I'd love to nock his arrow in my bow."

"Damn, girl." I grin at her. She shrugs. I am really starting to like Rada.

"I want to eat the flesh from his bones," Zahara adds in. Rada and I both turn to stare at her. "What? Harpies are not gentle lovers."

"I didn't prepare a speech, but I've got a question," Sora continues.

He is definitely the hottest of all the guys. I send a glance over at Alaric to make sure. He winks at me and I wink back, with an upper lip tongue touch thrown in for some extra sauciness.

As I turn my attention back to Sora, I realize he's looking at me. "Okay, so if a girl doesn't give you any notes after kissing, does that mean you totally aced it?"

"I'll rate your performance," yells someone in the audience and surprisingly there are a few catcalls and lots of laughter. So not all angry-girl man-haters, then.

Since a lot of the contestants are now standing, I get up on my feet once more. "Well, Sora, that depends on—"

On either side of me Rada and Zahara stand as well.

"You already spoke," Zahara objects.

"I had a follow-up question directed my way, Zahara." Geez, for a super-smart person there's a lot she doesn't seem to know.

"Why is everyone standing up and talking?" Rada adds. "You're all interrupting Athena. And now I'm doing it too. It's like a sickness."

"Yes," Sophia loudly agrees. She points a finger at me. "And that one is the main carrier and transmitter. Her rudeness is spreading."

"Ladies," Alaric stands. "I understand how you feel. I feel it too. As the heir to my father's dukedom, I was raised in a world of decorum and ceremony. But let's not be too hard on little Brandee Jean. As the only person on this stage without blue blood, we'll need to be patient with her." He tips another wink my way, like this is all just a joke, but his words aren't quite matching up with his face. "And let's at least give her credit for making it here. My poor bastard half-brother, Trevor, seems to have lost his nerve. As a blood relative, and in the tradition of succession practiced by English royalty for centuries, I would like to formally request that Trevor's powers be bestowed upon me."

"Absolutely not!" Rada's bow leaps from her shoulder. Is she going to shoot him? Escalation much?!

Sophia takes to the air. "I will not allow such an unfair advantage!" She hovers above us.

"Let him have it!" Malik says with a dangerous smile. "Take one down before the competition even begins!"

It's difficult to hear what anybody else says after that. Everyone bursts out arguing over who should get the missing Trevor's powers and whose turn it is to speak. I sneak a peek at Athena and she's watching us all like she's trying to figure out which one of us to murder first.

And then to top it all off, Constantine stands up on his chair. His boner points out at the crowd like an accusing finger. "Stop looking at me like I'm here to steal your virginity. I'm gay. Okay? I. Am. GAY!"

His announcement is followed by another crack of thunder, this one strong enough to shake the stage. Prisha looks totally mortified.

"Silence!" Athena shouts, and I guess goddesses are pretty used to people doing what they say, because she seems totally miffed when nobody settles. "That's it!" she says. "I'm putting everyone in time out."

"Whatever, lady," I say to her, my mouth getting ahead of my good sense. "You can't put BJ in a corner."

But beside me, Rada puts her face in her hands, her gorgeous red hair flowing over her shoulders. "Oh no," she moans. "Not time out."

"What's the big deal?" I ask, reaching out to comfort her.

"No," she shrieks, slapping me away. "It'll take your hand right off!"

Apparently, Rada's superpower is not mental stability, because I have no idea what the flip she's talking about.

Then, I see it. A black shadow is zipping around her feet, weaving an enclosure as it repeats the pattern. There's one around my feet, too, climbing rapidly. I've just got time to pull my arms close and get a glance at everyone else—Malik has shifted back into a lion and is trying to leap out of his box—when mine closes over my head.

The noise stops immediately.

I am completely and utterly alone.

8

———

I feel like I've been placed in an upright coffin.

My shoulders touch the box on either side of me, and there's barely enough room front and back to move at all. There is some ambient light coming in, so that I know *exactly* how little space I've got. And I can't hear a peep. Apparently, this thing is soundproof.

Athena just put all our asses in time out. Big time.

"Okay, Brandee Jean," I say aloud. "You've got this. Remember the old Miss America pageants that Mama had on VHS? They put those girls in an isolation box, so they couldn't hear the answers the other girls gave during the question and answer session.

"It's the same thing," I tell myself. "It's the same damn thing. And if Miss *Iowa* can sit in an isolation box and walk out smiling, you can bet your ass that the five-time district Miss Roller Derby Dare Devil can do it too. Ain't that right?"

And while I've always been really good at giving myself pep talks, and I definitely *do* bet my ass that I can get through this, there's a major—and very sudden—issue.

My ass is no longer the only one in here.

"Um… hi," I say.

I'm talking directly into the chest of a dude. And I do mean *directly*. Like, my mouth has his shirt in it. And I can't really do much to change that, because there's not enough room. I spit out a mouthful of Oxford and look directly up at the intruder.

"Alaric?" I ask. "What the—did you do your tele-porta-potty thing into my box? I hope you don't have any ideas about what kind of girl I am just 'cause we've been flirting a bit."

He stares back at me in this strange way. His eyes aren't doing the little sparkle at me that they were earlier. And… they're an icy gray. Were they that color before?

"Teleport is the word you were searching for, I believe," he corrects, sounding super proper and incredibly uptight. If he'd said it in normal American English, it mighta been just a friendly reminder. "Furthermore," Alaric continues, "I assure you, ending up here was in no way my intention."

Alaric wriggles around a bit, apparently not understanding that the space we're in is all the space we got. As he mutters something about, "one damn thing after another," I feel cold metal rub against the back of my hand.

Curious, I run my fingers along it. And holy Christmas cheeseballs—Alaric's gone and got himself in handcuffs. Maybe he extra pissed Athena off.

He yanks his hands away from my searching fingers.

"Who are you and how do you know my name?" he asks. "And where am I?"

I tilt my head, studying him. "Did you hit your head when you teleported in?"

"And how do you know my power?" His voice gets louder even though my face is still only a few inches away from his own.

"Okay, calm down. We met earlier today. Remember? You

fell into my arms. We flirted. I was delightful," I toss my head to accentuate this, and some of my hair goes into his mouth. "You were charming. There were definite sexy vibes between us and I didn't hate it."

"That wasn't me." He spits my hair out like I use AquaNet or something. "I don't flirt and you're not my type."

A gasp escapes me. "Excuse you. I'm a Wisconsin hot dish. I'm *everyone's* type."

"Don't be ridiculous. You are fish and chips after a night at the pub. Greasy junk that you consume and regret the next morning."

Oh. Hell. No. "Why are you being such a dick? Have you gone wacko?" I shift slightly so I can knee him in the groin. Unfortunately, I can't lift my leg high enough and just manage to barely kick his shin.

He grunts at the kick, then sniffs. "A man that does not find a woman of your caliber attractive has most certainly not *gone wacko*."

"A woman of my caliber? You barely know me!"

This quiets him for a moment. Then he clears his throat. "Actually, I don't know you at all, and you're right. I made assumptions based on a snap judgement. It was not gentlemanly of me." There's another moment of hesitation, before he stiffly adds, "I apologize."

It's the type of apology you get when a teacher or parent forces you to give one. Still, this guy doesn't strike me as the type to apologize much at all. "Fine," I say, "Those handcuffs on your wrist have something to do with your bad mood."

"I am not in a bad mood."

"So you always act like a junkyard dog when meeting new people?"

"Junkyard dog?" He sounds shocked to his core. "Is that your preferred type?"

"Nah." I smile up at him, knowing he's in a foul mood and having fun tweaking him to pass the time. "I prefer the charmers and sweet-talkers."

"A case of opposites attract, I assume," he says stiffly.

I can't help but laugh at that one. "My mama used to say the same thing." I give him a little poke in the chest. "So c'mon, we got nowhere to go. Tell me how you scored a pair of silver bracelets in the two seconds since we were on stage."

He goes red, which I first mistake for a blush, only to realize after a moment—it's fury. Between gritted teeth he spits out, "There was a misunderstanding."

"Ooh. You're mad about something. Spill it."

He raises his head an inch higher, giving me a great view of his nostrils. "I accidentally teleported into a girl's locker room. I tried to explain myself, but the officer called to the scene did not find my story believable."

I give a low whistle. "Not until you vamoosed right out of his cruiser, I'm guessing. Escaping from custody is a serious crime."

"I was running unforgivably late. I had to…vamoose. And then I ended up here. Which one is preferable, I'd rather not say."

"Oh please," I give a little snort to let him know what I think of that. "You'd rather be smiling for mugshots instead of sharing space with all of this?"

Normally at this point I'd take a good step back and put my hands on my hips so that he could get the full power of my silhouette. But that's not happening in our current situation, so all I can do is also stick my head up into the air, accidentally butting him in the chin.

I huff over the pain. "I don't know what your game is, Alaric, but I'm not playing it. You can't run hot and cold on Brandee Jean. Mama always said room temperature was best for chocolate and cheese and frosted cakes. I think that applies to boys, too. So, if you're going to like me, you do it. And you do it thorough, you hear?"

Alaric's eyes stare down into mine while I glare up, wanting him to feel the full heat of my words. Now we're looking into each other's eyes. And *man*—I swear they weren't that color earlier.

It's not a bad color, though. And I gotta say, despite his sniffy mood, my attraction seems to be growing. There's something about the width of his shoulders and how they bridge one side of the box to the other. Or how his height means he needs to stoop a bit.

Plus, he smells good. Manly sweat mixed with a cologne with clove undertones. It's like someone baked a pumpkin pie in a locker room, which sounds gross, but right now, I wouldn't mind trying a slice.

So I do.

I figure since I just showed him the sharp side of my tongue, it's just good manners to let him get a taste of its softer side too.

Sliding my hands up his chest, I curl my fingers around the back of his head, weaving them through his hair. A little gentle pressure brings his lips down to mine.

I flutter a soft kiss across his mouth.

Mama always used to say, "Brandee Jean, you don't always need to go in guns blazing."

I'm about to follow-up that gentle opener, when Alaric pulls back. Maybe he thought that was both beginning and end. He starts to say something too. Seeing an opening, I angle his head and go in for a little mouth to mouth.

His cuffed hands move between us, probably wanting to get in on the action. But Brandee Jean is running this show. Although that doesn't mean I don't want Alaric to contribute.

Pulling back slightly, I flick my tongue against his lips like they're an ice cream cone. My naturally competitive nature now demanding a response. "Come on, Alaric. Don'tcha like me even just a little bit?"

I peek up at him through my lashes. He stares down at me with stormy grey eyes.

"No," he says, his voice harsh. But even as he says it, somehow he gets low enough to scoop my knees into the V made by his joined wrists. I'm lifted so high my head bumps against the ceiling at the same moment his mouth smashes into mine.

He attacks without finesse, but a whole lotta hunger. Generally speaking, I don't like this messy sort of kissing. I try to keep my smooch sessions as choreographed as one of my dance routines. That way nobody gets hurt. But this right here feels a lot like running with scissors. It's dangerous is what I'm saying and I shouldn't like it.

But I do. I really really do.

Alaric suddenly breaks off. He drops me and then pushes himself as far back into his side of the box as possible. We're both breathing hard, like we've run a mile.

"Hell," I say, unable to decide if I want to do that never again or a million times more.

"Yes," Alaric agrees, clearing his throat. "I apologize again. I don't want you to get the wrong idea, and as I said before— you're not my type. Also, I believe..." He stops to clear his throat once more. "I believe you have been duped by my bastard half-brother, Trevor."

"Trevor?" I repeat, remembering Alaric's attempt to get his brother outed on account of his absence right before we were put in this time-out. "Trevor isn't even here. He's the contestant who didn't show."

"Actually, I'm fairly certain Trevor was one of the first ones here," Alaric says, his breathing more under control now. "You just didn't know it. Trevor and I were…having a bit of a spat when the lightning struck."

"Oh, so you were like, fighting?"

"Something like that," Alaric says. "Zeus's powers were dispersed to both of us, and I received the ability to teleport. My brother, however, received the ability to physically mimic others."

"Wait—so you're saying the guy that fell out of the tree and landed on me when I got here was actually Trevor… pretending to be you?"

"Quite," Alaric confirms. "And I'm guessing he was up in that tree in order to keep an eye on other contestants as they arrived, perhaps hoping to overhear conversations and gather information to use against you later."

My eyes narrow. "Or he was just copping a feel," I say, remembering his line about being a *master clothing adjuster.*

"Yes, well, Trevor's taste in women has always been…unfortunate."

"Unfortunate my ass!" I say. "Wasn't your tongue just getting friendly with my tonsils a minute ago?"

"A mistake," Alaric says. "It's been a trying day and I lost my self-control. Once again, I do apolo—"

I cut him off. "I don't want another apology. Trevor might be an underhanded little weasel, but at least he's not chronically stuck up. I've never met anybody so full of themselves and that includes the time I met the third runner up to Miss Northwest Wisconsin."

"Third runner up, you say? My goodness, a young woman of such consequence and humility. She must have been a gem indeed."

I narrow my eyes at him. "You know, Trevor tried to get you disqualified for not showing up on time. And he wanted your powers too. Maybe when we get outta here, I'll tell Athena *you're* the imposter."

Alaric is silent for a moment and I'm pretty sure he's rethinking his attitude. But then with a sigh he says, "I would advise against saying anything at all. My relationship with Trevor is ugly and it will not help your chances to get involved in it. He will not hesitate to use you or anyone else to take me down."

Now it's my turn to hesitate. His tone hasn't warmed up any, but that warning, though stiff, seemed heartfelt.

"So you two got some sort of blood feud going on, huh? Reminds me of the Sorbero twins. They were the identical type, so the only way you could tell 'em apart was by the scars they'd given each other. If it's anywhere near as bad as them, then I'm guessing you're here late cause Trevor didja dirty, huh?"

"Indeed," Alaric nods, his chin dipping against my head. He jerks away when I look up at him, like he's afraid I'm gonna kiss him again. "He had one of the servants give me the wrong information about where Amazon Academy was located. I was popping in and out of various places trying to find it, luckily remembering at the last moment that if I focused on a person instead of a place, I would be led to them. But somehow I ended up next to you, not Trevor."

"Aww…" I rest my head on his chest, unable to stop myself from teasing him. "We're supposed to be together."

He shudders. "Sorry, but the girl I marry will have no otherworldly blood. I'm guessing you're a shifter of some sort? I'm getting a very 'raised by wolves' vibe from you."

I slap his face. It doesn't have the impact I'd like, but with my strength I don't need to wind up in order to leave an imprint. "I was raised by my mama, may she rest in peace. And I'm the only human in the whole group, thank you very much."

Alaric swallows. "I apologize. You're correct. That was

out of line." There's a pause and then he adds, "You're truly human? No paranormal blood at all?"

"Well, my mama says the boy who knocked her up with me had farts louder than a gunshot. But I don't think he was any sort of magical being because of that."

Alaric makes a sorta choked noise in response, but his mouth remains flat. It's disappointing. Usually that fart story kills.

"What about you?" I ask. "So far, there's a lion shifter boy, an Amazon girl, and a harpy. I'm not sure what everybody else has got in their surprise bag."

"It's not spoken of in my family," Alaric says slowly. "But for centuries there's been a strain of fairy blood that does not dilute no matter how much time passes."

"Oh wow, that makes so much sense! When you said I wasn't your type, I didn't realize it was 'cause you prefer boys." I grip one of Alaric's hands. "You missed it, but one of the other guys—Constantine—is gay too. Maybe the two of you will hit it off. He's—" I'd been about to say he's cute, but now realize that I have no memory of his face and quite possibly never saw it at all since my attention was entirely focused on his lower half. "He's got two and a half legs," I finally say, 'cause it feels like some sort of physical description is needed. And then before Alaric can ask any follow up questions, I add, "I can put in a good word for you. Tell him you're not that bad a kisser."

"Not that bad!?" Alaric shakes his head. "Never mind that. I'm not—fairy is another word for fae, the fair folk and—okay, hold one moment—I heard that aloud and realize it's not helping to clarify."

"It's okay." I smile at him gently. "I once participated in the first annual outer outer Milwaukee suburbs Gay Pride alliance pageant. I didn't win, cause, well, we found out when we got there that it was only meant for drag queens. But damn we had a good time anyway. And those girls helped me up my contouring game to levels I never would've reached otherwise."

Alaric breathes out slowly through his nose and then in again.

"You're not claustrophobic, are you?" I ask. "'Cause you sound like you're maybe starting to hyperventilate."

"I am not hyperventilating," he says through gritted teeth. "I am trying to control my temper, which up to this moment has been remarkably steady!"

He shouts the last bit in my face, which I don't much appreciate.

Also, I can't really have him freaking out in here, and despite the stick up his ass, he's obviously had a tough day, so I decide to help him out.

"Look, Rick, let's get those cuffs off you and I bet you'll feel a lot better."

"My name is Alaric, not Rick."

"But you told me-oh, I guess that was your brother who told me to call you Rick."

"Yes, he knows I detest that nickname." I tug at the cuffs. "And I think it might be best to leave that for now," he adds.

"Listen, I know a thing or two about getting out of handcuffs," I tell him. Well, that came out wrong. Now, I'm the one blushing. Time to explain.

"Back on the junior beauty pageant circuit, Missy Jenkins was hard up for a talent. All the dance moms had their girls running around in tutus. There were baton twirlers, and tumblers, and my personal favorite, tap dancers. But Missy, she had her own special talent. She could escape handcuffs like she was made of butter. It was during the Little Miss Wisconsin Corn, Apples, and Potatoes Pageant that she broke the world record for being so quick at it. Got her picture in the Guinness books and all that stuff."

"Fascinating," Alaric says, in a tone that conveys quite the opposite.

"So anyway," I go on. "The trick was that she would throw her shoulder out, which means you're super lucky you didn't teleport into a time-out box with your bastard brother. You teleported to Brandee Jean for a reason, and that reason was for me to free you from these cuffs. I'm blessed with super-strength and can pop your shoulder out in a jiffy."

All the blood now goes in the reverse direction, rushing from his face and leaving him pale. "I don't think—"

"That's right," I say. "Don't think."

Then I snap his arm out of its socket. He releases this deep male groan that goes a little gaggy at the end. But I pay it no mind. Alaric sags back against the box, which actually gives me a little more room to maneuver.

I study his popped-out shoulder, wondering if it's supposed to look quite like that. Just so he's not worried too, I cover the silence with a little conversation.

"Now don'tcha worry, this is something I have some skill at. While Missy Jenkins had the escape trick down to a fine art, her nemesis—Alabama O'Keefe—had a tumbling act that blew people's minds. She also had an arm that liked to wander off a bit from her shoulder, and I'd popped it back into place more than once. It was at the same competition that Missy broke the world record that Alabama's arm went out right in the middle of her tumbling act, leaving her to land flat on her face and break her nose—which actually was a blessing since the one she was born with hadn't been doing her any favors. But she flat out refused to tumble anymore after the reconstruction. Which was a good call—that new nose was an award-winner."

"Alabama's mom was pissed, though, on account of her having sunk so much money into tumbling lessons over the years. But it's like Mama said, 'You can bring a horse to water, but you can't make it do backflips across a stage unless it wants to.' And ain't that the truth."

Alaric's eyes are closed. I run a finger along one of his sharp cheekbones, and he shudders. So he's not passed out then. That's a good sign. Okay, maybe I also wanted an excuse to touch him when he wasn't looking at me with those disapproving eyes. But also, I'm a bit worried.

The thing is, I'm not on the mats at the Little Miss Wisconsin Corn, Apples, and Potatoes Pageant. I'm in a time-out box on a secret island with a royal pain whose arm I just dislocated. And I just remembered something really important.

"Um, Rick?"

He's dead pale now, his skin waxy, mouth shut tight against the pain. "Don't call me Rick," he breathes.

"See… the thing is, Missy's act wasn't escaping from handcuffs. It was escaping from a straitjacket. I got confused on account of you just appearing like that and us being in such an intimate situation."

"I thought the idea was idiotic," he tells me.

"Well, that might be a *bit* judgmental, but I'm really sorry that I snapped your arm out for no reason."

He hisses through his teeth. Hard to say whether it's from annoyance or pain. "Do you know, I came here with the hope of getting along with my fellow contestants. And of keeping things civilized. Regardless of how things work out, I wanted to avoid any uncomfortable scenes."

"Hunh." I study him in the low light, wondering if he's kidding. But I'm pretty sure he doesn't even know what a joke is. "Yeah, that seems pretty unrealistic. Nice and competition where there's only one winner just don't go together. Even when the whole contest is centered around being nice! I once competed in the Miss Congeniality

Pageant sponsored by Kind CarKare and Lube. Us girls all started out—"

"No," Alaric snaps, cutting my story off. "Please, I cannot take one more pageant story. If this is your plan to wear down the competition, I must say it's an evil yet brilliant strategy. Which was my point. I honestly wanted nothing to do with this competition, but my family convinced me it was my duty. With such mighty powers up for grabs, we can't have some idiot off the street claiming them." He looks down his nose at me. "No offense."

"Offense taken," I inform him. "And I just decided, I really don't like you."

"Right," he nods. "Understandable. It's for the best, though. This way I won't have to pretend at remorse when I beat you."

"Beat me?" I cannot believe his nerve. "Turn around so I can pop that shoulder back in."

"Or finish me off?"

"I'm fixing you up so that when this is done, you and I both know that I beat you fair and square." I reach between us and grab hold of the chain connecting his wrists. With a squeeze of my fist, it crumbles.

Alaric's mouth hangs open. "You can do that, but you decided to take my arm off instead?"

"Don't be such a baby." Grasping his hips, I try to rotate him so his back is to me. But those wide shoulders of his keep him wedged in place. "You want to help me a little here?"

His good hand closes over mine. He's got a big mitt to match the sizing of the rest of him. But not strong enough to budge me.

"I got the strength of Zeus!" I grin at him while my hands slide toward his back shoulder. "Now just let me—"

Alaric's good arm comes around me, lifting me off my feet. "No. Don't touch my arm again."

"I'm putting it back!"

"I like it where it is!"

We grapple. My arms around his. His arm that still works trying to pin me down.

And then suddenly I feel the sun on my face.

9

The other contestants stare at us.

Alaric and I release each other at the same moment, and we both stumble back without the box there holding us up.

"Aw man, nice one!" Sora offers with a hand held high in the air for Alaric to slap. "Wish I'd thought to get stuck in a girl's box."

Alaric ignores Sora's hand. "Not this girl's box."

Honestly. Is there no end to his rudeness? "My box is everything a girl's box should be and more."

"Excuse me." Prisha steps forward. "I do not think box is a good word to describe the beautiful flower that is the female genitalia."

"Oooh!" Sora's eyes go wide. "Dude! I totally didn't get that until now. I just meant her like box, not like her *box*." He raises up the hand that Alaric refused. "C'mon, Prisha. Up top for the box."

Thunder rumbles all around us as Prisha shakes her head. I realize that things are once again getting out of control, and I really don't want Athena to put us in time-out again.

Except...Athena seems to have left the stage. The audience full of Amazon girls has cleared out as well. They must have been sent back to classes after there was nothing to see but a bunch of black boxes.

"Oh my gods," Rada says, taking in Alaric's arm dangling limply by his side. "What happened to you?"

Alaric looks at me. In full light, I can see how bad his color is. Yet he manages a sour smile. "Apparently, I was meant to be wearing a straitjacket."

Confused, Rada looks from him to me and then back again. I just shrug as if I don't have any idea what he's talking about.

"Prisha!" She calls. "You're a healer. Can you help Alaric?"

"Ah, I see you've arrived," someone says, and I look up to see another Alaric. Who then morphs into someone new...or, someone I've already met, but looks totally different now.

I can't say anything for at least a full minute. I am actually speechless, which has never happened to me before. But I've also never watched someone's face go through extreme plastic surgery in half a second.

At least I'm not the only one staring. Everyone is stunned.

Alaric gestures with his good arm. "May I present my brother and incurable prat, Trevor."

"The wily bastard," I add, giving him a hard glare so he knows I'm not happy with how he tricked me earlier.

He takes a deep bow and then grasps my hand. Pressing a kiss onto my knuckles he flashes me the same naughty smile as earlier—just on a totally different face. "At your service."

"So you're planning on winning this thing through trickery?" I fold my arms over my chest, pretending to be as judgmental as his brother, but the truth is, I admire his strategy.

Trevor is handsome but slight and the top of his head just barely reaches Alaric's shoulder. But the twinkle in his eye is still the type that makes me want to twinkle back. I haven't decided yet if I want to strike up an alliance, but if I do, he might be a good choice. Just so long as I ditch him before he backstabs me too.

"It's my faerie blood. They say Puck himself was inserted into our bloodline and there are definitely some offspring that are more puckish than others."

I can't help but feel a little disappointed. "So that means you're gay too?"

"Too?" Trevor's eyes dance. "As in Alaric and me?"

"And Constantine," I say, glancing toward where the boy in question is stretching out after his confinement. A quick glance is all it takes to confirm that he's still in an aroused state.

Trevor laughs out loud. He glances over to where Prisha is running her hands up and down Alaric's arm. "Hey, Ricky, I didn't know you finally came out of the closet."

"Just stand still," Prisha is saying. A warm, amber glow spreads out as she massages him. He leans his head into her shoulder. A low moan hums from his throat, it's the same sound he made during our kiss.

I frown. It's not that I feel jealous exactly. It just seems unfair that he's putty in her hands, while he was mister frosty with me. Except for that kiss.

"How come you're letting her fix your arm?" I can't help but ask.

"I'm a healer," Prisha says, not even looking up at me cause she's too busy petting his arm.

"Oh, and I guess that makes me a breaker."

Rada stares at me. "Did you do that to him?"

Malik, who I haven't even officially met yet, curls his lip. "Dirty play to harm another contestant during a time-out."

Everyone else sorta nods in agreement. I wait for Alaric

to explain how I was trying to help, but he's too busy turning to putty in Prisha's hands.

It's all I can do to keep my chin up. Even before the end of the world stuff, I was used to having people taking a swing at me. I've always been pretty good at swinging back. But this day has been a lot. At every turn it feels like I know less than everybody else.

"Darling," Trevor slips an arm around my shoulders and gives me a squeeze. I slip away and give him a glare that lets him know I still haven't forgiven him. He just smiles back and then turns to the other contestants.

"Let's not stone Brandee Jean quite yet. As Alaric's brother I can tell you all that he is the type of person who has a real knack for making one want to punch him. If he invaded her box—"

"Nice!" Sora laughs.

Without even looking in Sora's direction Trevor holds out a hand and Sora immediately high fives it. "If he invaded, then perhaps Brandee Jean was simply defending herself. You may not all realize this, but Zeus gave her super strength. She could have crushed him to bits. But she didn't. And that shows great restraint."

I side eye Trevor, not sure why he's sticking up for me. Also, I can't help but notice he's got himself a silver tongue to go with those laughing eyes. Between that and his general lack of trustworthiness, he's exactly the type of guy I tend to fall for.

"Darling," he says again. "Healers are witches. They learn how to use their powers to fix people."

"Like magic doctors?" I ask.

"That's it exactly." He's not mean like Alaric, but there's something in his voice that tells me he's making fun of me deep down. Honestly, I prefer Alaric's more straight-forward rudeness if I have to choose. "And," Trevor continues, "Faerie, or the fae, does not make one part of the LGBTQ community. Think of it more like…Tinkerbell."

"Still sounds gay," Constantine chimes in.

Alaric glances up at Trevor and then me. Trevor grins. "I like this one."

Alaric raises his eyebrows, looking the very definition of haughty. "She's remarkably ill-informed about everything, it seems, except the trivial details of provincial beauty pageants."

"Excuse you." I give him the hands-on-hips move now that I'm free to do it properly. I can almost see the internal struggle going on as he tries to keep his eyes on mine. But he loses the battle. His gaze goes down the length of my body and then back up again. When our eyes meet again, his jaw stiffens and he looks away.

"Thank you, Prisha," he says softly. "I believe you may have also solved the twinge from an old rugby injury as well."

She smiles up at him. "Well sure, it's no problem."

"You don't think healing the competition is a problem?" Sophia comes striding over and then conveniently stops right in front of me, effectively blocking me out of the group conversation. "I'm guessing you'll be second out. Right after this one." She flicks a finger over her shoulder, indicating me.

"I'm up for some betting!" Malik strides forward. "I've heard the Amazons are fearsome oddsmakers."

Rada nods. "It's true. Amazons love the art of the gamble."

"Perfect," Sophia practically purrs. "Now who wants to bet on Prisha going out early?"

Malik shakes his head. "I would never underestimate a witch. I'll put my money on Prisha lasting until round five at least." He reaches into his back pocket. "What amount are we betting?"

He and Sophia haggle over money for a moment. A few of the other contestants put in bets on each other as well.

"What about Ms. Plastic Crown?" Sophia asks with a smile, raising her voice for everyone to hear. "Care to back her lasting past day one?"

Malik throws an apologetic glance my way. "Um…no."

Sophia gestures to the rest of the contestants. "Anyone? It's not where I'd put my money. But there's always someone who likes the longshot."

No one answers. They all sort of shuffle their feet and glance at me sideways.

My throat goes thick with tears but I don't let them sparkle in my eyes. Instead I hold my chin up high the way Mama taught me. "For your information this crown is made of a high-level polymer compound. It could survive a bomb. And so could I."

I whirl around and prepare to exit the stage. But instead walk right into Athena.

"Contestants, due to your less than stellar behavior, the welcoming ceremony has been cancelled," she announces, skipping the niceties.

Athena nods at Alaric. "Glad you were finally able to join us. Going forward please be aware that tardiness is not tolerated at Amazon Academy." She levels a harsher gaze on Trevor. "The next time you speak to me with another's face, I will rip it off. Understood?"

Both Alaric and Trevor nod. Though Trevor's eyes—damn him—are still dancing with mischief. I really can't decide if I should hate him or throw myself into his corner.

"Now, as I was saying," Athena continues. "I am severely disappointed. As this is the first day, I am willing to allow some slight irregularities, but going forward I will expect the same decorum from all of you that the Academy students display. To that end, you will attend classes. You will not simply show up to class, but participate and be graded with the same rigor as any other student. Finally, should anyone tamper with my students, I will discover it and you will be sorry. That is all. You are dismissed."

Athena strides off the stage to be replaced by her assistant, Taylor. Someone has given her another clipboard and after glancing my way, she hugs it tighter. "I'm here to give out your dorm assignments. As we do not have facilities for the boys"—she wrinkles her nose—"males, you will be housed in a tent on the beach."

"Beach?" Malik asks. "And a tent? Surely you can do better than this. Won't the girls have an unfair advantage, with better sleeping quarters?"

"I think everyone here is perfectly fine with the girls having an unfair advantage," Taylor sniffs.

"No," Sophia says, stepping forward. "After I win this thing—" From behind me Zahara snorts loudly, but Sophia ignores her. "I will not have some thin-skinned little boy saying I only won because I slept better at night." She stomps her foot. "I demand equal housing for the boys."

I look around to find the female contestants nodding along, with various degrees of enthusiasm.

"They will have pallets and blankets," Taylor argues. "And since boys are not fussy about bathrooms, they'll have the whole ocean to do their business in."

"Hey, that's my home," Sora protests. I have no idea what he means but Rada leans in and whispers, "He's a merman."

"I don't wee where I swim," Sora continues, "I agree with the vampire. We need fair accommodations."

"And food," Alaric adds, stepping forward. "We'll eat what the girls eat, where the girls eat."

Taylor frowns, looking seriously put out. "We set up a spit

for you on the beach and we were going to supply you with all the rabbits you could roast. But…" she pauses to sigh heavily, "I can ask Athena about granting you cafeteria privileges as well. All right? Are you happy now?"

"That seems more than fair," Trevor says, shining an ingratiating smile in Taylor's direction.

She blushes and looks away. "Fine. Now that's settled…" Taylor starts going off about all the campus rules, but it's so boring I zone out almost immediately.

Anyway, I've got more important things on my mind. Leaning into Rada, I whisper, "If Sora's a merman why does he have legs?"

"He shifts into mer-form when he wants. It's not useful unless he's actually in the water."

I give her a nudge. "So, if his bottom half is fish what does that mean for his—"

Taylor's voice gets louder as she turns her scowl in my direction. "Finally, there will be no fraternization between the girls and boys."

"Frat what?" Sora asks. "There's a frat party?"

"She means sex," Zahara informs him. "Athena has prohibited any sexual activity between the males and females. Because, you know, that will totally work."

Rada puts her hands on her hips. "I think we can all keep our libidos under control."

Sora's eyes go wide. "Dude, that's racist! Malik is from Libido!"

"Libuya," Malik cuts it. "I'm from the African country of Libuya."

"Right, right," Sora nods like he thinks they're on the same page. "So you're cool with that chick telling us to keep you under control?"

"Okay, boys," Taylor continues, "After I get the girls

sorted, you'll have to come with me so that we can make some last-minute adjustments to your sleeping arrangements."

She rolls her eyes, as if they were being super high-maintenance by just asking for a roof over their heads. "Girls," she says, clicking her heels together and turning to us. "Let's get you settled in. Zahara, you're with Prisha; please collect your welcome package at the table." She glances down. "Sophia…" I pray to all the gods that I'm not stuck with that horrible girl. "You're the odd one out so you get a single."

"No fair!" I say.

"Don't talk to me about fair," Malik says. "They weren't even going to give us beds!"

I try not to get too upset over not having a place of my own where I can lick my wounds in private, when a freckled hand waves in front of my face.

"We're roomies," Rada informs me.

Rooming with Rada won't be so bad. She can give me the deets on the school and might have inside knowledge, and I can loan her some sunblock.

Putting my game-face back on, I grab her arm. "Come on, roomie."

She shakes me off. "You're very touchy-feely."

"It's from being a pageant girl." I go in to give her a hug but she ducks out of the way, turning so that instead I get a face full of arrows from her quiver.

I'm stung, though I smile through it.

I thought we'd bonded over gossip, but now she doesn't even want a friendly hug? What the hell? How am I supposed to relate to her if she won't take beauty tips, refuses to be my enemy, and then passes on being my friend?

I follow her to the table where a willowy woman is giving out duffle bags. She hands me one, but not Rada. "School uniform and books," Rada explains. "I already have mine… just need to move it to my new rooming assignment—with you."

"You do get one of these, though," the woman informs Rada, handing her a houseplant. "For your new room," she explains. "Think of it as a housewarming gift."

Rada steps aside and I am also handed a plant. I hold it like it's a bouquet of roses. I've never touched a plant before that wasn't meant to be used as an accessory.

"Oh…um…I am so honored to be taking care of this noble plant," I tell her. "I promise to… read to it every night."

I'm probably supposed to water it, too. And what do plants eat, anyway?

The woman eyes me; her bright green eyes twinkle. "Good luck."

"I'm Brandee Jean by the way." I've already blown my start with Taylor, but maybe I can get this assistant on my side.

"I am Demeter."

"Oh shi—" I hear Rada say, under her breath.

"Very pleased to meet you, Demeter." I say with a curtsy. "How long have you been Athena's assistant?"

To which suddenly the woman's face goes from twinkling to turd-eating.

"She doesn't know what she's saying," Rada cuts in. I realize I've stuck my foot in it again, so I follow Rada outside.

"You idiot!" She says. "Demeter isn't Athena's assistant. She's here for the trials. She's the goddess of agriculture."

"Oh. Crap. Like Athena, but…" I search for the right word. "Less muscle and more gardening skills?"

"Just…come on and keep your mouth shut," she tells me. "In case we run into any other gods on the sly."

We're a bit behind the other girls but I spot Zahara and Prisha, talking. Sophia is walking alongside them, holding her houseplant at arm's length, her nose wrinkled. As we pass a garbage can she throws it in.

"Rude," I say. I look at my own plant, patting the terra cotta container. "Don't worry, buddy. I'm gonna keep that mean vampire away from you. Unless you're garlic, then you can keep her away from me, right?"

Rada side-eyes me. "Garlic is a bulb," she says. "Not a plant. That is clearly an aloe plant."

"Are you a good little aloe plant?" I ask it.

"Do you always take to non-sentient beings?"

"Look, I'm a pageant girl. I talk to anybody, and anything. Usually with a big smile, big hair, and a great big personality. Not everyone can handle it. We're going to be living together, so you're gonna have to handle it. You either like me, or you don't. But I'm going to do my root-toot-toot-in-est to make sure you do. And the harder you struggle, the more I'm going to get friendly all over your ass. So you might as well just give in and like me now. Fewer people will get hurt."

"Fine. I like you," Rada says with zero enthusiasm or sincerity.

It stings. I never had trouble making friends and always considered myself a likeable person. But the people here are making me doubt myself.

We get to the building and find our room. It's small but clean. I've been in worse hotel rooms. Mama always said you can't judge a book by its cover, but you sure can judge a mattress by a black light.

I plop down on one of the beds. Magically, my carry-on and even my checked luggage is waiting for me.

It's nice to have the familiarity of my stuff in front of me. There's not a lot of closet space for my things, but that's okay. I figure hanging my dresses around the room will help brighten it up a little. Right now it has a prison block sort of feel.

Rada watches me as I hang my dresses on the wood moldings near the ceiling. Then I take up most of the bathroom counter with my make-up, since it looks like Rada only has a toothbrush and a bar of soap.

"You know, you don't need all that," she tells me as I check each dress for rips or lost bling. I lick my thumb, picking up a few sequins that have fallen to the floor.

"*You* may not need all that," I tell her. "You know what Athena is looking for. I need to look my best and be prepared for anything."

"No, that's not what I meant," she tells me, standing. She scrunches her face and suddenly her school uniform turns into a black leather catsuit. Then she sorta wriggles her nose and this time it becomes an emerald green bikini—and daaaaaaamn.

"Girl," I say. "If that's what all you Amazons look like I really hope there's not a swimsuit competition, because Zahara can just fly her harpy ass on out of here."

One more face-scrunch and now she's wearing a pair of comfy pajamas. She sits back on her bed, looking smug. "Our uniforms can change into anything we want."

Whhhhaaaaa? "Anything?" I ask.

She nods.

There are so many dresses I wanted that Mama couldn't afford. Not knock-offs, but actual designer dresses. I rip open the duffle bag they gave us and the plain uniform clothing spills out everywhere. Quickly, I change and then stand in front of the mirror. For all the Amazon's rah-rah you-go-girl attitude, this uniform was definitely chosen by a man. Short plaid shirt and a tight white blouse.

Nope, sorry. This is definitely not going to work for me.

Closing my eyes, I think about that dress I saw in *Cosmo*,

the one that was a hundred grand. I knew owning it was impossible, but at least it's free to look.

Except when I open my eyes, I'm looking at myself wearing it.

I turn toward Rada so the skirt of the dress swirls around my feet. "I have never been happier than in this moment," I tell her. "And I want to thank the Academy—"

"I really don't understand you," she says.

"But you like me," I remind her. "You really, really like me."

"I'm going to sleep." She lays back on her bed, and instantly seems to zonk out.

I'm left alone in the most perfect dress ever made...but all the fizz goes out of my soda.

I wish Mama was here. If only she'd held on for a little longer.

Or Shauna. My post-apoc buddy. My sister from another mister. She would've hated this dress, but she also would've totally understood why I loved it.

I promised myself I would find a way to rescue her, but instead I'm half a world away. And If I lose my power, then I'll return home with no freezer nest egg and super strength. I won't be able to take care of myself, much less think about going after Shauna.

With that thought, my dark mood gets darker yet.

I hate feeling this way. Sad and hopeless. It reminds me of Mama when she had her cement boot days. Those were times when she couldn't get out of bed 'cause it felt like she was wearing thigh-high boots made of hardened cement. It's hard not to worry that the same darkness that did Mama in might eventually track me down too.

It's one of the few things that can't be held back with a spangled baseball bat.

But thinking about that won't help me now. I imagine a

big fluffy bathrobe. With sequins. I need every pick-me-up I can get.

Wrapped up snug, I hustle off to find the bathroom to let all this sadness rinse off me and away down the drain. 'Cause tomorrow, I gotta go out there and show them all—nobody bets against Brandee Jean.

10

We wake at the butt crack of dawn for our first trial. I barely have time to apply foundation, cover-up, mascara, a bit of eyeshadow, and a dab of lip gloss. But my outfit looks fierce. Another dress I never thought I'd wear.

As we near the horse barn, I'm overwhelmed with stinky animal smells. It occurs to me that wearing Versace to a stable doesn't make much sense. After a moment of thought, I change into studded leather leggings and high heeled riding boots. There's no mirror nearby, but I don't need it to know I look fierce.

Everyone else looks like they chose whatever they're most comfortable in—mostly athletic wear. Except for Alaric who has on another polo shirt and a pair of perfectly pressed pants. Only Rada wears the uniform.

Athena eyes us. "While you're here you will follow the dress code," she tells us. I sigh and change, as do all the girls. The boys look bewildered. "All of you."

She waves her hand and suddenly the boys are wearing

white shirts and plaid kilts. Alaric has killer legs while Trevor's are a bit too skinny. They all look slightly put off, but whatever. Fair is fair. I think about what Sora said yesterday…how the boys were originally meant to sleep in a tent by the beach. Or maybe fair isn't quite fair at Amazon Academy.

Honestly? I'm not gonna waste my tears on them. They can deal with a little sexism this one time.

"Artemis has designed your trial for today," Athena announces.

"Goddess of the hunt," Rada whispers to me.

"It is a multi-part contest," Athena continues. "You will find that throughout this competition, not all trials will be to your liking. Some of you will find the tasks simple, due to your newly inherited powers, while others may find the same task nearly impossible. Do not be fooled by the simplicity of some trials. You may not be aware of all the elements at work. Indeed, you may not even know that some trials have already begun. And some of you"—her gaze sweeps us, betraying nothing—"have already been found lacking."

The ten of us exchange wary glances, as if the one of us found lacking might suddenly announce themselves and go home.

Sophia smirks and says in a low voice, "Brandee Jean, she was looking at you."

I glare at her, but say nothing. Today I'm working on keeping my mouth closed.

A woman who must be Artemis steps forward. She's extremely fit and looks like she could run down a deer.

"Follow me," she says and starts off at a jog. Is this a running competition? Good thing I kept up my pageant work-out schedule during the apocalypse. Cardio is very important for your heart and circulation. And your ass. We leave the stables and jog up a cliff path that overlooks a pasture. Below us are beautiful wild horses. A few of them rear up, showing off, and I quickly amend that. Stallions. These are definitely boy horses.

"The first part of your task is to catch one of these wild horses and bring it back to the stable. You have until the end of the day to claim your mount. If you do not, you will not be able to compete in the next phase of my trial."

I laugh…but no one else does.

"Are you the goddess of jerking my leg?" I ask, but Artemis only gives me a cold glare. Rada nudges me, and I remember how I was gonna keep my big mouth shut, but I can't help but wonder…how the actual hell am I gonna catch a freaking wild stallion?

Folding her arms over her chest, Artemis takes a step back. "Begin."

We all sorta stand there, waiting for someone to do something.

Alaric comes forward. Of course he does. He thinks he's the best. Jerk.

He scans the horses in the pasture below in this assessing sort of way and then with a blink—he's gone. There's just empty space where he was standing.

"Look!" Prisha says, pointing out toward the pasture.

Alaric is now below us, seated on a giant black stallion. With no saddle or reins, he struggles to stay on the horse as it rears up. But somehow he keeps his seat and the horse settles.

"Nice," Malik says.

I bite my tongue to keep myself from agreeing with him. But truth be told, it's an impressive display.

We're all still watching in amazement as Alaric gallops off across the field like some sort of fancy horseman. In a skirt, too! I try to pretend he looks ridiculous in the skirt, but astride the horse, it really plays up his powerful thighs.

"Don't be too impressed," Trevor says. "He was head of the equestrian league at school. But it's only because horses like him better than people do."

Malik nudges Trevor. "Sounds like you're jealous, man."

"Does it?" Trevor smiles in a way that has a slight edge, but then his eyes twinkle and the darkness fades. "Let me ask you, would you rather be riding a beautiful girl in the stables or a big ugly horse out round a ring?"

"Girl," Malik says with a grin.

"Ugh." I shake my head at both boys. "Gross."

I turn to ask Rada what her big plan is, but she's gone.

"What the…" She's wandered down into the pasture and is staring down a horse. She has her hands out and is speaking softly. The horse bows its head and she grabs its mane. She swoops onto its back and rides it over to us.

Artemis beams. "I am not surprised, my Amazon," she says.

"How did you do that? I ask Rada, as she neatly prances over to the eight of us, un-horsed people.

"I am an Amazon. One of our first tasks is to tame a wild horse," she tells me, then turns her stallion's head and races back to the stable. I fold my arms. I'm gonna have to wait and see how the rest of them get this done, because my horse-whispering roomie obviously isn't dropping any hints.

Zahara flies into the air and lands on a horse. It tries to get her off its back but she steadies herself with her harpy wings. Sophia follows suit, flying and landing on an unsuspecting mount. Prisha does some witchy mumbo jumbo and traps a horse in a magic lasso, pulling it to her.

Malik turns into a lion and sprints after a horse, who looks absolutely terrified. Malik leaps, shifting back into a human midway. He holds on for dear life and manages to stay on its back. Constantine, his erection *almost* unnoticeable in the folds of his kilt, walks out and a horse trots over to him. He doesn't even have to do anything!

"What the what?" I ask, aloud.

"Virility and charm," Trevor says.

Oh, that explains a few things. Like, I assume it's the charm that attracted the horse. But these are boy horses and Constantine is gay. I guess maybe horses can be gay, too.

I don't know about any of that, but what I do know is that I'm the only girl left. I glance at Sora. Then I lose about five minutes staring, because he's freaking beautiful. "What do you have up your sleeve?" I ask.

"I honestly don't know," he says. Then his face brightens. "Wait...." He takes off down to the meadow, and I don't know if I'm supposed to actually wait, or just check him out while he does his thing. And honestly, I'm okay with either. He's just as captivating from behind.

I turn to Trevor. "And you? Do you have any ideas?"

He shakes his head. "Not a one."

Artemis reminds us that we have all of today, then goes back to the Academy, apparently bored with her last three students—or maybe she's just assuming we aren't going to catch any horses before time runs out.

Once she's gone, Trevor smiles mischievously, then turns into the spitting image of her. He even has her voice. "You have one day to tame a horse, raid a village, kill a cave bear and wear its skin, eat a monkey, charm its mother, then conquer all of Westeros."

I laugh as he turns back into himself. "Very funny, but that doesn't help us any."

A bell rings, long and rolling, from somewhere back on campus.

"That's probably breakfast," Trevor says. He puts out his

arm. "Shall we? We have all day to think about how to solve this conundrum."

I take his arm, forcibly reminding myself that he's not to be trusted. But at least he can be fun. Unlike his brother.

"Conundrum," I repeat. "Is that a British word?"

"It's English, yes," he says. I think he might be making fun of me, as we make our way back down the path. "It means a problem that needs solving."

"Speaking of problems, what's up with you and Alaric?"

"Rick?" He coughs out a laugh. "Well, let's see. His mother is our father's wife, while mine was just our father's mistress. We are very nearly the same age. You see where I'm going with this."

I nod. "Secret love child drama?"

"Well, in my case, not so secret. My mother died when I was five. Our father decided that I was to be raised with his other son. He wanted us to be friends."

"But your stepmother was a wicked bitch?" I ask.

"Karen? No, she's a lovely woman. She knew I wasn't to blame for her husband's wandering eye. She treated me like I was her own son. The problem was Rick. He hated me right away. Thought I was there to usurp his inheritance."

"Oh, that's awful," I say as we get to the dining hall. I mean, awful relatively speaking. He did get to grow up the son of an English duke. He probably never had to barter for Quik Powder, or anything else for that matter.

Before we walk into the hall, Trevor stops me. "Shall we dress for lunch?"

I smile. "I think we should."

He changes into a leather jacket and white t-shirt combo that is very James Dean. It fits him perfectly. Meanwhile, I go back to my earlier dress since I didn't get to wear it nearly long enough.

All set, we enter the hall. Immediately conversation stops. All eyes are on us. I drop my hand from Trevor's arm.

"What?" I ask the room. "Haven't you ever seen Versace?"

"I think they're staring at me," Trevor says. "They're not used to males."

Oh. I look around and don't spot the other boys. But I do see Rada. I head over to her, Trevor in tow.

"Hiya roomie!" I say as we sit down across from Rada. Her fork pauses midway between her plate and her mouth. Eggs spill onto the table.

I stare. Eggs. There's a whole platter of them in the center of the table, along with pancakes and for the love of all that is holy, bacon.

Plopping into a seat, I fill a plate and shovel food into my mouth. I'm making little moans of pleasure but I don't even care. It just tastes so good.

"It's nice to see a woman eat with enthusiasm," Trevor says.

"Oh man, I've been living on Quik Powder and frozen beef," I tell him. "Plus, ever since I got my super strength, I seem to have super metabolism too. Wish that part could've happened when my favorite donut shop was still open." I pause and look around the table. Spotting salt and pepper, I pick them up to see if anything else is hiding behind them.

"What do you need?" Rada asks, curious.

"Where's the cheese for the eggs?"

She shrugs. "Not a lot of dairy on this island. Unless you want Goat Milk."

I put down my fork and level a look at her. "Milk comes from cows," I tell her. "Duh."

"Actually," Zahara chimes in. "All mammals have mammary glands. Milk can be had from any of them."

"First you need breasts," Sophia says, snidely. "Guess nobody will be getting a refill off you, harpy."

"Actually," Zahara says, not at all perturbed. "Not all mammals have teats. The exceptions are the two monotremes the Echidna and the Platypus."

"Actually," Sophia mimics back at her, "you're ugly."

"I'm about to *actually* shove this fork up your—"

But I don't get to hear what adventure the harpy has in store for her utensil. Trevor's hand slams down onto mine, effectively ending the conversation.

"I've got it!" he says, and pulls me away from the table.

11

"The conversation at breakfast has given me a wonderful idea," Trevor says, leading me back down the path toward the pasture. "I know how to catch my stallion."

I come to a halt. "I said milk comes from cows…"

"No, no," he waves his hand in the air. "Everything you said was inane, of course. It's what the other girls said that caught my interest."

I take a second, mentally replaying breakfast. "Oh," I say, hitting on it. "Boobs. Of course. Boobs is what caught your interest."

"Precisely," Trevor says. Except, he's not really Trevor anymore.

He's a horse…kind of. The head isn't quite right.

I squint trying to figure out exactly what about it is wrong—beside the fact that the boy I was just talking to is now a horse. Finally, I put my finger on it. Trevor isn't able to change the eyes. That explains why Alaric's stormy ones kept bugging me yesterday. But this is way more obvious. Human eyes in a horse's head are not a pretty thing.

Although, I doubt any of the horses will be focusing too much on his eyes. When Trevor said he was inspired by the boobs, well he definitely had a very specific vision.

"Um, I don't think boy horses are into girl horses with huge knockers." I tell him. "Also, I'm here to tell you, running with those things hanging lose is gonna be painful."

But Trevor can't hear me, he's already beating hell for leather down into the pasture. Well, he's kind of awkwardly shuffling, and tripping over his own boobs occasionally, ending up face first in a bunch of dandelions. A stallion comes over to investigate, and horse-Trevor struggles to his feet.

"Well God bless his triple E ass," I mutter. "Well, not his ass," I correct myself.

Because mother of all that is holy, it's working.

Another stallion has wandered over, curious as to what the first one found so interesting. Trevor tries to toss his mane, but this throws him off balance and sends him belly up...which is the best way to show off his attributes.

Now all the boy horses are coming over to investigate, completely ensnared, all conscious thought lost.

Trevor gets back to his feet...er...hooves, and seems to pick one stallion at random, giving him a slight nudge and leading him off toward a copse of trees. The others stare after them. Apparently voyeurism is a thing, no matter the species, and *boys will be boys* has never been more true than it is right now.

But none of that helps me, like, at all. Alaric teleported his khaki-d ass right onto a horse's back. Malik and Zahara both used their bodies Zahara her wings, Malik his shifting abilities—to wrangle their steeds. Me? I've got super strength, but that doesn't mean anything if I can't get within grabbing distance.

Going down into the pasture, I try talking low and

walking slowly, my hands outstretched and open, like Rada did. But the horses just chomp grass and move steadily away from me, so that I never get any closer.

Tired of the slow and steady I approach, I switch it up, lunging at the closest stallion. It rears at me, hooves flashing above my head.

"Gaaaah!" A terrified scream escapes me. I scrunch myself small, hands over my head, eyes scrunched closed, certain I'm a goner.

The sound of hoofbeats fills my ears and the ground trembles with them. Cautiously, I screw open one eye to discover that the horses are running away.

I decide in this moment that I hate horses. What's so great about horses anyway? Sure, when people needed them to get around, I can see why a person might keep them around. But now that we got vehicles with heated seats, it seems like the horse riding thing oughta just be retired.

"Success!" Trevor declares, as he approaches on the back of his clearly bewildered mount.

"How did you manage?" I ask, narrowing my eyes. "Did you *seduce* your horse, Trevor?"

"Preposterous!" Trevor shouts. "I simply used temptation as a ruse to draw my prey in." He heads off toward the stable, his mount kicking up dust behind him.

Unfortunately, he's forgotten to eliminate the evidence of all his horse shifting. That horse has two tails—and one of them is Trevor's.

But I decide not to tell him; I've got bigger problems. The most obvious one being that I'm the only contestant left standing in the meadow. The only one without a horse.

"Edie," I say under my breath. "Now would be a great time for you to fly in here and save the day…"

But my dragon mentor doesn't show. She'd warned me that her duties were strictly limited to giving advice. She wouldn't be able to help me during the trials in any way. But still…

Glumly, I survey the pasture. The remaining horses have moved away from me, ears flicking toward me as try one last time to approach. It's a half-hearted gesture, and they seem aware that I don't have much fight left in me. They trot away, completely unconcerned, knowing full well I'm not going to catch them.

"I've got until midnight," I say to myself, then repeat it again, more loudly for the horses. "You hear that? I'll be back!"

I'm kicking my way along the trail back to the stables when I hear a bell ringing, loud and clear, rolling over the hills.

Crap. I've got to get to class.

———

*A*rchery: *Arrows are a girl's best friend* is taught by a goddess named Devana, who is apparently on loan from a Russian school. The shooting range isn't far from the stables, thank the gods. I show up slightly sweaty.

All the Amazons are in their uniforms and I am so not, but manage to do the face squish thing and end up wearing something pretty similar to what everyone else has on—a version of the school uniform, except my little white blouse is cinched at the waist and my skirt is in violation of all dress codes, ever.

Sophia turns her nose up when she sees me, her own skirt ending demurely right above the knee. But I don't care. After not bagging a horse this morning, I need all the confidence I can get. And for Brandee Jean Mason, that means showing some skin.

"IIcy," Zahara whispers, as I grab a textbook entitled

"Assholes Get Arrows," along with a bow from the wall, and a quiver of arrows. "Any luck? Did you wrangle an Equus Caballus?"

"I think that's personal," I tell her.

"She means a horse," Prisha explains.

"Oh. No." I shake my head, but decide not to go into detail at the moment since class is starting and I really can't piss off yet another god.

Devana tells us to read through the first chapter as a refresher and then move onto target practice. I open the book, but only get through a few pages before my eyes start to glaze. The whole thing is about making your own bow and goes into detail over the different types of wood and…well, I don't know what else, because that's where it lost me.

Closing the book, I decide to try some target practice instead. Zahara is sitting with her book open, but her eyes closed, so she was obviously having trouble with the reading as well. I give her a nudge and we move over to one of the targets.

Devana walks the row of students, adjusting a bow here, correcting posture there. Like all the gods I've seen around her so far, she's got that whole 'Yeah, I really am this naturally gorgeous' vibe going on.

"I see zat I have a few of ze kontestants in my class," Devana says, eyeing me, Alaric, Zahara, Prisha, and Sophia. "Ave you shot bow before?"

I look stupidly at the weapon in my hand; it's almost as tall as I am. I have no idea how to hold it, how to use it, or even which way to point it.

Why couldn't this be a tap class?

Alaric and Sophia, however, nod confidently, each of them stepping up to take a shot at the targets on the far end of the green. Alaric does fairly well, landing three arrows in the outer rings of the bullseye, while Sophia shoots everything straight down the middle, even being a total show-off and splitting one of the already embedded arrows with a fresh one.

"Yeah, yeah, we see you, Robin Hood," I say, to which she tosses her mane of dark hair and gives me a nasty look over her shoulder.

"Let's see what *you've* got," she says, coming to stand beside me.

"Oh, I've got plenty," I shoot back. But words are the only thing I can shoot.

It takes me three tries to get the stupid arrow on the stupid string, then I fumble and it falls to the ground. Prisha also looks immensely confused, so Devana does a step by step tutorial while the Amazons giggle at how crappy we are.

It doesn't help that Devana's tone is one you would use on a toddler who didn't quite make it to the potty, but tried really hard.

"All right now, you, Ze Zhunder Girl. You give try," Devana tells Prisha.

Prisha and I exchange nervous looks. It stinks to be bottom of the class, but at least I'm not alone there.

I watch as Prisha actually manages to notch her arrow and hit the outside of the bullseye, accompanied by a clap of thunder. She grins at me and I can't help but grin back.

Devana nods. "Good enough, for beginner. You, Strong Girl. Iz your turn."

I can do this. I hope.

I notch an arrow and draw back on the string. It's the furthest I've gotten so far and I'm feeling optimistic about this arrow actually getting some air. Then something freakishly cold slides down the back of my neck. I yelp and twist around to see Sophia with one of her long vampire fingers extended and a nasty smile on her face.

Meanwhile, my arrow does get some air, but it goes so

wide of the mark that it hits a target belonging to the group next to us.

"Watch it." One of the Amazons turns, her face dark.

"I hit the target," I say. "No congratulations for the girl who never held a bow until today?"

The Amazon takes a step closer to me...and it's definitely not to offer a friendly slap on the back. "You're not an Amazon. You never will be. The only one we'd ever accept as our queen is one of our own."

"Right," I nod. "So you're rooting for Constantine, then?"

The girl obviously has no sense of humor, cause her eyes narrow even further as she spits at me, "I'm rooting for Rada." The Amazon snatches the bow right out of my hands. "You're not worthy of this weapon."

"Lilliana," Devana cuts in. "Is true, zis one has no talent for ze arrow. Perhaps she vill improve some, or perhaps she remain clumsy oaf. Ve vill see." With those crushing words, Devana takes the bow away from Lilliana and hands it back to me. "Ve must let her try and pretend to be good sport until she lose contest and go away. Okay?"

With that, Devana gives me what I think is meant to be a comforting pat on the shoulder before drifting off to another section of the room—presumably where she can help someone with natural talent.

Despite Devana's words, Lilliana is not appeased. She steps closer to me so I can see very clearly how overdue her eyebrows are for plucking.

"Sorry won't cut it when one of you accidentally shoots someone." Her eyes slide over us, the outsider contestants. "If an Amazon gets hurt they'll have to hold the rest of the trials at Underworld Academy after all." She grins in a way that is not pretty. "Because I'll send you there myself."

More thunder rings out and Prisha looks like she's about to pee her pants. This is bullshit.

"Well, now I know who to ask for advice if one of the trials is baseless threats and—" Before I can say more, a hand lands on my shoulder. A well-manicured one.

"She meant no disrespect, my lady," Alaric says, giving the Amazon a low bow. She eyes him for a second, then dismisses him and turns back to her group.

I'm about to go after her, but Alaric squeezes my shoulder, steering me away. "I don't think cracking wise at the natives is in your best interest."

"And since when are my best interests your business?" I ask, but it all comes out as kind of a sloppy mess of vowels because I'm about to cry.

I couldn't catch my horse. I can't shoot a bow. The mean girls aren't just mean, but armed as well.

How the hell am I supposed to compete here?

"Brandee Jean," Alaric says calmly, pulling an honest-to-goodness handkerchief from his pocket. "There is only one person that I want to see win this competition, and that's me."

"Watch it, buddy, assholes earn arrows, remember?" I point to a nearby textbook. But it's hard to keep an edge on my voice.

"And there's only one person I want to see lose," he continues. "Was Trevor able to capture a horse this morning?"

"Oh," I say, taking the handkerchief from him and blowing my nose, making sure to leave something nice and shiny right across his embroidered initials. "You're not being nice to me right now. You're milking me for information."

He says nothing for a moment as something unreadable flashes in those stormy eyes. Then he shrugs. "Of course. I am a cold fish, obsessed with the duty I owe my title and heritage. We bred nice out of the bloodline several generations ago and never looked back."

I frown. Did I hurt Alaric's feelings? Does Alaric have feelings? "Well, thanks for the hanky anyway," I say, folding it neatly so the snot's a nice little present waiting inside.

Alaric takes a step back, rejecting the handkerchief. I expect him to say *keep it*, but instead he says. "Please wash that before returning it to me."

I toss it at his chest. Even though I have the strength of Zeus, it's still just a hanky. It bounces off harmlessly as my temper flares.

"Clean your own laundry," I shout at him. "And don't ask me to do your dirty work!"

I stomp away from him back to the line of students, but my little tantrum has caught Devana's eye. "You, Strong Girl. Dress for class next time. Zis is not Stripper Akademy. And bring your glasses vith you! Da?"

"I don't wear glasses," I tell her, to which Devana turns and eyes my single arrow—still sticking out of the wrong target.

"Zen maybe get eyes checked," she says. "Or take job as magician's assistant. Pretty girls kut in half. Zip." She mimics a scissors with her hands.

Remembering Alaric's advice to not make enemies of the Amazon, I choke back my suggestion of where she can stick her arrows. Somehow, I give her a tight nod and manage a, "Yes, ma'am," before walking away, arms crossed. But her voice follows me as I head for the dorms.

"Is good pay! And benefits! Health insurance very important for girls being kut in half!"

12

———

Rada is in our room when I get there, her curly red locks spread across her pillow as I bury my face in my own, resisting the urge to sob. The only thing that could make this day worse is having to face the rest of it with red puffy cry face.

There's a weight on my bed as Rada joins me, and the warmth of her palm on my back.

"You okay?" she asks.

"No," I yell into my pillow. "I couldn't catch a horse, and the big Russian god-woman just told me to be a stripper's assistant."

"Strippers have assistants?" Rada asks, and I roll over, wiping away the last of my tears.

"Sorry, no. She called me a stripper, but she told me to apply to be a magician's assistant."

"Oh, yeah," Rada says, rolling r's and dropping her voice low like, Devana's. "Pretty girls, kut in half. Zip." She makes the scissors motion, just like the archery instructor. "That's kind of her go-to insult. Which is weird because it's not really that offensive."

I sniffle. "Yeah, but it's the way she says it."

"Like you're the most useless person alive. Yeah, I know. You're not the first person to run off the archery field in tears."

I sigh. "I bet. It's just…" I look up at Rada and her calm, freckly face. I know technically she's my competition, but I wouldn't mind coming in second to her, even if she is sporting more split ends than a homeless German Shepherd.

"I've had a sucky day," I admit. "I'm the only one who didn't get a horse this morning."

"Actually, I heard Sora is still trying to get one too," Rada says.

"I know that should make me feel better, but have you noticed he's maybe not the brightest guy ever? It's possible he just misunderstood the assignment."

Rada shrugs. "It's possible. I don't think anyone has seen him all day."

"Ugh." I hit my head against the mattress, wishing I could shake some sort of solution free. "If I can just get my hands on one it would be simple. I can sling one over my shoulder and take it into the barn."

"I would love to see that, so I'm going to give you a free tip."

Hope rising, I lift my head. "Please something. Anything."

"Well…" Rada hesitates before finally saying, "Horses usually go to bed pretty early."

I frown. "So I should go and tuck them in? Sing them a lullaby and make them like me?"

Rada shakes her head. In a harder voice, she adds, "You have until midnight. The horses will be sleeping well before then…" She looks at me like I'm supposed to finish that sentence.

And finally I get where she's going with this. "I sneak up on a snoozing horse and carry it away!"

"Yes! Exactly!"

"You're amazing, thank you for the hot tip!" I sit up, taking her hand. "Will you come with me?"

Her eyebrows come together. "I don't want any of the others to think we've formed an alliance…"

I fill in the rest for her. "And you don't want anyone thinking that, because you want an alliance with a better contestant than me."

"Sorry," she says. And she does look sorry, but she doesn't take it back. Maybe tough love is something they teach Amazons.

I sigh heavily and then add in a little moan too, hoping guilt might make Rada change her mind.

"It's okay, I understand," I say softly. "It's just…this girl, Lilliana, threatened me today after one of my arrows hit her target. I'm kinda worried about running into her after dark."

"Oh, that definitely sounds like Lilliana," Rada says, with a smile. "Just be glad you're not one of the boys. She said if she ever got one of them alone…well, let's just say Constantine's problems would be over." She makes the scissors snipping motion again.

I let out a shaky laugh. "Well, hopefully I can avoid her."

"Okay, if you need protection," Rada stands. "I'll come with you."

"Yay!" I yell, and throw myself into her arms. "Besties!"

"Let's not get ahead of ourselves," Rada says, pushing me away.

But my new sense of hope cannot be dimmed. Especially when this mission requires a total outfit change.

After giving it some careful consideration, I change into a skintight black burglar suit, complete with mask. Rada stares at me.

"What?" I say. "We're sneaking."

"Then maybe you should tone down the sparkle?"

I look down at the sequence I added for glitz. I squinch one eye closed and they disappear. "Fine. There. Super boring."

Rada changes into baggy dark sweatpants and a T-shirt. It's tragic. As we head for the door, I make a mental note to work in a makeover night. Out in the hallway, Zahara and Prisha stand outside our door.

I stare at them. "Um…hi…?"

"These walls are paper thin," Zahara says.

"We want to come with," Prisha adds. "I owe it to my all female coven to uphold the bonds of sisterhood, and that means making sure a girl isn't the first one out."

"I'm all about girl power," Rada says, "But Prisha, you might do more to hurt Brandee Jean's chances than help her. One thunderclap and the horses will be spooked."

Prisha reddens. Zahara nods. "Good point. We'll stay behind, but we'll be wishing you luck!"

I'm touched. I really am. I give each of them a hug before heading out with Rada to the pasture. We sneak along and I'm glad to find that a lot of the horses are lying down, sleeping. Rada gives me a little nod and whispers, "Go ahead."

Despite telling Rada I could use my strength to lift one of them, up close it doesn't seem too easy. These guys are huge.

Still, there's no going back now.

I finally choose a soft grey-colored horse, since grey is a good neutral color that will easily go with any riding outfit I put on.

The stallion has no idea what hit him. I come up from behind and put him in a full nelson—a move an ex-boyfriend taught me when he was trying to impress me with how big and tough he was. It's a sweet little maneuver where you come up behind somebody, lace your hands into their armpits like you're gonna give 'em a love squeeze from behind. But instead you loop your hands up behind their neck, interlock your fingers, and boom—you've got them hanging like a five-dollar dress on a wire hanger.

It works with horses, too. If you have the strength of Zeus.

"Now listen," I say as the horse bucks and tries to fight me. I've got him standing on his hind legs, his back pulled up tight against my chest, his mane in my face as I whisper into his ear. "You can be a good boy, or I can crack all your ribs. Your choice, mister horse." I give him a little extra squeeze, in case he doesn't speak English. Or British. Or whatever it is Trevor was trying to make me feel stupid about earlier.

Whatever my mouth is saying, my body language seems to be doing the trick, because my horse goes so limp I bet Constantine would be jealous.

"Be a good boy, or else." I set him back on all fours. "Okay buddy?"

He doesn't really respond, only looks at me, wild-eyed with fear, seeming to ask if I'm going to crush him like a stale Cheeto or not.

"You just let me carry you and nobody gets hurt," I say, feeling like some sort of mafioso. But the tough guy thing seems to be working, the horse doesn't try to get away, even when I take his face in my hands, and resting my forehead against his.

He's soft and warm, and surprisingly, the smell of him is less gross than I expected. His ears flick back and forth while I talk to him, but otherwise, he's gentle like a baby whose mama slipped some whiskey into the bottle.

"Whiskey," I say, tapping him on the nose. "I'm gonna call you Whiskey."

I pick him up like a baby and start across the pasture when suddenly, there's a low moaning noise from somewhere behind me. Awkwardly, I spin around and try to see around the armful of horse.

"Nggggghhaaaaaahhh."

There it is. Again. Like somebody moaning about a bad headache.

I stop to listen for it again, but it's hard to hear anything over the suddenly worried horses whinnying and shuffling their feet.

Then one of the stallions screams.

Whiskey flails wildly and no amount of threats are getting through this time. I'm so busy struggling to hold onto him, that I don't hear the pounding of hooves until the ground around me beings to shake. Quickly, I shift Whiskey onto my right hip to see what's going on.

Every single horse in the pasture is running at me full speed. It's an actual honest to gods stampede.

And I'm standing right in the middle of it.

Whiskey peddles his legs in the air, like he thinks he's on land. Clearly, he's ready to run. So I let him.

Keeping my arms locked around his chest, I lower him until his back legs connect with the ground. Almost immediately, his hooves dig into the dirt—and he's off. All I have to do is stay on.

Which is easier said than done.

My entire body bounces up and then slams back down the length of his spine with every stride. Eventually I manage to lock my knees around him, but it's still like riding in a car with no shocks.

After what seems like an eternity, Whiskey starts to slow and then comes to a full stop. I lay limp on his back for a while, too tired to move. When I finally find the strength to sit up, I nearly cry with the realization of how far we've gone. We're at the total opposite end of the pasture. The stables are just a speck in the distance.

Grabbing Whiskey's mane, I give it a little tug. "Okay, boy, let's giddy-up back the way we came now."

He ignored me, instead dipping his head to eat some grass.

Tilting my head back, I look at the moon overhead. Midnight is the deadline; I can't just sit up here on his back and hope he'll eventually go back.

With an exhausted sigh, I slide off Whiskey. My whole body aches, but I pick him up the way I did before and start walking back across the field.

I have to stop a few times to put him down and stretch my arms out. Each time the little speck that is the stables gets a little bigger. Each time it's harder to pick him up once more. And each time I remind myself of Shauna and how I gotta win this competition if I'm gonna help her.

Then I pick up the horse and get going again.

But still, it's definitely the hardest thing I've ever done, and that includes the time I had to compete in the bikini competition despite a bad case of the shits.

I am gritting my teeth as I carry Whiskey up the hill where the barn waits at the top. Rada has already laid fresh straw—or hay, I really don't know what's what—in the stall that has my name printed on a pretty brass plate overhead.

"Brandee Jean," Rada says her eyes wide. There's something in her tone I can't quite put my finger on until she adds, "That was amazing." Then I realize—it's respect.

I drop Whiskey outside the stall, but the asshole has apparently decided he's not taking one step he doesn't want to. Lifting my leg, I give him a kick in the butt that sends him stumbling into the stall. Whiskey turns to glare at me as I close the door between us.

Whatever got me this far wears off all at once. I slump against the wall.

"What happened down there?" Rada asks. "I saw the horses get spooked, but couldn't see what set them off."

I let my eyes drift closed for a moment before answering.

As I do, the sound I'd heard plays in my mind. "Nnnnnnnnggghhhhaaauughh."

I don't realize I've said it aloud until Rada's cool hand presses against my forehead. "Are you okay?"

"That's what I heard before the horses went nuts," I explain.

"Ooh. I thought that was you."

My eyes fly open as I swat Rada's hand away. "Why would I make that sound?"

Rada throws her hands up. "Brandee Jean, I don't know why you do most of the things you do."

I eye her, wondering if that's a compliment or not. "Well if I pass out, just so you know, it's because I'm exhausted. Or maybe dead."

"You're not going to pass out. You just gotta get back to bed." She holds out a hand. "Come on."

I'm practically leaning on Rada as we head back to the dorm, at least as much as she'll let me. If this were a pageant girl, I'd have my head on her shoulder, and she'd put an arm around my waist. But since it's Rada instead she just makes her body really stiff and pushes against me to counterbalance my weight.

Still, she smells nice, and I feel like we may have crossed a bridge. And maybe we did, because even though she won't let me put tiny braids in her hair before bed, I do spot a couple of sequins on her pajamas before we slide into bed, both of us exhausted.

"Nice flair," I whisper, but she shushes me.

"Go to sleep, roomie," she says. "Tomorrow won't get any easier."

And while I'm sure she's right, I'm smiling when I slip off to sleep, thinking of Whiskey in his stable, and wondering if Rada will let me tweeze her brows someday.

13

When I get to the stables in the morning there's a whole gaggle of people standing around.

"Brandee Jean!" Rada runs over to me, grabs my hand, and then pulls me to the center of the crowd where Taylor and her clipboard are holding court. Rada positions me directly in front of Taylor and then gives me a nudge. "Tell her about last night. And the noise you heard before the horses stampeded."

I quickly tell Taylor the whole story and when I'm finished lean into her. "Hey, is there a Keurig around here somewhere? It was a late night and I really need the caffeine."

"No, we do not keep a Keurig in the stables." She shakes her head in this disgusted sort of way, and then to my dismay adds, "Or anywhere else. An Amazon does not sully her body with chemicals."

"Okay, but I'm not an Amazon, so is there a way for me to sully my body?"

Rada leans closer and in an urgent voice tells me, "Not now, BJ! There's important stuff going on right now."

I turn to her and then back to Taylor. "Like what?"

Taylor sighs. "The noise you heard last night was a zombie." Her mouth twists as she says that last word, like she can't believe she's having to say it. "Nothing like this has ever happened here at Amazon Academy before. I knew having the contest here was a bad idea."

"It was a student who passed away last year," Rada says softly. "She was a witch."

"Of course, it's always the worst people who rise from the dead, right?" I make a little joke, trying to lighten the mood which has gotten super intense.

Rada jerks away from me. "She was a friend of everyone. Beloved. A true Amazon sister."

"This will not go unanswered," Taylor adds, her voice thick with unshed tears. "Thank you for giving me the details of last night. I will pass this along to Athena and she will make sure her uncle pays dearly for this offense against the Amazons."

With that Taylor pushes through the crowd and is gone.

"Rada," I put a hand on her arm and am encouraged when she doesn't pull away. "I'm sorry. I didn't realize. When I heard 'zombie' it sounded so campy. But if she was a friend…"

Rada's face softens again. "It's okay, BJ. I know you're kinda clueless."

Ouch. Just when I think Rada and I are friends, she tells me what she really thinks of me. And it's never good.

"Come on." Rada jerks her head in the direction of the stables. "Looks like everyone's starting to head in."

As we join the other contestants inside the stable, I can't help but notice they're all gathered around my horse's stall. Worried something is wrong, I quickly march over.

"Holy gods, she actually got one," Malik says, as he

watches Whiskey happily munching in his stall. The others look just as surprised.

I want to flip the other contestants the bird for not believing in me, but my girls, Rada, Zahara, and Prisha are there too, so I curtsy.

Turning to Whiskey, I reach over his stall door to scratch his nose, hoping to start our relationship off on a new foot this morning. But Whiskey is committed to being an asshole. He snaps his teeth at me and I only just jerk my fingers away in time.

"Well, you really cleaned up," Sophie says.

Assuming she's talking to me, I do a neat little pirouette in her direction, ready to rub her nose in my success. But it turns out her comment was directed at Alaric.

Sophie hands him a stack of bills and he nods coolly.

"I told you she'd pull through," he turns to Malik, "You owe me too."

"Wait, *you* bet on *me*?" I stare at Alaric in disbelief.

"It felt a little early to be getting against anyone," he says simply and then discreetly slips the bills into his inside jacket pocket. Because, of course, he's the kind of guy with an inside jacket pocket.

I wonder if there's a clean handkerchief in there too, and vow to myself I'll get through the day without needing it. Or, at least, refuse it if he offers it to me. I mean, I haven't even washed the first one yet. If I keep collecting Alaric's hankies eventually good manners will force me to just go ahead and offer to do all his laundry. Although I admit to some curiosity about whether he's a boxers or briefs kind of guy. I got my money on pure starched cotton boxers. Stiff and uncomfortable, just like him.

I whirl toward Sophia and Malik. "And you guys bet against me!" I switch my clothes into an eighties chic dress.

"Big mistake! Huge! Just ask this guy." I point a finger over my shoulder to Whiskey. "He let his guard down last night and then Bam! He got hit with a big old BJ!"

Malik covers his mouth, smothering a laugh, while Sophia does nothing to disguise a snicker. "So you seduced your horse?" Her eyes flick toward his stall where Whiskey has started kicking the walls. "Looks like he's having regrets this morning."

I take a threatening step toward Sophia with the idea of explaining to her with my fists that BJ is my power nickname and not some cheap and easy oral sex joke.

But then I notice Artemis marching into the stables and shelve the plan for later.

"This is excellent," Artemis says, eyes scanning the full stalls. "You have all passed my first trial. Now that you have chosen your stallions, you must become as one with them. Amazons are the best riders in the world, because the bond they have with their mounts is an almost psychic one. The rider anticipates their animal's needs and the animal knows what their rider desires before the order is even given. This is the bond all contestants must forge between yourselves and your stallions."

I groan, unable to stop myself. I figured with the nameplates on the stalls that there'd be more to this than just capturing the horse. But I figured we'd have to ride and, I don't know, maybe teach it to count by stomping its hoof against the ground. But a psychic bond? I can't threaten Whiskey to make him bond with me.

Artemis's laser focus is on me and I squirm, certain she can read my mind. Wanting her attention elsewhere, I throw someone else under the bus. "Hey, what happened to Sora?"

Artemis smiles. "Sora thought outside of the box. He chose a water horse and was just finishing securing it before joining us up here."

"I'll have to remember that creative problem solving is allowed," Trevor says.

Artemis continues. "You must train with your horses, forge the bond, and become proficient riders. Otherwise you will not survive the second part of the trial. You have eight weeks."

I breathe a sigh of relief. It's not like a "happening tomorrow" thing. But apparently I breathed too soon because Artemis continues.

"But do not become complacent. Tomorrow morning you will face a new task from a different god. One of you will be eliminated."

Oh crap. My elation dips. There's a rumble of thunder and Prisha blushes. In his stall, Whiskey lets out a high, nervous whinny.

"Hey! Stop freaking out, man," I tell Whiskey, figuring we need to get some sort of dialogue going between us. He instantly goes still and my spirits rise. Maybe I am already one with my horse? There's another rumble and I glance at Prisha, but she's watching Whiskey, who has just made a donation to the manure pile.

"Your steed is terrified of you," Artemis informs me.

"What? No," I insist. "He tried to bite me earlier!" I put my fingers out to demonstrate, but this time he shies away.

"Fight or flight," Artemis says in a total 'duh' voice. Like this is so basic she's annoyed at having to explain it. "If you show softness, he will fight for freedom. If you are hard as with your comment moments ago, he will try to get away."

I frown. "But if I can't be mean and I can't be nice...what option does that leave me?"

A small smile curls Artemis's lips. "Indeed."

With that, she walks away.

I turn back to Whiskey, wondering if Artemis is right.

"Hey sweetie guy," I coo at him. Immediately his lips curl back exposing his big square horsey teeth.

Oh yeah. Artemis was totally right. He totally hates me. And fears me.

"I'm screwed," I say.

"Maybe give him a minute," Rada says, pulling me away from my horse. "Why don't we grab some breakfast?"

I notice everyone else has left.

"No, I'm gonna brush Whiskey," I tell her. I mean, I don't exactly know what I'm doing, but I know how to brush some freaking hair. I gotta start bonding with him somewhere.

He freezes when I enter his stall and his whole body remains locked tight as I begin to brush him. This actually works out well when I start braiding his mane. A fishtail braid is complicated and I'd never be able to make it look properly pretty if he was wiggling around.

After about twenty minutes, the braid is almost done and Whiskey relaxes just enough to actually blink. Encouraged, I start singing the only horse song I know, "Save a Horse (Ride a Cowboy). He must approve of the message, because he melts further, bending his neck to nibble on his hay.

I think we're maybe actually bonding just a tiny little bit, when someone clears their throat. I turn to find Edie, my dragon mentor, staring at me with a half smile.

"Edie!" I shriek, causing Whiskey to emit a sound that pretty much matches mine. I bolt out of the stall and rush to her, taking her hands in mine. "I passed the first trial!"

"I knew you could," she says. "But…maybe less screaming around animals that are prone to stampeding?"

"Oh, I know all about stampedes," I assure her. "I was right in the middle of one last night."

Edie's eyes go wide with surprise. "What?"

Quickly I fill her in.

"Brandee Jean, did you tell anyone about this? It sounds

like maybe someone was messing with you." She leads me over to some straw bales and we sit across from each other. "Although it doesn't make sense why anyone would single you out."

"What do you mean?" I ask.

"Look, some of the mentors are talking," Edie says. "They thought you'd be out on this one. If I was going to sabotage someone, it would be the frontrunner."

"Yeah, well, what if you'd place a bet against someone? Sophia and Malik put money on my losing."

"Oh." Edie frowns, nonplussed for a moment. "That does complicate things. I guess that I shouldn't be so surprised. It is a competition. I assume Trevor bet against you? He seems the type."

"He's not all bad," I say, coming to his defense. I tell her about the boob horse incident from the day before, winning a smile from her.

"Well, at least he's not too proud," she says, but her eyes suddenly narrow. "We may need to talk strategy at some point. It's possible that alliances could be formed. I need to know who was betting *for* you."

"Alaric," I say, then adding. "Weird." I'd been too focused on who bet against me to think about who had my back.

"Why is that weird?" Edie asks.

"I don't know," I shake my head, confused. "He just plays it like he's better than everyone else. Like, he knows which fork to use first at dinner and doesn't pronounce the *h* in *herb*, or the *l* in *salmon*."

"BJ," Edie says. "Nobody pronounces the *l* in *salmon*."

"Then why is it there?" I demand.

"For now I think it would be wise to keep an eye on Alaric," she says, skipping over my phonetics question. "If he's interested in an alliance, you could do worse." She stands and I realize our little heart to heart is over. "I'm here today because I wanted to give you a hint about tomorrow morning."

"Oh thank god!"

"Gods," she corrects.

I shrug. "Whatever! Can you tell me which god is running the trial? What do we have to do? What should I wear?

"I can't tell you much," she says. "But in general I think sensible shoes are always a good choice. And comfy underwear. Nothing that rides up."

"Are you telling me to wear granny panties?" I demand, hands on hips.

"Listen to me," Edie says, suddenly serious. "You don't have to win to not lose."

I nod slowly. "That's all you can say?"

"You don't have to *win*," she repeats, "to *not lose*."

"Yeah, I still don't get it."

She sighs. "That's as specific as I can get, okay? If you were to succeed because of cheating, the gods will find out. And you don't want them angry with you. Trust me on that one. There's not much you can do to prepare yourself for the next trial, if I'm being honest. Your time would be better spent on other pursuits." She eyes Whiskey. "And maybe less braiding."

I nod, still not understanding but I don't want to look as clueless as I feel.

"I'll be in touch when I can," Edie says, rising from the straw bale. "Good luck, Brandee Jean."

She leaves the stables, and I can't help but be impressed when she shifts into a dragon, flying away to go do whatever she does all day. Maybe dispense vague wisdom to other confused beauty queens.

I return to Whiskey and rest my hand on his back. He instantly freezes, no longer chewing away at his breakfast. "Buddy," I say. "We gotta figure this out."

Artemis had said someone would be eliminated tomorrow, and Edie isn't willing to bend any rules to give me an edge.

I guess it's like Mama always said—whiskey isn't my only problem.

14

———

Bright and early we're brought to a round stone room. It's eerily quiet even though every noise reverberates. I'm scared to say a word, like maybe a loud noise might bring everything down around our ears.

There aren't any chairs so I sit on the hard stone, going full on criss-cross applesauce. Edie's advice on footwear hadn't been off base, and I'd extended it to my wardrobe as well. I'm wearing a super cute fuchsia tracksuit and my favorite no-show underwear. Prisha follows me to the floor, but everyone else stands.

"Hello," someone says and I jump. There's a guy standing beside me, his kneecaps at eye level. I hadn't even noticed him. He talks very softly, with a whisper that forces you to lean in, because it feels like what he's saying is probably important and you don't want to miss it.

I cough and everyone stares at me.

"Sorry," I say and wince as my words sound like a shout in a church. I notice Trevor across the room with a cup of something. He offers it to Constantine, who sneaks a glance at the rest of the guys, and then gulps it down.

What is going on with that?

"I am Harpocrates, the god of silence," the whispering man continues. I scramble to my feet, Prisha following course. I wouldn't have tagged him for a god. He's small and weaselly looking.

"As well as the god of secrets," he continues, which actually makes me feel a little better. The god of secrets I can relate to. You can't live a life on the pageant circuit without noticing who's had dental work, a nose job, or some cool sculpting on their floppy bits—but everybody knows better than to talk about it.

"The trial I have set for you today is to see who can remain the quietest, the longest."

So…we're playing the quiet game?

After having to wrangle a horse, this almost seems too easy. Like child's play. Except, now that I think about it, I always lost that game.

From across the room Constantine breathes out a sigh of relief. "I'm gonna scream so loud the moment this starts. Then I can lose this boner, and go home."

"Wait, you want to quit?" I ask, to which he nods emphatically.

"Catching a horse was easy enough," he says. "But riding one in this state? No, thank you. And besides, I can't lay on my stomach anymore." He hiccups loudly and then smiles in a sort of cross-eyed way. "Get ready to make some noise!"

He sounds a bit drunk. What was in that cup that Trevor gave him?

"Excuse me," Harpocrates says in a soft voice. "It matters to me not at all if you wish to purposely lose, but wait until the contest begins before you start to chatter."

"Oh no, I'm not trying to lose," I quickly say.

Harpocrates lifts a single eyebrow. "Nor are you trying to win."

I open my mouth to object, but Prisha nudges me. Hard. Okay, so maybe I sometimes don't know when to shut up. But if he saw me carrying that horse last night he'd know how hard I'm trying to win this thing. Although...now that I think about it, I wasn't really trying to win, so much as trying not to lose. So maybe quiet guy has a point.

"Now," Harpocrates turns back to the group. "The person who makes a sound first will have to give up their powers to the person who lasts the longest. You have five minutes to prepare."

Across the room, Trevor lies down. Constantine joins him, slipping down to the floor in a way that makes me think Trevor most definitely put something in that cup. Malik shifts into his lion form and pads over to an empty area with a circle of sun, circling twice before settling in. Like a true cat, he's out in seconds.

"Unfair," I mumble but I try to get comfy too. Rada sits with her legs crossed, maybe trying to do some kind of meditation. Zahara flies to the roof and settles in on a rafter. Sophia levitates a few feet off the ground looking a bit bored.

Alaric takes a paperback book from the back pocket of his pants. It's worn and yellowed. He leans against the wall, letting his long legs stretch out in front of him, and starts to read.

Harpocrates whisper rings out through the room. "We will begin in five, four, three, two, one. Silence."

It's so quiet the silence is loud. My ears fill with a ringing and I'm afraid to swallow much less adjust myself. I don't have a lot of padding on my butt and I'm already uncomfortable on this stone floor. I shift awkwardly, doing my best not to let my sneakers squeak. Harpocrates hadn't just said that we couldn't talk—we aren't supposed to make sound.

Oh my gods...what if I have to sneeze?

I glance around, suddenly nervous.

In his corner, Constantine struggles into a sitting position, his mouth falling open as if he's trying to say something. He seemed sincere about being ready to say buh-bye to his boner and hello to his homeland. But he can't seem to manage it. His eyes roll back into his head and he looks on the verge of collapse. Trevor neatly catches Constantine just before he would've—loudly—crashed to the floor. Gently, but most importantly—silently—Trevor eases Constantine down to the stone floor, slipping me a wink when he sees I'm watching.

But why would he do that? Why would Trevor help Constantine when he wants to go home and eliminating him puts all of us one step closer to winning? I don't understand what's going on, but it almost feels like Constantine has been slipped a roofie, and that's not okay with me.

I shoot my hand up into the air, wondering if there's a special dispensation for tattletales, when suddenly the room is filled with a deafening roar of thunder.

My eyes snap to Prisha, who has a horrified look on her face. She shakes her head as Harpocrates approaches her.

"No," she says. "It's not my fault."

But Harpocrates doesn't answer. Apparently, he's playing the game with us. Instead he clamps her arm securely to her upper arm and leads her out. As Prisha's pleas for a re-do grow softer, I lower my hand.

This is clearly an all or nothing version of the quiet game, and anything I say—even a warning that Constantine may need a doctor—will be counted against me.

My eyes flick to Rada, but she's out in deep meditation, probably concentrating on smooth talking more horses, or maybe thinking about the perfect symmetry of an archery target.

Poor Prisha. She's the loser so she's out. It's single

elimination so the rest of us are safe, and who really wants uncontrollable thunder as a power, anyway? I mean, I've spent enough of my life stitching on a smile while holding farts in.

What Edie told me last night comes back to me. You don't have to *win* to *not lose*. I get it now. That girl deserves a medal for mentoring.

I stand, stretch, slap my butt a few times to wake it up, then announce, "I'm out."

I'm not gonna win this thing and in the process lose my damn mind. No way is that a good trade-off. I'd rather get out of here and bond with Whiskey. Maybe I'll check in on Prisha. I know she'll be bummed that a girl was the first one out after all, and doubly bummed that it was her.

On my way out, I stop beside Trevor. Leaning down I grab a handful of his hair and bring him close, my lips against his ear.

"You drugged Constantine," I say.

His eyes go wide with pretend innocence. I tighten my grip on his hair.

"I saw you. All I want to know is he's okay or if I should get one of those healer type people in here?"

Trevor gestures to where Constantine is sleeping, his mouth hanging open slightly and a little bit of drool making its way down his cheek. Reaching up, Trevor taps gently on my hand that's holding his hair. After a moment, I release him. He smiles at me and then crawls toward Constantine and gestures for me to follow.

Taking my hand in his, Trevor guides my fingers until they cover Constantine's wrist. After a moment, I feel the solid beat of his pulse.

I look up at Trevor and our eyes meet. His hand still holds mine. Slowly he lifts my hand and brings it to his lips. Without a sound, Trevor kisses each of my knuckles. Then flipping my hand open, he peels open my fingers and places one last kiss in the center of my palm.

The whole time his eyes continue to stare straight into mine. Pure naughtiness is in them, along with a dare. Or a promise. I'm not sure which.

As I'm still deciding Trevor's other hand drifts across my collarbone and then further south, skimming the v of my T-shirt.

Abruptly, I pull away and scramble to my feet, glaring down at Trevor. Did he really think I was gonna let him silently feel my up in front of all the other contestants? What sort of girl does he think I am?

I glance around to see if anyone was watching. Sophia smirks at me and mouths something that looks like whore. Everyone else seems to be in their own world...except Alaric was watching too. Right now he's looking down at his book, but the tips of his ears are fiery red and there's a stiffness to his posture that tells me he saw everything.

"You're a jerk," I tell Trevor just as Harpocrates grabs hold of my arm to escort me out. Trevor just smiles at me, so I give him the finger too, and add, "You'll get yours, buddy."

Honestly, though, I don't know if that's true. I've been around long enough to know that assholes don't always get their comeuppance.

But if Brandee Jean has anything to say about it—Trevor will.

———

I can't find Prisha anywhere. I think she's been spirited away.

I guess they had us clear the day for the competition, 'cause there's nothing on my class schedule. I enjoy a leisurely breakfast and then make my way to the stables.

Whiskey manages to shit himself upon my arrival, which is not exactly encouraging. Luckily, not all the Amazons are like Lilliana. A few teach me the basics of horse care and show me how to slowly start training Whiskey. First, I'm supposed to rest a blanket across his back to let him get accustomed to having weight there, and slowly work up to him wearing a saddle.

"Slowly is the key," a black-haired Amazon tells me. "It will take time. But…" She eyes Whiskey, who hasn't even flicked his tail, his eyes locked on my every breath. "With this one the problem might be getting him to move."

I really hope the second part of Artemis's contest isn't a race. It would be awesome if she took a page from Harpocrates and we were asked to see which mount could be quiet the longest.

"You and me, boy!" I say, flipping Whiskey the peace sign. I hear his teeth grind, but that's about it.

I take my lunch to the Harpocrates temple and find a few more contestants have been eliminated. Apparently Constantine started to snore and that made Sora giggle. I join them, all of us gathered outside the closed doors of the quiet room.

"What happened to you throwing the trial?" I ask Constantine.

"I wanted to!" he says. "But I couldn't even talk. It was like I was paralyzed."

Yep. Roofied.

"You had the right idea, anyway," Sora tells me. Gods, he's beautiful. I look away so I'm not just staring at him open-mouthed. "I wasn't going to win that," he goes on. "But I'm competitive so I wasted four hours of my life."

The door opens and Zahara is escorted out, along with Trevor. Trevor is covered in…something white and black that looks like it belongs on my truck's windshield. Oh my gods is that...?

"This is totally unfair," Trevor is saying. "I get covered in harpy excrement and I'm the one who's disqualified?!"

Zahara laughs wickedly. "I really had to go and I thought I could slam a doot quietly but…"

"Nice!" I hold my hand up for Zahara to high-five it. As her talon connects with my palm, I turn to Trevor. "You deserved that."

He grins at me, unrepentant and unabashed. "My dad does always say that I'm a little stinker."

I try to hold back a smile, but can't. Trevor is awful, but I do love a guy who can laugh at himself.

"So everyone in there is now basking in your turd smell?" Constantine asks. "You are evil."

Zahara shrugs. "Those stuck up jerks deserve it. Not Rada, though. I feel bad for Rada."

The door opens again and Alaric is let out. "Foul, disgusting, disgraceful," he mutters.

"So it's down to Malik, Sophia, and Rada, right?" I ask.

"Well, no use crying over spilled…whatever this is," Trevor says, raising his arms. "I'm going to go clean up."

"I'll walk with you," I tell him, keeping a few feet between us.

When we're out of earshot I ask him about the drink he gave Constantine. "What are you trying to pull? You could have seriously hurt Constantine."

"Please. You were just talking to him. Obviously, he's fine." Trevor gestures behind him toward where Constantine is now sitting. It's true, he does look fine. And actually less miserable than I've ever seen him before.

"Well, he did say he hasn't been sleeping well. Maybe that's why he passed out so quickly."

"Exactly," Trevor quickly agrees. "I was just helping him

out. The poor guy wants to throw in the towel because of the unfortunate side effects of his power but he needn't."

"Why the hell would you want to help him?"

"Would you believe that I'm a good person?" He gives me that devilishly wicked grin.

"No, absolutely not."

"You have wounded me," he tells me, hand on heart. "I think we should hug it out."

"No way," I squeal. "You just want to cop a feel."

"And I think you'd let me if no one else was around." He makes a big show of looking in all directions. "We do seem to be alone now."

"Actually, we're not. I count you, me, and a whole lot of stink lines."

"What's a little feces between friends?" he asks, arms wide, coming at me.

I back up and run right into someone. Oh my, someone with one heck of an ab pack. I raise my face and realize this Oxford is familiar.

"You two are such children,"Alaric says.

Trevor changes into Alaric, mimicking his expression. "I am an arrogant prig with the sense of humor of a boiled egg," he says.

"How droll," Alaric says.

Trevor changes back into himself. "At least Rick didn't win either," he says, his gaze clashing with his brother's.

It's clear Trevor's trying to get under Alaric's skin, but it doesn't work. Alaric just shrugs and turn away.

Trevor, after a moment, shifts his attention back to me. "Alright love, now I really have to get in a shower." He gives me a wink.

"Yes, you do," I agree, thinking about Trevor in the shower. I shake my head. Get it together, girl. I've got a competition to win, and that won't happen if I'm thinking about the boys' bums.

Or about boys who are total butts.

For some reason Alaric is still standing nearby. I give him my haughtiest glare and then spin on my heel, heading back to Harpocrates's shrine to find out who else couldn't stand Zahara's bird bomb.

Alaric falls into step beside me. "He's playing with you. It's because he doesn't take you seriously as competition."

My stomach clenches. That's sorta why I assumed Trevor was helping Constantine. Help the weaker competitors through the early rounds, so they're easy pickings in the later ones. But Trevor hasn't helped me. He's just flirted and...played with me.

But I'm playing with him too, right?

"I know you're just jealous of him," I say, because I gotta say something. "You're worried he's gonna steal your title."

Alaric laughs in this brittle sort of way. "No, I'm worried that one day he'll push me in front of a bus so he can steal the title. Honestly, the title would be of little concern to me at that point, as I'd be dead."

"He would never!" I say, although honestly, I'm not entirely sure. "You're just being paranoid."

"Perhaps," Alaric nods. "We were only children the time he nearly drowned me in the lake behind our estate."

I gasp. "He didn't."

"He said it was a joke. That he didn't mean to hit me in the head with the boat ore."

"Well maybe it was an accident."

Alaric slants a look my way that makes it clear he thinks I'm a fool. "I don't like to meddle, but I felt honor-bound to warn you about Trevor. He will not forget that you are his competition. You should not forget it either. Also, this morning I saw him having a tête-à-tête with Hades—" Alaric stops and shakes his head. "Never mind."

"Hold up," I grab hold of Alaric's arm and pull him to a stop.

He looks down his nose at me, obviously frustrated by my superior strength. "Please resist the urge to dislocate my shoulder again."

"Don't change the subject. I wanna know more about this titty-tits he had with Hades. They got some sort of sex thing going on?"

"Tête-à-tête is French."

"Oooh. So super kinky then, huh?"

Alaric sighs heavily. "It means a private conversation between two people."

I throw my hands up in disgust. "Then why didn't you just say that to begin with?"

"I apologize. In truth, I shouldn't have mentioned it at all. I only saw them for a brief moment. I heard nothing of what was said. It could have been an innocent chance meeting."

"But you don't actually believe that, right?"

Alaric glances at me and then away. "I don't want to pass along half-baked theories based on something I saw."

"But you don't trust him. You told me not to trust him. And he once tried to kill you and you're afraid he'll do it again."

"Not afraid," Alaric corrects. "Just wary."

I frown up at him, realizing there might be more there than I suspected. "I don't get it."

"He's my brother," Alaric says in his stuffy way, that for some reason is starting to grow on me. "I don't like him. I don't trust him. Even though he would not hesitate to toss me under a passing bus, I will not do the same to him. He's blood."

I don't say anything to this. I don't know what to say. It's a pretty impressive little speech. And I can't help but think, with that sort of loyalty, Alaric would be a pretty great guy to have on one's side.

In bed, my traitor brain adds.

I quickly shake that thought away. Alaric is so not my type.

Anyway, as he himself pointed out, he and Trevor are blood. And I bet there's some things they have in common.

Neither of them is gonna forget that I'm the competition. And both of them are determined to win.

———

Rada carries the day.

Malik's lion form almost gave him the win. He was planning on sleeping through the whole contest. But Zahara's amazing asshole exodus was too much for his sensitive nose. He sneezed in his sleep.

That left Sophia and Rada. Pissed at losing and at having his nap interrupted, Malik zapped them both with lightning on his way out. He insists it was no worse than a little static electricity. Sophia cried out and was eliminated. She walked out with all her hair sticking straight up, which was a damn pleasure to witness.

Rada was so deep in her meditative trance that Harpocrates had to raise his voice to rouse her, which only impressed him all the more. He walked out of the quiet room holding one of her arms in the air, pumping it viciously, a silent celebration of her…silence.

As word went around campus that it was down to the final three—and one of them was Rada—the Amazon students had begun gathering outside. Obviously, all of the Amazons are entirely behind my roomie, shouting and stomping as Harpocrates quietly declares her the winner. A few of them even send arrows flying, narrowly missing her head, and landing with a thunk in the wall behind her. This must be some sort of high compliment, because Rada bows deeply, blushing.

I'm clapping too, jumping up and down. I stick my fingers into my mouth and let out a wolf whistle. Beside me, Alaric stops his polite golf clap to give me some side-eye, but I don't let his attitude bother me.

Nobody's going to poop on this parade. My roomie just inherited thunder.

15

———

The transfer of power ceremony is after dinner.

I was sort of hoping us girls could have a little celebration for Rada mixed with some commiseration for Prisha.

But no one's seen Prisha all day.

Zahara disappeared with Sora after they were whispering and giggling together. She told me they were going to check out his water horse, but she gave me a wink that told me it was code for something else. And I think that something else was sex. I've gotten used to Zahara's appearance, but still my mind is struggling to understand how she managed to hook up with the hottest guy here.

Not that I'm jealous. I don't like kissing with my eyes open, but if I was with Sora, I can't imagine closing my eyes to his beauty.

With my other two girls gone, I've stuck by Rada as much as possible. The Amazons have been jostling me, anxious to claim her as their own. We're surrounded by well-wishers at dinner. Including Lilliana. She actually has the nerve to shove herself in between Rada and me. Then she points at the table where the rest of the contestants are sitting and suggests I might be more comfortable over there. Rada intervenes and tells Lilliana to be nice.

I definitely do not want to sit with the other contestants. The atmosphere at their table is gloomier than a January afternoon. Nobody even laughs when a still drowsy Constantine falls face-first into his plate, spattering Sophia with mashed potatoes. After screeching something about commoners, Sophia levitates with anger and flings a gigantic glob of potatoes in Rada's direction.

Lilliana, without hesitation, puts an arrow straight through it. Which would be cool, except she jabs me hard with her bow as she moves it into position, and I'm pretty sure it's not an accident. Also, the mass of mashed taters rains down on us and instead of just Rada picking it out of her hair, we all gotta do it.

I guess it's sorta a girl-bonding type thing, but not really what I was hoping for.

Finally, everyone starts to make their way from the dining hall to the auditorium where the ceremony will be held.

"So, does anyone know what the transfer ceremony is like?" I lean into Rada, before she gets snatched away again.

"No," she admits, her smile losing some of its shine. "I hope it's not something that will hurt Prisha."

"Or you," I add, squeezing her wrist as Taylor pulls her away from me, double-checking something on her clipboard as she leads Rada to the stage.

I spot Zahara and make my way to her, but as I spot what's sitting on her other side, I can't help but hesitate. But Zahara is already waving for me to join them.

"Hey," I say to Zahara. "Did you have a nice afternoon visiting Sora's water horse?"

"Oh yeah," Zahara grins. "I saw the water horse. I rode it too."

I smile back, but honestly I have no idea if we're talking about Sora's horse or his merman dick.

"This is my mentor, Shehelb," Zahara says, introducing me to the thing sitting next to her. "She's a manticore."

"She?" I'm about to ask, because that's not the pronoun I would have picked first. But I'm smart enough to tamp down on it. "Pleased to meet you," I say, but I have no idea whether to attempt a shake or not. Shehelb has the face of a human, but the body of a lion, and is sporting a pair of wings that would look at home on something I'd spray Raid on.

"Where is your mentor?" Zahara asks.

"Oh, Edie popped in yesterday," I tell her. "Are they supposed to be here for the ceremony?"

"Quite a few others are. Malik's in particular is hard to miss," she admits, her eyes following the easy stroll of a panther as he prowls through the crowd. I mean, it's a nice looking cat, but I'd think having spent her whole life in the paranormal world it would take more than a sharp set of claws to impress Zahara.

Then he shifts into his human form, and I totally get it.

"Seriously, how is everyone here not pregnant right now?" I ask, and a bunch of Amazons toss me dirty looks. I couldn't care less, though. I'm straightening my clothes and making sure my hair looks good. Because Mr. Cat Man is coming my way.

"Hey Zahara!" he says first, and then to my amazement, he leans over the seats to kiss her cheek.

"Jordan, I just found out that you're Malik's mentor," she says in a voice that's definitely different than the one I normally hear. It's husky and totally flirtatious.

"Yeah." He shrugs. "Small world, huh?"

Zahara turns to me and her mentor, including us in the

conversation. "Jordan and I went to summer camp together ages ago. It was this one-time thing to try and broker peace between monsters and shifters. Of course, us kids were way more into spin the bottle than politics. At first no one would kiss me. Except Jordan." Her eyes go soft as she looks at him.

"Hell yeah, I did," Jordan says with an enthusiastic nod. "You used tongue. Nobody else even tried, but you went for it. You totally blew my mind."

Zahara smiles and gazes up at him through her lashes, cranking the flirt factor up to its highest power. "I was hoping we could catch up, find out if you've learned anything new in that department, but I hear you've got a pretty serious relationship now?"

Suddenly bashful, Jordan shrugs and shoves his hands into pockets. "Yeah, I got hit with Hepatitis and never looked back."

Looking a little deflated, Zahara sinks back into her chair. "By the way, this is one of the other contestants, Brandee Jean."

"Hi," he says, looking me right in the eye, gaze not wandering anywhere else. "I'm Jordan, Malik's mentor."

"Hi," I say, and then not caring about the whole girlfriend thing, I drop my voice into a sultry tone I only use for contest judges and police that pull me over. I need to have a talk with Zahara and explain that flirting isn't something that's done with an end goal of getting into a guy's pants. Sometimes just the flirting itself can be fun.

If you do it right.

"You're Brandee Jean, Edie's mentee, right?"

"You know Edie?" I ask. "I just love her. I mean, not like that. I'm into guys."

"Cool, me too," Jordan says, and I'm instantly deflated. "I mean, I love Edie," he clarifies.

"Oh?" I perk right back up, only to realize what he just said.

He smiles, following my thoughts. "Platonically, I love Edie," he says. "I took a swipe at her, but she wasn't into me."

"Um, how?" I ask, and next to me Zahara makes some sort of guttural noise of agreement.

Malik shows up beside Jordan, and they both shift back into cats, threading their way to the aisles, where they can stretch out. On stage, Athena approaches the podium. Behind her, two chairs are arranged facing each other, the length of the stage in between them. Other gods start to come up to the front. I spot Artemis and Hades, Demeter, Harpocrates, plus a handful I don't recognize. They line the back of the stage. When Prisha is brought out, a hush falls over the crowd.

"Ladies and…gentlemen," Athena still struggles getting the phrase out. "Welcome to the first transferal ceremony. Before we begin today, I want to address the zombie situation. I appreciate that you ladies resisted the urge to speculate and discuss the topic amongst yourselves. As I always say, 'Not everything you hear is good for talk.'"

Around me, several Amazon heads nod in agreement with this.

I gotta admit, this is the most impressive thing I've seen from the Amazons yet. The pageant scene practically ran on gossip, but not once today did I hear a single peep from anyone about how one of their own got zombiefied and then trampled by horses.

Athena continues, "My uncle, Hades, wants to offer an apology for this incident and his assurances that this will never happen again."

There is a threat in Athena's voice as she announces this and from the way Hades scowls and drags his feet as he approaches her podium, I'm guessing she already made some pretty big threats to his face.

"Hey, uh, girls—" he begins, but Athena quickly cuts him off.

"Not girls. They are Amazon warriors."

Hades looks at her with ill-disguised annoyance. "Fine. Amazon warriors, sorry about the thing with the zombie girl —er, zombie Amazon warrior—this morning. Okay?"

He turns to Athena. "So that was the part where I apologized. You got that, right?" She nods regally and he continues. "Anyways, it wasn't my fault. As you all know, the world's a mess right now, which means it's busy season down in the underworld. Lots of people dying and needing to be sorted out. Meanwhile, I'm up here, because this is where Athena wanted the contest, so I can't be directly overseeing everything that's going on. I put a new assistant in charge while I'm gone, this bat shifter kid. Frankly, he's not underworld material, but he's there, so we work with what we got. Anyway, zombies gotta be kept on a tight leash, but obviously the kid let a few slip. He oughta be the one apologizing, but he's not here, so really when I said that I was sorry, I really meant that he was."

This is seriously the worst apology ever. First off, it's not my fault, secondly, zombies gonna zomb.

Once more Hades looks to Athena. "Okay, that what you wanted? We good?"

Her lip curled in a sneer, Athena flicks a hand at him. "Begone, Uncle. I've had enough of you for today. We'll complete the ceremony without your help."

He looks like he's gonna object, but he must see something in Athena's eyes that makes him think better of it. With a shrug, Hades disappears from the stage.

A serene smile on her face, Athena turns back to the crowd. "Now Amazons, let us give our full attention to Rada.

It is no surprise that one of our own is the first to claim two of Zeus's powers for herself."

There's polite clapping as Prisha makes her way to one of the chairs, a woman I presume to be her mentor walking alongside her.

The gods lined up at the back of the stage watch impassively as she passes them. If any of the gods gathered here are disappointed by Prisha's loss and Rada's win, they're doing an excellent job of disguising it.

From the other side of the stage, Rada emerges, towering over her mentor. In the aisle, Jordan roars, then remembers himself and shifts into a human form.

"That's my girlfriend!" he announces. "Hey, Hepa! I love you, baby!"

The mentor with Rada covers her face, apparently embarrassed. By what, I certainly don't know. She's cute, for sure, with girl-next-door good looks. But I wouldn't rate her above a California four. Jordan shifts back into a panther when a few Amazons draw a bead on him for being so openly enthusiastic about Hepa. He skulks lower to the ground, where he'll be less of a target, but his eyes never leave Rada's mentor, and he's openly purring.

Rada and Prisha face each other, both of them holding their heads high. Athena begins to murmur something, and at first I think the mic system must have gone out, but then I realize it's not words…not English, anyway.

The other gods join in the chant, and a light begins to glow in Prisha's chest. Alarmed, she looks down, her hand going to the spot. I grab Zahara's hand, but Prisha doesn't appear to be in any pain. As the gods' volume grows, so does the brightness inside of her. They extend their arms, and motion to it, beckoning the light to come forward.

It travels up Prisha's throat and into her mouth, her skull

brilliantly lit like an X-ray in reverse. The gods move their hands in unison, directing the light toward Rada.

Hepa leans down and says something to Rada that makes her eyes go wide with surprise. At first, she looks worried, but Hepa puts her hands on either side of Rada's face, and must give her some kind of mentor pep talk.

Rada nods, faces the light, and opens her mouth as widely as she can.

I notice that some of the gods' arms are shaking with effort, as if holding Prisha's power in a sustained manner is difficult. I can't help but wonder what it would do to Rada if it simply went full tilt into her mouth. The light gets closer to her lips, and then it's in her mouth and sliding down Rada's throat. Every muscle in her body is taut, spectacularly outlined as the light settles in her chest.

The gods lessen their volume and the light begins to fade.

Everyone lets out a sigh of relief. Even Rada. Except it comes out like a thunder clap.

"Sorry," she apologizes to the auditorium. "Sorry everybody, sorry!"

Laughter answers her, and even Prisha seems a little relieved to be free from her disobedient ability. She gives Rada a hug, and there's another rumble, this one reverberating the entire auditorium.

"Oh gods," I say to Zahara. "I really hope she gets that under control soon, or neither one of us is going to be getting any sleep."

"Maybe she'll get lucky and the next winner will be whoever is the loudest," Zahara says, winking at me.

"Oh, Brandee Jean can get loud," I tell her. "No special powers necessary."

Zahara laughs, and we're both on our feet, clapping for Rada. When she raises her arms, the auditorium goes wild for her, her fellow Amazons thrilled by her victory.

I'm happy for my roommate, I really truly am. But a small part of me can't help but worry how that feeling might change if it were to come down to just the two of us.

All those Amazons would be behind Rada, cheering her every step of the way.

And then there'd be poor little me, who even my own mentor considers a long shot.

16

Even though I've been at Amazon Academy for a bit, I have yet to master my riding class. A lot of that is due to the fact that I've been competing for Zeus's crown.

The few classes that I've attended I've spent on the sidelines, watching the Amazons, like Rada and Lilliana, be outright badasses. Meanwhile, I cast forlorn glances at Whiskey, while he side-eyes me like he's secretly plotting a prison break.

Rada has a mount she's trained since childhood, but for the purposes of the competition, that mare is sitting out while Rada trains the stallion she captured in her trial—Madathan. He's an impressive dappled gray, and Rada keeps bragging that he's eighteen hands. I nod and try to look impressed even though I have no idea what that means.

The riding class—Bareback Ride & Shoot—had me snickering when I saw my schedule, but the instructor—a goddess named Epona—wanted nothing to do with my jokes. When I couldn't get Whiskey to leave the stables, she informed me that a girl with no horse was not welcome in her class, and neither was my sense of humor.

The next class, I dragged him out of the stable (quite literally—he refused to move his legs), leaving ruts that looked like someone had taken an ATV to Epona's immaculate equestrian field.

My last few attempts in class have not impressed her, either. Even though Rada told me we should train our mounts to a saddle for the purposes of the competition, the first time I'd carried one out to the field, Epona actually gave me a welt across the cheek with her riding crop.

I went after her, ready to pull Epona off her horse by her big, blonde braids, but Rada held me back, whispering urgently into my ear a reminder that this is a bareback riding class, which means no saddles. Later in our room, she explained that in general Epona likes horses better than people, but she really hates anyone who misuses a horse. And she definitely hates me because of how messed up Whiskey is. You'd think maybe the lady could focus her ire on Artemis, who decided to make bagging a horse part of the competition. But no, I'm the bad guy. And so I find myself at the top of yet another god's shit list.

The welt faded, but the damage to my pride remained, like the time that Prissy Highbanks lined my Diva cup with Icy Hot. I'd made it through my tap routine in record time, but the burn lingered.

Today the rest of the Amazons in Epona's class are exhibiting how very well they can do exactly what the name of the class implies—ride bareback while shooting their bows. It's astonishing. Rada wraps her long legs around Madathan, muscles tightly defined as she swings low, hiding most of her body behind his as he gallops past the target. I can barely see her red hair skimming the ground as she releases an arrow from under the crook of Madathan's neck.

It whistles through the air and then lands with a thunk in the center of the target's bullseye.

"Nice," Lilliana says, admiration in her voice as she brings her own mount—a white mare—into the ring. "Rada will send these *napos* back to where they come from in no time."

"What's *napos*?" I ask Zahara, under my breath.

She pretends to think for a second—something she does as a special favor to me, since she knows how much it freaks me out every time she can just instantly recall the answer to just about anything, with the gift of Zeus's knowledge.

"It's Greek for *shit head*," she tells me.

"Hey, we're not all *napos*," I shout back at Lilliana. "Trevor is the only one Zahara slammed a doot on."

It's not the right thing to say. Pretty much me saying any words at all to Lilliana immediately make them not the right ones, because she circles her mount back around to where I and the rest of the contestants are standing with our horses, most of them still too skittish to be ridden. I silently swear at myself for drawing her attention.

Like Mama always said, if you can't keep your legs shut, at least keep your mouth shut.

But it's too late now. Lilliana is eyeing me and Zahara, as Rada circles back around the other side of the ring, her brow furrowed as she watches her fellow Amazon.

"So," Lilliana says. "You can run your mouth, but not your horse. That about right?"

There's a smattering of giggles, the loudest coming from Sophia, who has been feeding her horse sugar cubes since she caught him. He nuzzles her snazzy riding jacket, looking for more.

"I can run my horse just fine, thank you very much," I sniff at Lilliana. "There is absolutely nothing wrong with Whiskey," I insist, walking my fingers up his snout, and emphasizing his name with an affectionate tap between his eyes.

He falls over into a dead faint.

Laughter rises all around me, mostly from my fellow contestants—I easily pick out Sophia's and Trevor's among them. But Alaric frowns, his eyebrows coming together in a little peak above his nose. He probably has more money riding on me for the next trial and is now doubting the wisdom of that choice.

Well, he can kiss my hair-sprayed ass. And everyone else in this paddock, too. Without thinking, I square my shoulders and grab Lilliana's reins just as she's about to ride away.

"I challenge you to a race!"

"You what?" Lilliana asked, her eyes wide. "Are you serious, *napos*?"

"Oh I'm dead serious, *napos*-eater," I say, which technically translates as *shithead-eater*, but it must sound good enough because everyone around us goes, "Oooooooooo."

"Very well," Lilliana tosses her hair, unconcerned. But she should be. She is in desperate need of a hot oil treatment. "Shall we?"

She nods her head toward the track, and I agree with a tilt of my own head. Rada slips off her horse, landing next to Whiskey, who is still out cold on the ground.

"BJ, are you insane?" she asks. "You've never even sat on Whiskey… and I think he might be dead."

"Oh, he's not dead," I say, giving him a casual nudge with my toe. "He's taking a nap."

Alaric joins us, his serious gaze following the rest of the crowd as they head toward the track, most of them cheering Lilliana, and a few looking back at me to see if I'll follow.

"How about if we all participate?" Alaric suggests. "Might be good for the rest of us to get a taste of what it's like."

Easy for him to say. He already sits his horse like he was born in a saddle…which, come to think of it, he might have been. I'm sure his family's English estate probably has all kinds of things like flowers and ponds and geese and horses that don't fall down when you tap their heads.

"Go ahead," I say, trying not to be jealous when Zahara and Malik easily swing up onto their own mounts, guiding them toward the track. "I'll catch up."

I say the last thing like it might be a real possibility, but the truth is that I have to manually get Whiskey to his feet, which involves a lot of propping and relying on gravity and physics to get him on all fours. Once that's done, he just kind of side-eyes me, like he's hoping I'll forget that he exists. Which is not going to happen.

He exists. I exist. And the two of us need to become one if we're going to not look like absolute *napos*.

"Okay, Whiskey," I tell him. "I'm going to get onto your back now, and you're going to let me."

Sounds simple enough, but without the saddle I don't have a stirrup, so I just have to get my leg as high as it'll go, which is not a problem. Brandee Jean Mason did not win the Straight Razors and Straighter Women contest three years in a row with a pair of stubby little nub grinders underneath her.

Once I'm on Whiskey, I start to feel a little better. He's a big fella and I can see far from up here…too bad the first thing in my line of sight is the track, where everyone is waiting on me to start the race.

And also too bad that I don't know how to make Whiskey go over there. I kick him a few times in the ribs, which only makes him shudder. I slap his bum a couple times but there's no response. Guess he's not into that type of horseplay.

I try everything I've watched the Amazons do to make their mounts go, and none of it is working.

It reminds me of Chessy Jamison, a girl from the All-Midwest A-Cups Extravaganza. It was supposed to be for the less endowed, and technically as a C-cup, I wasn't eligible. But Mom made me not drink anything for three days and then Saran-Wrapped my chest, squeezing me in at the last minute. Chessy, on the other hand, was an all-out A. And by that I mean there was no chance of anything falling out. She was so flat-chested she went without a shirt at the pool all through seventh grade. With her pixie cut, nobody knew any better until they spotted her tampon string one time.

Regardless, Chessy should've had Miss A-Cup all wrapped up. But she balked—and hard—during the talent portion. They announced her name twice, but Chessy refused to take the stage. Her mom showed up behind the curtain and told her she'd better haul ass or she'd *make* her haul ass.

Chessy had this whole Victor/Victoria act that really played up her androgynous look. But in the All Midwest A-Cup Extravaganza, she wasn't the only girl who could sometimes pass for a boy, and as luck would have it, the contestant before her did a number from the exact same show. She did it better than Chessy too. The crowd went wild. Some of the fathers actually woke up enough to clap.

Absolutely panicked at the idea of doing the same thing, but worse, Chessy had frozen. Gone dead still, just like Whiskey.

Until her mom gave her a wet willy.

She'd popped her finger in her mouth, slicked it up good, and just jammed it right into Chessy's ear. The girl had gone onstage like it was the only place on Earth she wanted to be.

"Alright, Whiskey," I say to the immobile horse underneath me. "It's like Mama always says, sometimes you gotta stick your fingers places you'd rather not." And I spit on my fingers, and dig them into his ears.

The reaction is immediate, and impressive.

Whiskey takes off like a bolt, all of the muscle underneath me bursting forward with a speed that would have thrown me off if I didn't have my fingers buried so deep. It's useful for steering too, so I point him towards the track. The assembled crowd scatters, and Lilliana screams, "Are we starting?" as I fly past her.

I have time to yell back, "Yes!" But that's about it.

I'm being thrown about like a rag doll with half her stuffing, and it takes all I've got to catch my breath. We round the first bend before I figure out that I'm clenching my legs too tightly. With the power of Zeus in every part of me, Whiskey is starting to flag because I'm cutting off his oxygen. I release a little, and he rewards me with a burst of speed, his mane flying into my mouth as all the careful braids I put into it fall apart under the breakneck pace.

I bend low over Whiskey's neck, like I've seen Rada do, and peek under my arm to see if anyone is behind me. There's a cloud of dust that we've kicked up, and only one shadow breaking through it. Only one rider even close to me. They break through the cloud and I see that it's Sophia, her eyes bright despite the dirt.

"*Napos,*" I say under my breath as we clear the second turn, more riders gaining on us.

I got Whiskey to take off by giving him a wet willy, but I don't know how to tell him to keep going, or to speed up. And suddenly, I realize why that is. I've got my fingers buried so deep in his ears, he has no idea what I want from him. I pull one out. It comes free with a horrible popping noise I'd rather not think about, but I lean closer to his neck, my mouth near his ear.

"Hey Whiskey," I say. "If we win, I'll get off you."

His speed doubles like I'd just given him fresh batteries. We break through the finish line with no one even near us, Epona standing watch to mark me as the winner.

But I don't have time to relish the victory. I promised Whiskey something, and he wants it. We come to hard stop right away, and I go sailing over his head, rolling ass over ankles.

Still. We won. I get up before anyone else finishes, and go to Whiskey, cradling his head in my arms.

"Good boy," I tell him. "You're a really good boy."

He nods his head, like maybe he agrees, and maybe we've reached an understanding.

Epona walks over, eyeing us like we're something she found at the bottom of a thousand-year-old manure pile.

"Very good," she says, eyeing me up and down.

"Thank you," I say, shaking dirt from my hair. "Guess I'm not so bad at this after all."

She sniffs. "The class is not only Bareback Ride," she reminds me. "It is Bareback Ride & Shoot. You can do only one of the two things. I would say this gives you a solid C."

I nod happily, pleased with that result.

But as I walk away, I remember what Harpocrates said about trying not to lose not being the same as winning. It also occurs to me that if I somehow win this thing, the Amazons are not gonna accept anyone who got a C in riding and shooting.

With a sigh, I turn back to Epona. "So is there any way I could get that grade up with some extra credit?"

17

———

I feel like Whiskey and I have reached an understanding, and my good mood follows me the next morning when the remaining contestants gather before a field of corn for the next trial. No, not a field, I realize after a moment.

It's a maze.

I adjust my pink camo hoodie and change my high heels into silver sparkly sneakers instead. I mean, I *can* traverse a maze in heels and look fierce while doing it, but when given the option, I might as well be stylish *and* comfy.

I hum a little as I spot shine one of the sequins. Good outfit. Good mood.

I think this is gonna be my day to shine.

"You're perky," Rada says.

"Corn," I tell her, sweeping my arms out to encompass the maze in front of us. "You could not put a Wisconsin girl in a more natural habitat. The rest of you might as well quit and go home now. I got this one."

Rada shushes me when a small woman appears before the opening to the corn maze. She's petite and perfect, with alabaster skin and flowing blonde hair. It looks like someone made her out of porcelain. She's too short to be a model, but she could definitely be an actress. Or in a reality TV show about tiny houses.

Artemis towers next to the woman, her height and muscles emphasizing the other woman's diminutive beauty. They look about the same age but Artemis gives her a nod when there is silence and says, "Go ahead, Mother."

"That's Artemis's mom?!" I ask loudly.

"Yes," Rada tells me, adding another shush.

Alaric leans in. "Leto's one of Zeus's conquests."

"Mother to Artemis and Apollo," Zahara confirms.

"Wait, if Zeus is also Artemis's dad, then Athena and Artemis are sisters, right?" I ask.

"God family history is almost as confusing as the aristocracy," Trevor says with a wry smile. "Mostly we just all bang each other and let the plebes sort it out."

"That's…charming," I say. I was going to say *incest*, but then Rada dug an elbow into my ribs. You really do have to be careful with the incest jokes around the gods.

"You will show my mother the respect and courtesy due her," Artemis says, hitting me specifically with a look of intensity, even though everyone was talking. I guess I did start it. I decide to shut up.

But even in the silence that follows, it's hard to hear the tiny goddess; her voice is small and fragile. She sounds almost scared.

"I am Leto, the goddess of hidden things." She stops and pulls Artemis's arm. "You explain it, dear. You're better at"— she waves her hand in the air — "all this."

Artemis steps forward and her booming voice echoes around us. "This trial is about hiding and finding. My mother, Leto, will be somewhere in the maze. In order to win, you have to find her."

Okay, so far so good. Easy peasy. The quiet game. Hide

and seek. It's starting to feel like the gods think humans really are just children...

Artemis continues, "While you are searching the maze for my mother, you will be hunted by a minotaur."

"There it is," says Alaric, almost to himself. When I lean into him, he cups my ear and says, "We're not just seeking Leto; we're hiding, too. You don't want to be caught by the minotaur."

I nod like I know what he's saying and then lean to the other side.

"Minotaur?" I whisper to Rada.

"Head of bull, body of a man. Serious anger issues."

Okay. *Not* so easy then.

"If you get caught by the minotaur you will be returned to the start of the maze," Artemis continues.

"The first one out loses?" Constantine asks, probably thinking how he can easily get caught.

"No. If you are caught and end up back here, you will have to begin again. Points will be added to your total score."

"There's a point system?" Alaric questions.

"Points are bad?" Malik asks.

"Like in golf," Trevor adds.

"Yes. Points are bad. The more you have, the lower you are in the rankings."

"Now there's ranking too?" I ask. My brain is starting to hurt.

Artemis continues her explanation. "The amount of time you remain in the maze will be divided by the times you are caught, made a variable of x, then subtracted from the points you accrue."

"Why does this have to be so complicated?" I sigh.

"The Amazon Algorithm is a time-honored equation," Rada tells us.

"You understand it then?" Trevor asks.

"No. No one really does." She eyes Zahara.

"Don't look at me," Zahara says. "Nobody's cracked it yet.."

Sophia sniffs. "Whatever. It doesn't matter. I'm going to win this in five seconds flat."

"What, like you know something about corn?" I ask, hands on my hips.

"No," she sniffs. "More like altitude."

Oh, duh. Sophia can just levitate over the maze and spot Leto from above. Not to mention easily go aloft anytime she needs to avoid the minotaur. I'm about to complain that this is completely unfair, when her expression of extreme self-satisfaction fades into quite the opposite.

"What's wrong?" Malik asks.

"I can't fly!" Sophia looks panicked now.

"You didn't think it would be that easy, did you?" Zahara asks. She flaps her wings in a half-hearted attempt to become airborne. "I can't fly either."

Artemis booms at us. "No flying over the corn maze. No going through the walls of the maze. No climbing over the walls of the maze. No setting the corn on fire." She runs down the list of things we're not allowed to do, or more accurately of things we won't be able to do.

It quickly becomes obvious to us all that we've been temporarily stripped of our special powers.

"Dammit!" Constantine yells, looking mournfully at the front of his pants, which still stick out a solid five to six inches. "Why do I still have my power?" he demands of Artemis, who only shrugs.

"I don't see how a massive erection will help you in a corn maze," she says.

"A massive erection helps you in only one situation," Constantine says. "And when that trial comes, gods help you all."

"Questions?" Artemis asks.

We stare at her blankly. She turns to Leto. "Go ahead, Mother." Leto nods and disappears.

Artemis looks back at us. "Your time starts…now!"

There's a pause, then a mad rush for the maze. Rada is first to enter and I'm left in her dust. Sophia, still pissed about not being allowed to fly, stomps in. Everyone else runs toward the entrance and I follow, but I have a thought and turn to Artemis.

"Is your mama staying in one place? Or is she moving around like us?" I ask.

Artemis looks me up and down. "You talk too much, Brandee Jean, but in this instance you have used your words well." Something sorta like respect makes her face a little less disapproving. "Once hidden, she'll remain still."

I nod once and enter the maze.

Even though the others were only a few seconds ahead of me, there's no one else around. I turn and the entrance has disappeared. Even the walls seem taller. Looking up, the previously sunny sky is a solid blue-grey. There's a guttural moan from deep inside the maze and it makes me shiver.

This is all the worst horror movie moments rolled into one. Except I still have my shirt on. That's a good thing. As soon as you see a flash of nipple, you can bet its owner is a goner.

If there's one thing I learned by competing in Miss Mighty Maids at the Maize Maze, it's how to navigate the twists and turns of a corny labyrinth. In order to get where you want to go you can't run around all willy nilly like a chicken with its head cut off. You have to go about it a certain way.

I place my left hand on the maze wall and hope the layout doesn't shift on me. If I follow it ceaselessly, I'll go the length of the maze, ending up in the center eventually. It might take for-freaking-ever, but at least I know I'll get there at some point. Like my mama always said, "You can do something right or you can do something fast, but you can't do both."

I start to walk, letting myself meander through the rows, always keeping my hand on the wall. In the distance there's another guttural moan, then a deep cry of outrage. One of the boys must have been caught and forced to start over. I search for them, hoping for a glance of someone else. An arm. A leg. A moving shadow.

But there's nothing. If I hadn't heard that cry, I could almost believe I'm in here all by myself.

Despite being completely alone, I can't stop looking over my shoulder. I got this feeling I can't shake that someone is near. Glancing back once more, I turn a corner and slam straight into Alaric. He also has his hand on the wall.

I scream, then laugh. He actually has a slight smile on his face.

"I must admit," he says. "You gave me quite a fright."

"You?! I almost just peed my pants!" I put my hand to my chest. My heart is racing.

"Oh no you don't!" A voice that sounds like Sophia carries across the maze. "If you put one meaty hand on me I'll remove it from your arm." The silence returns.

"I'd sure hate to be that minotaur," I tell Alaric.

"Certainly. He thought he was the scariest thing in the maze, then he came face to face with Sophia."

I tilt my head. "Alaric, was that a joke?"

He looks put out. "I thought some humor would lighten the tension."

"No, it was really funny," I assure him. It's the least I can do, since I didn't actually laugh at the joke, and it actually was funny. I nod to his hand on the wall. "You know the same trick, huh?"

"We had a hedge maze at the manor. Trevor and I would

sometimes play there." His eyes look kind, like maybe it's a good memory he has of his brother. Suddenly I'm imagining the two of them as small boys, happily running through the grass together. Funny though, I definitely know which one is Trevor in my imagination, because his smile is more of a smirk.

"It's nice you have some good memories of the two of you," I say. "I guess when you were little kids it was easier."

"Yes, I suppose it was a bit easier as small children," Alaric says. "But often it seemed as if Trevor was aware of his bastard status from the moment he was born."

"Trevor told me about his mom dying when he was little."

Alaric stiffens, his hand dropping off the wall. "Did he?" he asks tightly.

"Yeah. He said you were…" I guess there's not a nice way to put it. "He said you were pretty hard on him."

Alaric takes a deep breath. "Not that it's any of your business, but it was *my* mother who died when we were five. My father moved Trevor and his mother into our home before the body was even cold."

I gasp. "Why would he lie about something like that?"

"Why indeed?" He elbows past me. "Your sympathy is misplaced. My brother is a liar and a rogue. He made my childhood hellish, making up perceived slights to tell my father. He wanted to be what he never could—our father's heir."

"Wait," I say, putting a hand on his firm shoulder. He turns to me. "I like you better than him. That's probably not something you care about, but well, I always know where I stand with you. I mean, that place is always miles below you, cause your blue blood elevates you way beyond mere mortals and wannabe beauty queens, but—"

"Brandee Jean. Stop." Alaric holds up a hand.

"Thanks. I was having some word diarrhea there."

"Indeed." Alaric wrinkles his nose. "Well, on that note, we should probably each go our own way."

"Right." I nod and put my hand back on the wall, while Alaric does the same. Carefully we maneuver past one another.

'Brandee Jean," Alaric calls my name once more and I turn back. "Thank you," he says simply and then he turns the corner and is gone from sight.

I think about going after him and telling him that before he stopped me I was about to say I'd really liked kissing him too. But nah. He'd probably just wrinkle his nose and look disgusted again.

With Alaric gone, I'm alone once more. I stretch and shake both arms out, then put my hand back on the wall and move forward—it's the only way I know how to go. Around every bend and corner I think I'm going to run into the minotaur. I don't know who else has been caught and forced to start over.

Strange noises reverberate; there's even a sound of a scuffle. Who would be stupid enough to try and fight the minotaur? I shake my head. At least half of the contestants, that's who. There's more than pride on the line, I remind myself. There's a crown and a lot of power behind it.

I shake off the tension in my shoulders as I continue walking. Being scared of running into the minotaur isn't going to help me. I take several deep calming breaths—in through the nose, out through the mouth—when I realize there's another sound.

I pause.

Yes, a constant in and out sound. Like someone else is taking big deep breaths.

Fear shoots through my body

I know the minotaur isn't going to kill me—it's just

supposed to return me to the mouth of the maze—but holy hell, I don't want to come face to face with it.

Rada's description of it was not flattering, and if running into Alaric almost made me pee my pants, I don't want to imagine what bodily function I might lose control over during a close encounter with the minotaur. And while Artemis didn't specifically say that crapping your pants figured into the Amazon Algorithm—I'm not taking any chances.

The breathing is getting louder and I shrink into the wall. My pink camo tracksuit sticks out like a sore thumb. I think of proper camouflage. Normal green won't do. I picture the perfect outfit made of corn, and my clothes transform. Stalks grow up to cover my face and down to hide my legs. My super strength might have been taken from me for the time being, but it seems our magical uniforms still work. Thank gods for that.

Sometimes it takes a beauty queen to know that the key to survival is a wardrobe change.

I am one with the corn, I think as the breathing grows louder. *I have become the corn.*

The minotaur turns the corner and I try not to scream, or even budge an inch. It has the head of a bull, great and terrifying. But his chest and upper arms belong to a bodybuilder who went all out on the steroids. He stomps forward on cloven feet, pausing right in front of where I'm hiding.

His large head studies the spot where I am doing my best impression of a corn stalk. He knows I'm here, but can't quite find me. The minotaur snorts, sniffing. The warmth of his breath makes me feel ill and the smell makes my eyes water. It's like a barnyard and a graveyard all at the same time.

From far away there's the sound of an argument. Sora and, I think, Malik sound like they're fighting over the correct words to the Scooby Doo theme song. It seems like they're trying to change the words to sound more like "Leto Leto loo, where are you?"

It seems like we've officially reached the point in the competition where some people are getting a little loopy.

For me, the timing couldn't be better.

The minotaur's head turns, then he sprints off in that direction. I stay hidden for a several moments after, my knees shaking with relief. Then I slide to the ground and softly sing under my breath, "Leto Leto loo, where are you?"

By the time I get through all the words I can remember, I feel better. Back on my feet, I change into an explorer's outfit, all tans and greens and earth tones. I even give myself a safari hat and imagine my hair up into a jaunty ponytail, just to boost my confidence.

Mama did always say I should stretch my long graceful neck out more and swing my bottom less if I wanted to be taken seriously. And I'd always tell her I didn't see why I couldn't do both.

So that's what I do now as I start again with one hand on the wall. I raise my chin up high and let my hips swing to the beat of Scooby Doo. Eventually, though, my shoulders sag and my feet drag. It feels like I walk for hours, my hand grazing one wall of the maze while I move forward. I hope my plan is working and I'm not just stuck in an endless loop, wandering the maze forever.

At least I haven't been caught, so even though the Amazon Algorithm may be confusing, there's no way I'm losing this thing.

I round a corner and find someone face down in the path, my toe catching in their ribs. I stumble, falling forward, my knees going into the softness of a stomach. I roll, coming up on my elbows to discover it's Sora.

"Sorry," I say quickly. "I didn't mean to kick you. At least it wasn't your face, right? I mean if I broke your nose or knocked out some of your teeth, I'd never forgive—"

I stop, my words coming to a halt as I realize he's not moving.

"Sora?" I ask, crawling closer to him. "Are you playing dead for the minotaur? Cause he's not anywhere around here, I don't think."

I put a hand on his chest, which doesn't seem to be rising or falling.

Nervous, I start to babble. "Hey, um, I heard you singing the Scooby Doo song and I really liked it and—"

I continue talking as I give Sora a little shake, certain he just got bored and fell asleep. As his head falls back, unblinking, unseeing eyes stare back at me.

Once more, I find myself at a loss for words around Sora. But this time, it's not because he's beautiful.

It's because he's dead.

I might be speechless, but I'm not soundless. I can still scream. Real loud too.

In fact, it's really hard to stop.

18

Screaming doesn't bring help.

I don't know if that's an indication of how little my fellow contestants care about me, or if everyone is too far away to hear. I try calling out again, less frantically, but no one comes. I'd even welcome the creepy mouth breathing minotaur right now, anything to get me back to the start so I can tell Artemis what has happened.

Still no one shows. Not Alaric, with his thin-lipped sarcasm. Not the minotaur, with his cloven hooves. Not even Sophia, with her award-winning side eye. I'm on my own... with a corpse.

Tears start to form, but they're not entirely for myself.

Sora was a nice guy. A total bro, but sweet.

How did this happen? Artemis said the minotaur wouldn't hurt us, which doesn't leave me with any pretty options. Either the minotaur doesn't know his own strength, has a grudge against us that Artemis doesn't know about, or

worst of all—another contestant did this. Any of those would mean that I'm in a lot more danger than I thought.

I wipe my tears and stand, ready to get the heck out of

here. But then I see Sora's beautiful face with his beautiful dead eyes. Crouching down, I help his eyelids close. There, now it just looks like he's taking a nap. I just need to tip-toe away before he wakes up.

Except I don't move. Because Sora isn't sleeping. He's dead. And I can't just leave him here.

Shit.

Without my strength, carrying Sora won't be a picnic. But beauty queens aren't exactly made of fluff. We gotta have good musculature underneath, or all the dieting just makes us look like a sad, plucked chicken. "Stringy," is what Mama used to say of a girl who was nothing but bone and skin.

I pull Sora up into a sitting position and then get behind him and wrap my arms around his middle. Then I stand. He comes up with me, but his feet drag in the dust.

I end up walking backwards, so my legs don't get tangled up with his. It doesn't take long before my arms start to ache. Even worse, I have no idea if I'm going in circles or not. I really need to find Leto or the minotaur or some other person before I completely lose my shit.

Finally, I come across Constantine sitting in the middle of the path, tossing pebbles.

"Oh thank gods." Tears of relief fill my eyes. "Another person."

"Hey BJ. Guess how many times the minotaur has caught me?" He tosses a pebble into the air and catches it. "Ten times. I'm losing this thing if it kills me. Last time *it* actually ran from *me*." He looks up from the ground, for the first time really seeing me—and what I carry. "What's wrong with Sora?" He scrambles to his feet.

"I found him like this. He wasn't breathing and..." My legs give out and I fall to my knees, Sora's body rolling to the ground.

Constantine backs away. "You're messing with me, right? This is a prank?"

"I wish," I tell him, starting to cry again. "So the minotaur didn't ever hurt you, right?" Looking confused, Constantine shakes his head. "That's a relief. Do you think the minotaur will take us to Artemis?"

"Of course, he—" Constantine stops talking as we both hear a snuffling sound from the other side of the corn. With it comes the particular stench of a boy's locker room…if the boys had all been dead for a week.

I say, "I smell him," right at the same time that Constantine says, "I hear him."

"Hey! Hey you, Mister Minotaur!" I start yelling. "Come and get my corn-fed ass!"

I don't know if it's my ass, the corn part, or the fact that it's just his job, but I can just see his bull horns above the corn stalks as he does a complete one-eighty. Half a second later, all eight feet of him is barreling toward us. His giant bull head is fierce and his eyes bright.

I really hope he didn't take my ass comment too literally, but I don't have time to take it back…until he spots Constantine.

The minotaur's face takes on a bull's version of "oh shit." He screeches to a halt, spins around, and immediately runs the other direction.

"Ugh," Constantine sighs. He looks at me apologetically. "Sorry."

But I hardly hear his apology; I'm charging after the minotaur, screaming at him to stop. Utterly panicked, the bull can't hear me. Luckily, the dude obviously spends all his gym time working the weights and none at all on cardio. Even though I'm worn out, but I force my legs to push harder and am able to close the distance between us. Unsure how to actually stop him once I'm close, I take a flying leap at him.

We roll, my cute little safari hat getting crushed and my outfit totally suffused in minotaur musk. He gets to his feet, realizes that I'm not Constantine, and makes a grab for me. I dodge, holding my hands out.

"Wait! Please, Mr. Minotaur. I'm not trying to stop you from doing your job. In fact, I want to get back to Artemis. But I need your help."

He cocks his head at me, interested, like he's listening. But his eyes are going places they don't need to in order for him to hear me.

This might be his maze, but I know this game. I flick my ponytail, bat my eyelashes, and deliver the weirdest come-on line I've ever had to utter. "Can you please carry a body for me?"

His head goes back in the other direction, like a puppy that was just told to poop inside. He's surprised, but after a moment of hesitation, he reaches out a strangely gentle hand. Taking it, I lead him to Sora's body. He stares down at it with a furrowed brow. And then sighs.

Leaning down he scoops Sora up easily, then, he touches my elbow at the same time that Constantine grabs on to my other arm—

Suddenly we're standing before Artemis where she waits at the front of the maze. Catching sight of Constantine first, she huffs loudly.

"Honestly, how many times are you going to get out?" Artemis asks him, clearly frustrated. "You're already losing by a huge margin."

"I don't think I'm losing this one," Constantine says motioning to me and Sora's body, which the minotaur has deposited at my feet before going back into the maze.

"I found him like this. I don't know what happened," I tell Artemis. She barely glances at the body.

"Leto is still not found. You need to return to the maze," she says.

"Excuse me?" I say, in the same tone that Marilyn Montgomery used when the judge of the All Around All Organic Competition accused her of having breast implants. It stopped that judge in his tracks, but Artemis doesn't even blink.

"Your mentors were supposed to explain how dangerous this was," Artemis tells me. "You must compete until there is a winner."

"Someone dies and you don't even care?" Constantine says exactly what I'm thinking. But then he adds two words that were not on my mind. "I quit," he shouts. "I've been trying to quit this whole time! I should never have agreed to participate in the first place, but my sister said it would be good for the pack."

"There is no forfeiture," Artemis tells him, blowing on a small silver whistle that hangs around her neck. Taylor appears, her expression not changing when she sees Sora's body. Instead, she makes a notation on her clipboard, then motions for the Amazons that accompanied her to step forward and carry away Sora's body.

Artemis turns to me. "Whatever your intentions were, this counts against you. The minotaur tagged you, regardless of the circumstances."

"I don't care about that right now," I shout. "Sora is dead, and the minotaur didn't kill him. That means one of the other contestants did."

"You are competing to become the next head of the gods. It comes with a price. Some will pay with their lives."

Constantine and I eye each other. I see the same resolve in his that I feel within myself. I sit right down on the ground and refuse to budge. Constantine does the same. Mama always said you gotta fight for what you believe in. And if you don't believe in it, get in a good crotch shot before you go.

"I'm protesting," I tell Artemis, and fold my arms.

It's just like when the organizers of the Miss Bee's Knees competition were going to require all contestants to use only razors as a form of hair removal, since bees didn't receive a fair compensation from the sale of wax in the beauty industry. We'd all camped out in front of their offices for almost seventy-two hours, tweeting pictures of razor burn and ingrown hairs until they caved.

Artemis snaps her fingers and Taylor puts down her clipboard. She stands in front of me, clearly enjoying what's about to happen.

"Taylor, please physically return BJ to the maze."

Taylor stoops to pick me up, but I didn't grow up on the pageant circuit for nothing. I can throw a fit as well as the next girl, and every toddler knows how to avoid being picked up. I let all my muscles relax, and I fall right through Taylor's grip, slithering to the ground.

"Go limp!" I yell at Constantine, as his own Amazon attempts to move him.

"That's what I've been trying to do this whole time!" he yells back at me.

Before I have a chance to clarify, Trevor suddenly tears through the maze opening, carrying Leto over his shoulder like she's a bag of flour. The other contestants magically appear around us.

Trevor places Leto before Artemis. "Three cheers for me! Hip hip huzzah!" When no one joins in, he shrugs. "I'm the winner. Which one of you losers is the loser?"

He spies me sitting on the ground and gives me a quizzical look, while Artemis announces in her booming voice, "Sora has lost this trial."

I stand up. "That's not all. Tell them what happened."

"Unfortunately, Sora is no longer with us," Artemis says, as if she's RSVPing to a children's birthday.

"Sora is *dead*," Constantine yells. "And this is bullshit. I'm calling my sister and seeing if she can get me the hell out of here."

"Even the Queen of the werewolves cannot stop this competition," Artemis says. "And I advise any of you who still believe this is child's play to revise your opinions.

"Hold on," Sophia says, ignoring Artemis. "Let's go back to the part about Sora being dead. How did he die?"

"How *exactly*?" Zahara adds turning to me.

"I don't know. I just found him in the corn," I tell her. "He didn't even look hurt. I tripped over him. I...I accidentally kicked him." I start to tear up again and Trevor comes over to me.

"Oh, love. Don't worry. It will be okay." I shake him off.

"And you're a liar and a...a dick!" I tell him, wiping away some of my tears. I look up to find Rada staring at me, unfazed by what's going on.

"It was always likely that some of us would die," she tells me. "You should have expected this."

I don't know who to go to for comfort. Trevor is a liar. Rada is stone cold. I feel alone.

Then Alaric's hand is on my shoulder. He gives me a squeeze, like maybe he agrees that all of this is completely insane. He doesn't say anything, but his hand stays in place.

"Trevor has won, Sora has lost. The particulars are not for you to sort out," Leto says in her small voice.

"Athena will let all of your mentors know what has happened. If they feel you are emotionally fragile and need coddling, they will be in touch," Artemis tells us.

Wow. Way to gaslight, Artemis.

I don't want to be alone, but I don't want to be around any of the competitors either. As far as I'm concerned,

Constantine is the only one who's reacting like this is a big deal. But the thing that really makes me want to keep my distance is that I'm convinced one of them killed Sora. It's the only thing that makes sense.

And that sucks. Cause now it's not just the Hunger Games, it's the Hunger Games murder mystery. And honestly, that feels like a little too much.

I go to the stables to sit with Whiskey. His warmth and strong breathing are comforting as I rest against him.

I expect Edie to show up, but she doesn't. Maybe she thinks I don't need the extra support, or that her warning me before the contest about people dying was good enough.

I don't want to go to the power transfer ceremony, but I have to. I owe it to Sora.

Later that evening in our room, I refuse to speak to Rada as I settle on what to wear. I decide to treat the ceremony like a funeral, choosing a tasteful black dress with a long train.

Word of Sora's death has spread, making the ceremony even more of a "must see" event than it was last time. It seems like everyone is there. Gods that I've never seen before line the stage, eager to help with the transfer of power. The audience is full of Amazons, some of them forced to stand in the back. Constantine was nice enough to save a seat for me, so I slip in beside him.

"Any luck getting out of the contest?" I ask.

He shakes his head. "Not yet."

Trevor is on the stage, waiting near the chair that Rada sat in last time to receive Prisha's thunder. With him is a sharp-faced man with cheek bones to die for and shimmery golden skin.

"Who's Trevor's mentor?" I ask Constantine.

"A gorgeous man with shimmery golden skin."

I elbow him. "Yeah, I know that. But who or what is he?"

"He looks like a faerie of some sort." Constantine gives me a wan grin. "Definitely my type."

I reach over to pat his hand, knowing he's trying to keep things from getting too heavy. Somehow we end up holding onto one another as we wait for the ceremony to begin.

It's comforting having him there beside me, especially as I focus on the loser's chair. It's empty, but a willowy girl with bluish skin stands near it, openly weeping. She must be Sora's mentor. After a while, people start to get restless.

"What's going on?" I ask Constantine and he shrugs.

Taylor comes in and all the gods huddle, whispering. Finally, Athena steps forward.

"I am sorry, but there has been a delay."

"What delay?" Trevor asks. "I'm supposed to be getting extra gorgeous."

Athena sighs, the sound carrying though the auditorium.

"Sora's body is missing."

19

———

There is chaos. The gods shouting, Amazons screaming, contestants looking worried.

Except Trevor. Trevor looks remarkably calm for someone who was just told their prize went missing. The shimmering man leans in to discuss the matter and Trevor waves him off.

Constantine actually gets up and leaves. "I've had enough," he tells me. I'm tempted to follow him, but I stay, wanting to see what happens next.

I expect the black boxes to start knitting up around us for another time out. Instead Athena raises an arm to quiet us. The Amazons immediately obey. The gods follow a moment later.

"Trevor," she says. "We have failed in our duty to you. We will find Sora, and we will bestow upon you the powers to which you are entitled."

Trevor nods. "It's okay, really. I mean, my personality plus amazing good looks? It's too much for one mere mortal. I'll wait 'til I'm crowned as a god."

Sora's mentor takes a step toward Trevor and it seems possible she might murder him there and then.

Thankfully, there's an interruption as Constantine walks onto the stage. He's holding a plant, of all things.

"I want to go home!" he says, throwing the plant on the ground and stomping on it. What the hell? What did that poor thing ever do to him? "I. Am. Done." He punctuates each word with a leap as he flies up into the air, coming down on the plant with a heavy thud each time.

"He has actually lost his shit," I say. In front of me Rada nods.

"Talk about slamming a doot," Zahara agrees.

Constantine flicks the hair out of his eyes, a sheen of perspiration on his face. "I know this wasn't a welcome plant. How welcoming has this place been, really? I've had arrows fly at my head. Also, nobody is even a little concerned that Sora was killed. You people don't care about any of us, except maybe Rada. Which makes it pretty obvious that this plant was a test. And I'm betting if our plant dies, we lose." He stomps down again, smearing green goo all over the stage. "Well, it's pretty damn dead. Tell me—did I lose?"

Demeter steps forward out of the huddle of gods. "Yes child, you are correct. It was a test."

Sophia looks like she's about to shit a brick, and I remember that she tossed her plant in a dumpster on the first day. Was it still alive in there?

Demeter continues, "Though I mourn the destruction of this plant, you have achieved your goal and lost the trial." She zooms in on Sophia. "While others have only neglected their plants, you, Constantine, have utterly destroyed yours."

"I'm sorry," Constantine tells the aloe plant at his feet. "But I really want this to be over."

Demeter nods. "We will have a ceremony after all." She

motions to me. "Brandee Jean, you are the winner of my competition."

"What?" I croak the word in a totally not pretty way. But honestly, you can't just declare someone the winner without first announcing the second and first runners up.

"How was that determined?" Alaric asks, frowning.

"By the plants themselves," Demeter says. "Each has been reporting back to me about the level of care and concern that their owner has bestowed upon it. Brandee Jean has not only been giving her aloe plant excellent care, she has treated it like what it is: A living thing."

"I guess talking to my little plant wasn't so goofy after all," I say to Rada.

I go up to the stage with mixed feelings. Sora is dead, his body missing, and I just won a competition no one knew was happening.

Once I set foot on that stage, though, I go into pageant mode. Shoulders back. Tits out. Smile plastered on.

I walk across the stage as if I'm about to take my crown, instead of Constantine's virility. I nudge Trevor away from the winner's chair, speaking out of the side of my smile—a much-treasured pageant skill. "Move it, mister," I tell him. "Brandee Jean's about to get a boner."

Trevor's own smile stays plastered on, and he also speaks through his teeth like a pro. "I'll slip you one of those any time, my lady."

"You too, shining fairy man. Beat it."

Trevor's mentor bows to me. "My lady," he says as he cedes the stage. Now that's a classy gentleman.

I look out across the audience. I might seem confident as hell, but I'm rattled as I take my seat. I have no idea what having Constantine's power is going to look like, or how it could possibly benefit me in any way throughout the rest of the trials. Of all the powers to win, I might just be getting a big dick. And, let's be clear, Brandee Jean doesn't need any help landing one of those.

Across from me, Constantine takes his own seat, a look of pure exultation on his face. The audience settles, and Rada gives me a double thumbs up as the gods stretch their arms out, their discordant hum filling the air. Just like with Prisha's thunder, a glow begins in Constantine's body… except this one is located slightly lower. His face betrays a little panic as the light travels, starting at his crotch and then as it moves up to his chest, leaving him blessedly deflated.

I don't have time to be happy for him, though; I've changed my mind. I definitely don't want that light coming for me, and I don't want to know where it's going to land. I've seen some drop-dead-gorgeous drag queens, but there is a hell of a lot of tape involved.

I decide to cede my power…maybe to Alaric. I'd love to see him retain that cool and calm manner with a raging 24/7 hard on.

But I can't get up. My body is rooted to the chair, my arms and legs totally inert as the glowing orb comes toward me, the gods transferring it slowly across the stage.

"Wait," I try to say, but my mouth won't move, either. The light comes for me, glowing so brightly I close my eyes. I feel it settle on me, and my panic subsides. It's not between my legs, and I definitely don't have any new appendages. This dress is cut to fit and if there were anything extra in here with me, I'd know it by now.

"You can open your eyes," a soft voice says in my ear.

I do, and see Constantine on the other end of the stage, happily rising to show his flat front end to a crowd of Amazons, who—for once—are rabidly cheering him. I turn to find Demeter standing next to me, her smile beaming down on my upturned face.

"Congratulations," she tells me. "Your virility is ensured. No birth control will ever be a match for your fecundity."

Wait. "What?!" I shriek, coming to my feet.

Rada is by my side in a moment. "She thanks you, kind mother," she says, grabbing me by the arm and pulling me off the stage as Demeter frowns at my reaction.

"Did I just get blessed with baby-making?" I ask Rada, my head falling onto her shoulder. "Tell me I didn't."

"Sorry, roomie," she says, patting my shoulder. "But you might want to keep the flirting to a minimum for now. And maybe raise some of your necklines. Also, I know where you can find some chastity belts."

We weave our way through the crowd, congratulatory pats landing on my back.

"BJ," a warm hand clasps my elbow, and I turn to find Jordan—Malik's super-hot panther-shifting mentor—beside me. "Congratulations!"

I stare at him in horror.

This is like when Mandy James found out she was lactose intolerant and had to drop out of the pageant circuit. Any time she ate dairy, her belly puffed out like...well, like she was pregnant. But the girl was a sixth generation Wisconsiner and made the choice to give up pageants before she'd stop consuming cheese.

I feel like I'm facing a similar decision.

"Edie's gonna be so bummed she wasn't here," Jordan adds. "Let me give you a hug from her."

Screaming, I run from the room, protectively shielding my ovaries as I go.

———

"I'm never going outside again," I declare.

I'm curled up with my arms around my midsection, lying on the floor of our dorm room.

"BJ, you have to go outside," Rada reminds me. "We've got another trial in two days."

I reach up, grab a random pillow off my bed, and throw it at her. "I don't care," I say, as she easily swats it out of the air. "I'll get pregnant if I go out there."

"Okay," Rada settles onto the floor beside me. "You do know how babies are made, right?"

"Yes," I say, sticking my tongue out at her. "But I also know that I like boys…a lot."

Rada makes a face. "I really don't know why."

I sit up, curious. "You don't?"

She shrugs. "Not really. I mean, I can look at them and think they are attractive, but I've never felt like kissing one."

I nod, understanding. This is exactly how I feel about girls. And I've spent my entire life around really, really hot girls.

"Do you think about kissing girls?" I ask Rada.

"Sometimes," she says. "But mostly I'm focused on being the best Amazon I can be."

"Yeah, I noticed that about you," I say, protectively covering my ovaries again. "Would it bother you if someone else got the crown?"

Rada thinks about it for a second, clearly wanting to give me an honest answer. "I want to win. But if I can't, I want it to be a woman. Men have been in charge for way too long."

"Preach," I say. "So…which of the girls left do you want to see win?"

"Other than me?" she asks, raising an eyebrow. A low roll of thunder sweeps across our room.

"Nice," I say. Rada had bent the thunder to her control

pretty quickly, something that makes me think maybe she is fated for the crown, after all.

Rada puts a hand on my shoulder. "If it can't be me, then I'd like to see Zahara win."

"Oh," my good mood quickly sours. "I mean, cool. Yeah. Ugly queens are the best queens."

"Don't be hurt, BJ," Rada says. "Zahara exhibits many of the qualities of an Amazon woman. I wouldn't be surprised if she were able to pass the entrance exams for Amazon Academy."

"What's that like?" I ask. "Kick a guy in the balls and the gate opens?"

"No." Another roll of thunder reverberates, the floor shaking underneath me. "The spirit of Hippolyta, the original Queen of the Amazons, judges whether or not you can enter by looking into your soul and weighing whether or not you deserve entry."

"What happens if you don't?"

"Not much," Rada says. "You are turned away. But many choose to fall on their swords rather than face a life as anything other than an Amazon."

"Fall on their swords?"

"They kill themselves."

"Oh…" I think back to Lilliana, and many of the other Amazons. They share an intense pride in being part of that sisterhood. One they've made very clear that I am not a part of.

"So, this Hippolyta lady looks in your soul, and then what?"

"If you are cleared to pass through the gates, you have been accepted as an Amazon, and your training begins." Rada says. "She wanders through the Academy at times. Hippolyta is not a goddess, so she cannot take a physical form. But you can feel her, hovering over her daughters."

Rada looks wistfully around our room, as if hoping Hippolyta might drop in any second.

I suppress a shudder. "I definitely don't want any spirit woman weighing my soul. Thanks, but no thanks. I've done enough weigh-ins on the circuit."

Rada laughs, her mood broken. "It's not like that at all. Having Hippolyta accept you is a huge rush. There's even a lingering of her power. For a few hours afterward I had heightened vision, better reflexes, and my aim…" She sighs, as if recalling her first kiss. "I could not miss."

"I've never seen you miss now," I tell her.

"Yes, but that's after years of training. Now it's a skill. On that day, it was a gift."

"Like my gift of baby-making," I say, coming back to my own problems.

"You'll be fine," Rada says. "Just don't have sex!"

"Ugh…" I say, burying my face in my knees. "You make it sound so simple."

"Well, at least Sora is gone," Rada says. We both laugh, then catch ourselves, remembering why he's gone.

In the silence that follows, there's a knock on the door.

"Hey ladies," Zahara says, sticking her head in. "The rest of us are having a campfire. We thought it might be nice to—"

"Remember Sora. Of course," I say, gathering my shoes.

"Actually we were going to talk strategy," Zahara says. "But no reason we can't do both."

I stare at Zahara, unable to understand how she can be so cold. "Aren't you at all sad about Sora? Didn't you and he…" I trail off, uncertain now. Maybe she did just ride his seahorse.

"Oh yeah, we absolutely had intercourse," Zahara says without hesitation. "But it's not like we pledged our eternal love or anything. I have needs and sex is one of them. I don't really understand why it has to be this taboo thing. Sex is no different than slamming a doot. Sometimes you gotta go, and sometimes you gotta get some."

"Wow." Rada stares at Zahara, fascinated. "Did you just go up to him and say, 'Bone me?' Athena advises us to be as direct as possible when dealing with the opposite sex."

Zahara snorts and I can't hold back a giggle.

"Men are fairly simplistic," Zahara says. "I'm not saying that strategy wouldn't work, however, I'd suggest something a bit more alluring."

"Yeah," I add, "like lingerie."

"It's true that men are visual," Zahara agrees. "But studies have consistently shown that the brain is our largest sex organ. Which is exactly what I told Sora." Zahara smiles wickedly and her eyes sparkle. In that moment I can see why Sora would've looked past the scarier parts of her appearance. "Then I added that I'd been using my super-powered brain to think up new sexual positions and I could really use some assistance trying them out."

"And he volunteered?" Rada guesses.

Zahara shrugs. "He did. Actually he was very sweet about it…" Her smile fades and I can see her actually remembering Sora and now fully processing the fact that he's dead. "When we were done, he said, 'Science experiments are so cool!'"

There's silence after this, as we all remember the beautiful, but not super bright boy.

"To Sora," I say, raising an invisible glass.

Rada follows suit. "To Sora."

"To Sora," Zahara stands, her eyes wet with unshed tears. "He was a good lay and now may he lie in peace."

20

———

Rada, Zahara, and I crest the hill to see the flames from the campfire below. Alaric, Trevor, Malik, and Sophia are already sitting around it.

I notice right away that Sophia is next to Alaric, and a sudden flare erupts in my stomach. It almost feels like jealousy, but that's not possible. Sophia can have his ice-cold ass. Besides, I've got to keep my distance from anything with a penis until I know for sure that I can trust myself—and my ovaries—to stay under control. With that in mind, I ignore Trevor when he pats the ground next to him invitingly, choosing instead to sit in between Zahara and Rada.

"So," Rada says. "Zahara claims we need to talk strategy— as a group. I would like to say right up front that I don't think it's a good idea. There's only one crown, remember?"

"There is only one crown," Alaric agrees. "And only one winner in the end. But there's no harm in looking out for one another until then."

"I wish I could say the same, brother," Trevor says. "Unfortunately, I don't trust you any farther than I can throw you. And given your size—have you put on weight by the way?—that wouldn't be far."

"Hey," I object, "Don't fat shame Alaric. Especially since he doesn't have any fat. My hands were all over his chest earlier today in the maze, and he is rock solid."

"Oh really?" Trevor's eyebrows go up. "A little playtime in the maze, brother? And I thought you didn't believe in mixing business with pleasure. Or indeed, in adding pleasure to anything at all."

I wait for Alaric to tell Trevor that my touching him was totally icky and gross. Except he'd say it in his snooty Alaric way. But instead he just says, "Brandee Jean and I quite literally bumped into one another in the maze. It was a nice break from the monotony of the maze to exchange a few words with her before we both went our own ways."

"Oh man, what a lost opportunity." Malik shakes his head. "If Brandee Jean and I met in the maze, we would definitely have exchanged more than words." He sends a wink my way. I give him my middle finger in return. Malik just laughs.

"Sora died," Zahara reminds us, stopping Malik's laughter. "Did your mentors warn you that could happen?"

"Yes" I nod. "Edie told me things would get rough. But it felt like our first few trials were so simple…"

"That was on purpose," Malik says, his eyes sliding into cat form, and glowing in the firelight. "They wanted us to get comfortable, to feel safe before they attacked."

"They?" I ask. "Exactly who do you think killed Sora?"

"The gods," he says. "Humans are just their playthings. Until one of us has the ultimate power, we're just pawns to them. Sora's death is their way of reminding us who really has the power."

"You don't think it was one of us?" Sophia asks, her vampire skin alabaster white in the fire's glow.

"Who else?" I respond. "We were the only ones in the

maze besides the minotaur. And he was being really careful with us."

"But there's no motivation for one of us to kill him," Zahara argues, her methodical mind at work. "The maze did not require a death in order for one of us to be stripped of our power, and for it to be awarded to someone else. No one had to die; they just had to lose."

"What about the zombie in the horse paddock?" Trevor asks, and I shiver as I remember the horrible noise I'd heard the night I'd captured Whiskey. "Could a zombie have attacked Sora?"

"But I thought a zombie couldn't attack unless it had orders from Hades," Rada says.

"Who says?" Trevor asks. "You heard Hades; he's lost control of his army of the dead."

"His body did disappear," Alaric says, thinking aloud. "It's certainly possible that he was bitten in the maze, and reanimated before his power could be transferred to one of us."

"Does that mean there's a really hot zombie out there, wandering around?" I ask, suddenly doubly concerned. Not only do I have to be scared of a zombie, now I have to worry about it being a super hot undead version of Sora that may or may not get me pregnant, depending on my mood when our paths cross.

"I didn't see any bite marks on Sora," Sophia says. "And believe me, I can spot a bite mark a mile away."

"Guys, it doesn't matter how Sora died," Zahara interrupts. "What matters is that one of us is going to be the next king or queen of the gods. They will have the ultimate power, and it must go to the right person."

"You sound almost like you don't care if you win," Malik says.

"I don't," Zahara shrugs. "As long as whoever does

deserves it."

"So basically…not a murderer," Alaric says.

"Yes," Rada agrees. "I will not have it said that a competition taking place at Amazon Academy was unfairly won."

Trevor holds out both his hands. "But is murder against the rules?" Sophia smacks him, but he keeps going. "Seriously? I'm asking. Did anyone explicitly say that we weren't allowed to kill each other?"

"I definitely don't want to form an alliance with you," Rada tells him.

"Understandable," Zahara says. "However, if you did ally with Trevor and then were the next to die, the rest of us would know that your back wasn't being properly watched, and would have good reason to suspect Trevor."

"Does everything come down to logic with you?" Rada asks, her feelings apparently hurt.

Zahara considers this for a second. "I would be emotionally moved if you were to die, however, I would find comfort in knowing who I couldn't place my trust in."

"So, yes?" Rada says, in a sulk. Zahara reaches across me, her palm upward in Rada's lap.

"If it makes you feel better, I choose to align myself with you," she says. Rada takes her hand, her eyes shining in the firelight. It would all be very moving if they weren't the two people I like best…and they both just passed over being my partner.

"Malik," Sophia pronounces, suddenly coming to her feet and crossing the distance between them. She settles onto the ground beside him, and he slips an arm around her. Together, they look like two sleek animals, and I feel a flutter of unease in my stomach. There's more cunning between the two of them than in the rest of us put together. If there ever was a power couple, this is it.

And speaking of couples, it occurs to me there are three people left to pair off—me, Alaric, and Trevor. My mouth hangs open, unsure what to do. I don't know if I can entirely trust Trevor, but Alaric is so stuffy. Plus, it's also possible he'd turn me down flat.

It's all well and good for Zahara to say that she wants the right person to win the crown, but if others are willing to cheat to win, anyone playing by the rules won't stand a chance.

I'm debating my choice when Trevor makes it for me.

"I always was a fan of threesomes," he says, coming over to Malik and Sophia. He wraps his arms around both of them.

"There's strength in numbers," Malik agrees, and Sophia nods.

"Well," Alaric's eyes meet mine over the fire. "I guess that leaves you and me."

I've never come in last. Never. Brandee Jean Mason might be first-runner-up, and—on one memorable occasion—the bronze medalist in the Bronzer Competition, but I have never been last. Even in gym class, my well-toned legs often earned me first pick at kickball. But here at Amazon Academy, no one wants to trust me with their lives.

No one except the boy who got stuck with me.

Tears blur the firelight as I get to my feet and run into the darkness.

Once I'm away from the group, I get myself under control.

Mama always called me Brandee Jean the drama queen when I cried. She'd say, "Unless someone died, I don't wanna see you with bloodshot cry eyes."

I guess with Sora dead, allowing myself a good cry right now might actually have been okay with her. But probably not, because the truth is that I really just want to cry for myself.

Closing my eyes, I mentally summon Mama. What would she say if she were here right now?

"Buck up, BJ. You're tied for first right now. Do you understand that? So what that you don't like your new power. Keep your ankles crossed the way I taught you and deal with it. And stop expecting the other contestants to be your friends. Your soft heartedness is holding you back and that's the good hard truth. You aren't gonna make it in the pageant world or any other one if you don't toughen up."

Okay, so maybe it's not so hard to imagine what Mama would say. She lectured me enough.

"Hey," a soft voice says, interrupting my thoughts. It's Alaric, his dark form silhouetted against the moonlight. "Am I to assume from the way you ran off that none of the remaining options for alliances were to your liking?"

"Huh?" I say.

He smiles. "Do you want to form an alliance with me? I'm not sure if you noticed, but we are the only ones left who haven't paired up."

"No, I noticed." I scuff a toe in the dirt. "I thought you'd join up with Rada and Zahara after I left. The three of you all got that sensible and logical thing going on."

"That's true. However, it seems to me that it might be more clever to diversify. If I'm smart and logical—"

"Sensible and logical," I cut in. "I never said you were smart."

"My mistake." Alaric actually laughs at this. "As I was saying, I would rather team up with someone who is my opposite."

I put my hands on my hips. "You calling me insensible and illogical?"

"Brandee Jean, are you trying to pick a fight with me?" Alaric tilts his head, studying me like I'm a curiosity he can't quite figure out.

"Yeah. No." I sigh. "Maybe. I've just been rethinking this whole alliance thing. My mama always used to tell me not to cozy up to the other contestants. I was supposed to be frenemies with the other girls, but once I got to know someone the enemy part of it usually went out the door."

"That's why I want to be in an alliance with you." Alaric takes a step toward me and I quickly take a matching step back, my hands automatically moving to cover my womb.

"Don't impregnate me!"

"Of course not!" Alaric's eyes go wide and he takes another step away and then one more, just to be safe. We eye one another across what has become a slightly ridiculous distance.

Alaric shakes his head, like he knows this is absurd. "As I was saying, the reason I want to be in an alliance with you is *because* of your friendliness. You are not a person who needs to be taught honor, you are inherently loyal to those around you. I saw that in the way you took care of Sora's body."

My throat thickens. "They just treated him like trash. Like he didn't matter. I didn't even really know him, but Sora deserved better than that."

Alaric nods in agreement. We're silent for a moment, and then he gestures to a nearby log. "Might we risk sitting side by side? I swear to you, I have no desire to be a father. I will keep a safe distance."

After thinking it over, I shake my head yes and head over to the log. I sit and Alaric sits an arm's length away from me.

He clears his throat and then says, "So what do you think? Shall we team up?"

I fidget with my hands, still unsure. Not about Alaric. The more I get to know him, the less I mind his stuffiness. But I still got Mama's voice in my head and I'm not sure if an alliance will make me weaker or stronger. I take a deep breath and try to explain it to Alaric.

"The last contest I won before the world went kablooey was this little podunk one. Miss Westside Dairy Express. It was for a new store and the prize was a twenty dollar gift certificate. Still, I won and I thought Mama would be happy. But instead she went off, talking about how many more crowns I'd have if got serious and competed like my life was at stake."

Alaric laughs softly. "I think you have a pageant story for everything."

Ouch. That hurts. It's like he didn't even hear what I said. "Yeah and pageants are dumb and I'm dumb too. I know."

"Actually, I've come to realize from your stories that pageants are a fascinating subculture." Alaric's arm crosses the distance between us and his big hand settles on top of mine. "And I understand about your mother. My family has always been hard on me as well."

I shake my head. "She just didn't want me to make the same mistakes as her. And I just wanted to make Mama happy. But sometimes...sometimes it feels like I've spent my whole life pretending to be tougher than I actually am."

"And I," Alaric says, "sometimes feel as if I've spent my whole life squashing any part of me that isn't perfectly genteel and polite. Do you know, I was terrified of accidentally winning Constantine's power? I couldn't imagine what my family would say if they heard I was walking around with a—" Alaric clears his throat, leaving the rest unsaid.

"Boner," I fill in for him. "Or as we call it in Wisconsin, a hardwood smoked sausage."

"Indeed."

I giggle. "But don't they want you to win the whole thing? Would they overlook that you're constantly at full salute if you got the powers of a god?"

"Full salute," Alaric mutters with a small chuckle. Then he goes quiet. "They want me to win. Or Trevor. Either of us claiming the crown would add to our family's consequence. And for Trevor, well, he'd no longer be the bastard son. He'd be a god."

I frown at him; the way he talks about winning doesn't sound very enthusiastic. "Do you even want to win?"

On the wobbly log, Alaric straightens, back lengthening, chin up. You'd think he was on a throne instead of a worm-eaten old tree. "It is my obligation."

"Yeah, but that's not what I asked."

Alaric turns to look at me. His eyes are intense. "I want to do my duty. It's what I've been taught."

I shrug, realizing that's all he's gonna say.

"What about you?" he asks. "Surely you have enough crowns in your collection?"

"Yeah, I got lots of crowns, but it's not really something a girl can have too many of."

"But it's obviously more than an accessory that's driving you." He reaches over to give me a physical nudge to go with the verbal one, obviously wanting to hear more. "You're not that shallow."

I answer by pushing him back. Except my push isn't playful. He falls off the log and onto his back. Pushing to my feet, I stand over him. "I spent every dollar I had to get here. Also, I've been living on my wits since the world went wacko, and before you can tell me those aren't the sharpest, I'll admit that having super strength has helped too. In fact, if it wasn't for my super strength—"

My throat goes tight as the night Shauna and I got grabbed plays through my mind.

"If it wasn't for my super strength, I wouldn't have gotten away from some super bad guys who grabbed my friend and me one night when we were out scavenging deserted houses."

I laugh, remembering the only good part of this story.

"It wasn't food or anything like that we wanted, but music. Shauna had found an old CD player that took batteries. It came with some old Madonna and Tiffany discs that I loved, but Shauna said she'd kill herself if she had to listen to them one more time. So we were on the hunt for her type of music." I look down at Alaric, who's still in the dirt at my feet. "Can you guess what it was?"

"Shauna loved Beethoven."

I scoff. "Please. Shauna was cool. She was total rock'n'roll all the way. She found some Van Halen and nearly pissed herself with joy. This one house that had frilly curtains and pictures of Jesus on the wall amazingly turned out to be the motherload. Journey, Whitney Houston, Prince, and a bunch of old movie soundtracks." I hold out a hand to Alaric and he takes it. "Now here comes the bad part."

I pull him up so we're standing face to face. "We were walking home and not being as careful as we shoulda been. Actually, we were loud. Shauna made up a game where we read a song on the back of a CD and the other person had to sing it. Whether you knew the song or not. Shauna's made up lyrics were the funniest thing I ever heard. We were dying."

I'm smiling, not just remembering, but almost back in that moment once more. If I could only pause it there. Take away the part that happened next.

But I can't.

I take a step closer to Alaric. He holds his arms out. I shuffle my feet forward until my nose touches his shirt and then my forehead falls so it's resting against his hard warm chest. After a moment his hands land lightly on my back. Not pulling or demanding, but just resting there if I need them.

"These guys came out of nowhere," I tell the buttons on Alaric's shirt. "Six of them on foot, and then more on bikes. Maybe they'd been following us for a while. I don't know. They got Shauna pretty easily. She was on the back of a bike and gone. I couldn't even see what direction they took her. I had three guys on me, after I punched the first one out cold. You know, those CD cases, when they break, are pretty sharp. I got the plastic clenched in between my fingers, the way they teach girls to do with their car keys if they're out late at night by themselves. And I just went all Wolverine on their asses. Then I ran."

I shake my head, still disgusted with myself after all this time.

"I was winning. I beat the shit out of them, and then I ran like a scared little girl."

"You *were* a scared girl," Alaric says gently.

"But I was stronger than them!" The words burst out of me. "Than all of them! I could've held them down and made them take me to Shauna. I could've threatened to cut off their balls if they didn't return her."

I pull away from Alaric, needing to stand tall as I repeat my pledge.

"I promised myself I would get her back. No matter what. And I'd make those assholes pay too."

Alaric stares at me. He doesn't crack a joke. Or make any comment at all. Finally, he just points a finger at me. "That's honor. The very definition of it."

I'm a little embarrassed by this. I've been told I'm beautiful, talented, cute, and even quirky. But honorable is a new one for me.

I think I kinda like it.

"Also," Alaric adds, "you definitely have the better 'why I want to win' story."

I laugh, the sound rough after all that talking.

He holds out a hand. "Brandee Jean, would you like to form an alliance with me?"

I hesitate before sliding my hand into his. "I will watch your ass like no one else has ever watched it before. And you better watch mine too."

"Indeed I will." Alaric clears his throat. "Perhaps our meeting within your box was providential after all."

Coming close I give his upper arm a little punch. "Does that mean you forgive me for your shoulder oopsie?"

Alaric tilts his head, obviously thinking about it. But then he grins. "One cannot hold a grudge against their ally. Which means that this one time I will give you a pass on dislocating my shoulder."

"And it's all better now?" I reach out to pat his arm, checking to make sure it's okay. And maybe also copping a feel.

"The healers here are quite extraordinary. The arm is better than ever." Alaric flexes his arm as I hold on. It's possible he's showing off a little. But I can't say that I mind.

"Aww, isn't this sweet?" a voice from the shadows says and I jump away from Alaric.

"I will straight up kill a zombie," I yell.

Alaric shakes his head. "It's not a zombie. It's Hades."

Hades steps forward. He's fit and attractive, like all the gods, but in a greasy way. Like an older dude who will offer to be your talent agent and the audition involves a seedy motel and some Polaroids.

"I've been watching you," he tells us.

"Okay creeper, what do you want?" I put my hands on my hips and push out my chest.

"I would like to help you," he tells us. I realize he's not talking to us, but only to Alaric.

"Help us what?" Alaric scoffs. "Cheat?"

"No. Nothing like that. Just help push you toward the winning spot. I had backed another contestant, but he's a bit of a loose cannon."

"Who?!" I ask, then think, *oh duh*. "Trevor?"

"Yes. He's not meeting my expectations but you..." He focuses on Alaric. "You can actually win this thing. You've got the talent and the breeding..."

"And what am I?" I ask. "Cheese curds? I just want to point out that I've won a trial. Alaric hasn't." I point to myself. "Me win. Alaric no win."

Hades ignores me. "Alaric my boy, join me. Pledge your loyalty to me. We can rule this world together."

Alaric narrows his eyes. "You think that I would betray my brother like that?"

Hades scoffs. "You hate each other. He was very eager to throw you under the bus."

"Regardless of what Trevor does or how he feels, I am not him. I would never cheat."

Hades finally turns to me. "Will you talk some sense into him?"

"Oh, now you care I exist?" I ask. "Why the hell..Hades... whatever...would I tell him to agree to your devil's bargain? My mama always said you can sell your soul, but ain't nothing gonna buy it back."

"You could see your mother again," Hades tells me.

My hands drop and I almost sink to the ground but Alaric is there, holding me up.

"Go away," he tells Hades. "I'm not making a bargain with you. I'll win fairly or not at all."

"You didn't even hear my offer," he says.

"I could talk to my mama?" I ask. Is it really possible?

"Get Alaric to agree to be my champion and to share the power he wins, and yes. I will bring you to the underworld."

Alaric whispers in my ear, "He can't be trusted."

I regain my footing. "Bring me to the underworld? So, I'd be dead?" No. Nope. Nah Ah. "When my mama took her own life I promised I would never do that. I can wait to see her."

"You do not want the god of death as your enemy." Hades puffs up and does this weird shimmering thing. The air around him smokes.

"I'm not getting in bed with death," I tell him. "And I wouldn't let any of my friends either."

"You hear the lady, begone," Alaric tells him.

Hades disappears and Alaric is still holding me. I look up at him. "That was very good of you to refuse Hades. Trevor…"

"Is my blood, whatever else he is." He places his hand on my cheek. "What about you. Are you okay?"

"Fine," I breathe. I force a tired smile. "I guess we just found out we make a pretty good team after all."

21

My alliance with Alaric does me zero good in the horse paddock.

Whiskey is still only willing to listen to me so long as I keep the promise that I'll be leaving him alone in the near future. Unfortunately, I don't have much control over that promise. Or over my horse. He still refuses to take a single step unless I stick my fingers in his ears. And then he runs like hell.

Epona spends an entire day giving me personal one-on-one help. We work on the apparently must-have Amazon move of slipping down the horse's side and then clinging to him with my legs while I shoot at targets from under his neck.

Of course, I'm terrible at it.

After a while, Epona sits down with a book and doesn't even look up at me—she just waits until there's the thud of me hitting the ground once more—and then offers the helpful advice, "Get up."

So I do. Over and over again. I climb up on my damn horse. He shivers beneath me and waits for me to slide off once more. Finally after the thousandth time falling on my face, I sulk in the dirt at Whiskey's feet, too disheartened to do much more.

It doesn't help that Malik and Sophia come cantering past right then, their horses trained so perfectly that they even crap on cue.

Archery class doesn't go much better.

I manage to miss the target and somehow the arrow rebounds and pierces Rada's shoulder. She's a champ about it, of course. No screeches for Rada. Not even a rumble of thunder. She simply grimaces and then pulls it out. Once the arrow's out, she calls everyone over so we can all see the hole closing before our eyes.

I'm totally jealous in that moment. Although I'm quite fond of my super strength, being able to heal yourself is amazing. I bet Rada doesn't even need to worry about putting her SPF on every day. She can simply heal any sun damage each night before she goes to bed.

Rada easily accepted my apology for the whole arrow incident. But Liliana lost her shit. She yelled that if I'd struck anyone else, they would've been seriously injured. Then making sure to get right up in my face, Lilliana suggested that I remove myself from the contest, the Academy, and for good measure the entire western hemisphere.

Devana was kind enough to insert herself between Lilliana and myself. Even though I could totally crush the little bitch with one hand, I don't think it would improve my standing with any of the other Amazons—including my roommate, Rada.

Once Lilliana was swept away to help someone restring her bow, Devana took me aside for some, "Extra help for the extra helpless."

This extra help mostly consisted of her insisting that I'm

left-handed. This apparently means that my left eye is my dominant one, and the one I should use for aiming.

"Right hand person teach you everything you know, ya? Zey teach you wrong. Listen to Devana. Devana knows," she says, looking glumly at my target's perfectly smooth and unpunctured surface. "Poor virgin target. You now use correct hand, which is the left one and break target's hymen."

"That's gross and I'm not left-handed," I yell, throwing my bow on the ground. "Mama told me I got my finger stuck in her diamond-studded hoop earring when I was just a baby. Hoops were her signature piece, 'cause Mama said every woman needs a signature piece. But she lost the left diamond hoop years ago, so she wore rhinestones on the right. But I went right for the real thing."

Devana stares me down for a second and then coolly asks. "Vould zat be her right or yours?"

Beside me, Lilliana snickers. I march out of class, head high, but my cheeks burn with embarrassment.

Now, at dinner, I'm trying not to be too annoyed while Zahara and Rada talk about tonight's trial. Since declaring their alliance they've been stuck to each other.

I'd almost think it was a romantic thing, except now that Zahara doesn't have a roommate she's got some boy sneaking into her room each night. The walls are thin, so I hear everything.

Rada mostly sleeps through it, but last night she woke up just long enough to say, "Did that grunt sound a bit like Alaric? I think it did?" Then she drifted off once more.

So there I was left lying in my bed, hoping for another grunt so I could positively identify it as not Alaric

Not because I wanted to be making the mattress squeak with him. But because we were in an alliance and it'd be hard to completely trust his loyalty to me if he's also secretly part of Zahara's nocturnal activities.

"Another night trial," Zahara says now as she stirs soup. "Do we know anything about it?"

"Only that Aphrodite designed it," Alaric says, staring into a cup of coffee.

I study the two of them, trying to see if they make eye contact or show some sign of being mutually disappointed at having their nightly plans interrupted.

Relief goes through me when I can detect absolutely nothing there.

"Ohhhh, Aphrodite," Sophia says, a naughty smile spreading across her face. "Not too difficult to figure out then, is it? A test in the dark, designed by Venus herself? Too bad Constantine bowed out so early. This might have been his moment."

"Don't count the rest of us out," Trevor says, stretching his arm to give Sophia an affectionate squeeze. She laughs, and I roll my eyes.

The other alliances have apparently reached the touchy feely stage; meanwhile I can't even get Alaric to meet my gaze over the table.

"What are you even talking about?" I ask. "Why does everyone seem to already know what the test will be?"

Rada clears her throat. "Aphrodite is the goddess of love," she explains.

"Lust would be more accurate," Trevor says, wiggling his eyebrows at me. "I seriously doubt we're expected to make someone fall in love with us. No, I'm guessing tonight will be all about who bags someone first."

"Puts you in a tough spot, doesn't it?" Sophia asks me. "With your overactive ovaries."

"Oh gods." I put my forehead down on the table, and feel Rada's hand on my shoulder, giving me a comforting rub. But it's not Rada's voice in my ear as the others file out of the dining hall.

"Come on, BJ," Alaric says. "Let's see if there's a way for us to get through this trial without losing our dignity."

———

My dignity is the last thing on my mind as we all hunker on a street corner back in the real world. Athena sent us through a portal—next to a fountain of a weird naked dude with ankle wings—letting us know that Aphrodite would be meeting us.

"How will we know who she is?" Malik asked, to which Athena only laughed.

And when Aphrodite shows, it's obvious why.

Even though it's cold, and we're all congregated on a dirty street corner in a questionable part of town, I can feel everyone's minds turn to one thing and one thing only.

Sex. The thing is sex. We're all thinking about sex.

"Good evening," Aphrodite says, as she comes to a stop in front of us. She's wearing six-inch spiked heels and a black trench coat. Something tells me that's all she's wearing. Oddly, something else in me desperately wants to get closer, so that I can unbelt it and see for myself.

I told Rada I've never been interested in girls. And that's true. But this isn't a girl. This is a woman...and suddenly I feel like my worldview might be expanding. Sexuality is a spectrum, after all.

That's not the only thing expanding.

Malik and Trevor shuffle uncomfortably, their hands in their pockets as they try to hide their arousal. Alaric is the only one of us who meets Aphrodite's eye, apparently unfazed by her aura...which seems to be soaked in pheromones.

"Good evening," Alaric replies to Aphrodite's greeting, his voice even.

I feel a sudden rush of affection for him and his icy restraint. Stepping closer to him, I tuck my arm into his elbow, and accidentally brush my chest against his bicep.

Almost immediately, I'm assaulted by a whole new wave of impulses, none of them directed at Aphrodite. They are most definitely about Alaric. A graphic technicolor scene starts to play in my head and it starts with me throwing him down on the sidewalk right here and finding out how many buttons I can pop off that Oxford with my teeth.

I hear Malik purring, and turn to find Sophia scratching behind one of his ears, her eyes focused on his mouth. Trevor has a hand curled in Rada's hair, and while she normally would bounce his ass halfway to Detroit for that, she doesn't seem bothered at all. She's staring at Zahara, who looks like she might actually be in the middle of an orgasm. She's not even touching herself or anyone else—her eyes are just focused on Aphrodite in this half-lidded sort of way. I actually snicker a little, remembering Zahara telling me that the brain is our most powerful sexual organ, 'cause it looks like her super brain is getting her super off right now. I'm so amused at this thought, that I barely pay attention to the fact that I've started to take off my clothes.

"Oh dear," Aphrodite says, and brings her hands together with a loud *crack*. We all jump, our minds suddenly clear. "I apologize. I do tend to have that effect on humans," she adds, with a knowing smile.

I shake my head, clearing away the images I had of me and Alaric redefining the meaning of Epona's Bareback Ride and Shoot class.

"Tonight's trial will test your ability to influence others, an important quality for a leader to have."

"I don't equate seduction with influence," Alaric says, his voice cold.

"Then you haven't tried it," Aphrodite says easily. "Sex is a weapon—one that you can wield to your advantage, if you know how."

"Or," Alaric shoots back, "sex is a physical expression of affection between two people who care for one another. Not a power struggle."

"Ass," Trevor whispers under his breath. Sophia giggles, but I can feel a little warmth spreading in my belly. Aphrodite had turned her power off as quickly as she turned us on. No, it's not the goddess arousing me right now. It's Alaric.

"Okay, so what's the deal?" I ask, stepping forward as I gain more control over myself. "Can we just get this frat party started already?"

"Most definitely," Aphrodite says, in a tone that tells me she might have been following my thoughts about Alaric. "Across the street you will see a bar—one of the only businesses still flourishing these days. You will go in, and procure partners. The first of you to seal the deal will be the winner."

"Seal the deal?" Trevor asks. "Does that mean what I think it means?"

"Sadly, no," Aphrodite says, a pretty pout on her lips. "As you are all minors, Athena would not allow me to design this trial to my own specifications. A kiss will do."

"A kiss?" Sophia repeats, baring her fangs. "That's easy enough."

"They have to kiss you," Aphrodite clarifies. "And I heard about your alliances. No kissing each other to win. The first one to get a kiss from a *stranger* will be the winner, and will get to choose who they wish to be the loser."

"That's a pretty prize," Malik whistles.

"But is it worth the herpes?" I ask. Rada groans.

"See you, losers," Sophia says, crossing the street with confidence.

Zahara is the next one to go. She wears a black dress and her wings are folded to look like an elaborate cape. She is followed by the others, Rada trailing slightly behind, her battlefield swagger somewhat diminished.

I should be pumped, jazzed, ready to go and already planted on a barstool. But I'm not.

I look up at Alaric. "This sucks and I don't want to do it."

"I know." He sighs. "However, as your ally, I feel honor bound to point out that as one of the few contestants with two powers, you will almost certainly be a target for the winner of this contest."

I groan, knowing he's right.

"Furthermore," Alaric continues. "I cannot help but notice that Sophia seems to particularly dislike you. I think she would take great satisfaction in stripping your powers from you."

"Fine." I throw up my hands. "Mama did always say that those fairy tales about having to kiss frogs to get a crown weren't totally wrong."

A teleporting aristocrat and a crazy strong beauty queen walk into a bar. It sounds like the set-up to a joke. But nope, it's just a totally normal weeknight.

We stand inside the entrance as a miasma of smoke rises above us and tinny music blares from an old jukebox.

Rada is at the bar, a very large pitcher of beer in front of her that's already half gone.

Malik already has a lady love engaged in conversation, As we watch he trails his hand up and down his conquest's leg. She looks old enough to be his mother and totally flattered by his attention.

Sophia's confidence was not misplaced. She's got three guys at the pool tables talking her up, while their game has definitely come to a halt.

"Where's Zahara and Trevor?" I ask, craning my neck. I

spot Zahara by the restrooms, leaning against the wall, one arm casually hanging off the shoulder of a guy who has more metal in his face than the front of an eighteen-wheeler.

"Do you want a drink?" Alaric asks, but I shake my head.

Alcohol might make this easier, but it won't settle my stomach, which is doing flips. I've got to get someone to kiss me, and while I know that might be an easy task, there's no one here I want to consider making a run for. Not without my obvious disgust showing.

"I think our strategy here is obvious," Alaric says, turning to me. "I'll be your wingman to make sure that you get the kiss. As allies you won't choose to take my power as your winnings."

"Wait, what?" I glare up at him. "Why is it obvious that I should get the kiss?

Alaric seems surprised. "I have to say, I thought you'd be relieved at a trial that plays to your strengths."

"My strengths?" I ask, as a man approaches Rada, his buddies egging him on from their table. "And what are those? Being easy?"

"No, not at all," Alaric says, and he sounds honest. "What I'm trying to say is, I would think that a woman of your…" He clears his throat, and colors a little. "A woman of your natural attractiveness would thrive in a situation such as this one."

"Oh…" He's not being snarky, or mean. Which leaves me not knowing what to say. "Well, thank you, Alaric. I…the problem is, I don't want to kiss any of these guys. I might come off as a certain type of girl, but Brandee Jean Mason doesn't kiss just anybody. I have—"

I stop mid-sentence as someone across the bar catches my eye. "Alaric," I grab his arm. "What are the chances that Ryan Gosling would be at this dive bar tonight?"

Alaric looks in the same direction and then goes

absolutely still. "Zero. Damn it. I should've guessed Trevor would use his powers. It's evil and brilliant."

"He does seem to like that combo," I agree. "But you know what this means?" I stab a finger into Alaric's chest. "I'm gonna be your wingman, so you can get the kiss. If Trevor wins, we both know he's coming after you. Which means you need to win this one, buddy." I slide my hand down his chest and grab hold of his hand. "C'mon, let's go find someone desperate."

Alaric pulls away from me. "Hold on. I don't believe this is our strongest strategy."

"Oh, c'mon. You're acting like you're so shy, but you locked lips with me two seconds after we met."

"A kiss you instigated."

"'Cause I thought you were Trevor."

"Whom you'd just met earlier that day. He was still essentially a stranger."

I cross my arms over my chest. "Let's not get bogged down in the details here. The main point is that you put your tongue in my mouth before you even properly introduced yourself."

Alaric groans. "Yes, thank you for the reminder. It wasn't exactly my proudest moment."

Ouch. That stings. I thought things were maybe changing between us, but clearly he still sees me as the trashy girl he regrets swapping spit with.

"Fine." I stick my hand down the front of my shirt and give each of my boobs a boost so they're just barely within the confines of my demi bra. Then I tug down the neckline.

Alaric watches silently, his eyes wide. "Brandee Jean—" he starts to say, but I cut him off.

"I don't need a wingman, thanks. I've got the twins here to help me out."

With that I turn on my heel and stride into the crowd. I

am desperately aware that the clock is ticking as I scan the crowd. Finally, I locate a boy who looks relatively clean and seems to have a sweet face despite the black gun tattooed across his left cheekbone. Putting a swing in my hips, I head in his direction.

But before I can reach him, Alaric steps in front of me. "Not him," he says.

My hands go to my hips. "How do you even know who I'm heading towards?"

"It's the man with a pistol inked across his face," he responds in this know-it-all tone.

I hate that he's right, but refuse to let him see it. "Yep, that's the frog I've chosen. So what do you think, partner?" I force myself to smile up at him. "When he kisses me, should I return the kiss with a closed or open mouth?"

Alaric's giant hands close around my upper arms, at the same time he leans down to growl in my face, "You are not kissing him."

I jerk away from Alaric, my heart racing. For a moment there I was tempted to kiss Alaric again. But that would not help me win this contest. More importantly, I don't want him calling it another mistake.

"I gotta kiss someone," I say at the same time that someone cries out at the bar.

I turn in time to see Rada break her pitcher of beer over a guy's head. Whatever his come-on line was, it obviously doesn't work on Amazons. His buddies rush to his aide, and Malik shifts with a mighty roar. His date screams and falls right out of her chair, but Malik is already leaping away, his claws leaving drag marks on the wooden floor.

Meanwhile, a slap rings out. I turn just in time to see that Trevor is now wearing George Clooney's face. Maybe the girl prefers older men. Or maybe he just couldn't resist showing off. Either way, the girl is not impressed.

I look over just in time to see her reach for Trevor's neck. He struggles, but can't seem to pull her off.

"Bit off more than he could chew," Alaric mutters as he pushes past me and starts to move in Trevor's direction.

If Trevor was my brother, I'd be going over there to see if the girl needed help finishing him off. But it's clear that Alaric is planning a rescue.

A rescue that Trevor doesn't need.

In the blink of an eye, he changes into a snake and slips between the girls hands, onto the floor.

Even though it's Trevor, I quickly jump onto a chair. I really can't stand having creepy crawlies wiggling around my feet.

I'm not the only one moving for higher ground, Sophia leaps onto the pool table. It's not Trevor she's trying to escape, though. I watch as she breaks a pool cue over her knees and then points the jagged pieces at the men she'd been flirting with.

Her eyes flash as she addresses them. "You think it's a kindness to tell me I look like an expensive whore and you're not sure if you can afford me?"

There's a rumble of thunder that almost sounds like a chuckle from Rada, but on second look, she's cracking beer bottles over heads left and right. So maybe not.

Malik's been helping her, but when he hears Sophia, he whirls around and charges to her side.

"Come on, lowlifes!" Sophia yells, leaping onto the floor while jabbing at the men with her improvised weapons. "Grow some balls and fight me. Then you'll see how blue my blood runs!"

"Gods," Alaric says as he teleports back to my side. He pushes me behind him so that his body is between me and the riot that's breaking out.

I search the crowd, scanning for Zahara. The harpy has

her date completely entranced, his gaze not even leaving her face.

From behind me, there's a scream. I glance over my shoulder and see that Sophia has stabbed one of the guys with her pool cue.

"Bitch!" he snarls.

I glance back at Zahara as she gives her date a slow, practiced smile. In response, he leans in, presses his mouth to hers and—

We're all back on the corner, Aphrodite giving us a quizzical stare. Rada is self-healing a bloody welt on her hand, the internal glow almost immediately closes up the gash from the broken beer pitcher.

"Not what I would have expected," she says. "Well done, harpy. The repulsiveness of your face is only testament to the powers of your seduction. To get a man to overlook that…" She shakes her head. "I'm impressed."

"How did this happen?" Trevor asks, just as the fight we'd started in the bar spills out onto the street. Fists are flying and someone shouts, "Over there!" when they spot us.

"Time to go," Aphrodite says, snapping her fingers once more. We're instantly back at Amazon Academy, standing on the archery field in our late night clothes.

"Now Zahara," Aphrodite says, "It is time for you to choose the loser. The field is yours, my dear. You may pick which power you find most useful."

But Zahara only shakes her head. "I don't want to take a power. My win was not accomplished in a fair way. I would rather choose a different prize."

"What do you mean it wasn't fair?" Aphrodite stomps her foot, her temper rising. "You kissed a stranger and you won and I declare you the winner. You will take a power and you will like it!"

"Nonsense," Athena's voice booms out across the archery

field, as she appears from behind one of the targets. "Sister." She smiles sweetly at Aphrodite, but there's no love in it, or her words. "You created this trial. You declared they must kiss a stranger and that is indeed what Zahara did." Athena turns her hard gaze on Zahara. "But it was not the first time you kissed this stranger, was it?"

Athena snaps her fingers and Zahara's boy from the bar is suddenly among us. Now, up close, with better light on his face, I immediately recognize those cheekbones. And the sparkle.

Trevor does too.

"My gods! It's my mentor!" He stalks up to the faerie. "You traitor. How can I trust you knowing that you've been bumping uglies with that ugly?"

"Trevor!" Alaric snaps, a clear warning in his voice that he's overstepped.

"Wait a minute," I say, trying to understand this. I'm pretty sure Trevor's mentor is who I've been hearing visiting Zahara's room at night. But if that's true... "If Zahara already knows him, exactly how does he qualify as a stranger?"

The faerie smiles and gives a small courtly bow to us all. "Colin Stranger at your service."

"You're fired," Trevor snaps. "I don't want your help anymore."

"Oh dear, how dreadful," Colin replies in mock despair. "When you never listened to a word I said or bothered to share your plans with me? What a loss to us both."

"That is cheating!" Aphrodite screeches. She advances on Zahara. "You have made a mockery of my trial."

"And we're done here," Athena says, smacking her hands together. Aphrodite is suddenly encased in a time-out box. Rada hides a smile, and Athena turns to Zahara.

"Well done, harpy," she says, then to the rest of us. "Now what is the alternate prize you desire?"

Zahara smiles at all of us. "Return us to the bar, but with all the other patrons removed. We deserve to have a night off and a little bit of fun too."

Athena considers it for a moment and then claps her hands once more.

Instantly, we are back in the bar, although it's now almost completely emptied out except for a small group gathered around the jukebox. One of them turns and I recognize Malik's mentor, Jordan.

"Who wants to macarena?" he asks as the music starts to play.

The girl beside him laughs, and I realize that it's Edie.

All our mentors are here. Including Stranger, who slips an arm around Zahara, pulling her close to his side. She smiles softly and rests her head on his shoulder. I know Zahara said sex was no different than slamming a doot, but whatever she has going on with Stranger seems like it might be something more.

"Come on," Edie says, grabbing my hand and pulling me across the bar.

"Strategy, advice, or hints?" I ask.

"Advice," she laughs and releases me. I realize we're now in the middle of the dance floor. "I'm going to show you the proper way to shake your booty."

And then Edie starts to dance. For all of her talk about booty shaking, her rear end is barely moving. Did no one ever teach her that dance starts with the hips?

I shake my head and head over to the jukebox. It only takes me a moment to find what I'm looking for.

As 'Baby Got Back' begins to play, I step in front of Edie. "This is where the student becomes the teacher," I inform her.

As I show Edie how it's done, I look around to see that

everyone is now on the dance floor, shaking what they got and just generally having fun.

We keep the jukebox hopping all night and the drink flowing too. It's one of the most amazing nights of my life.

For those few hours, we leave our rivalries behind and lose ourselves in the smoky haze. In short, we party like there's no tomorrow.

Because for some of us, there might not be.

22

At dawn we're transported to our beds without even being given a last call warning.

I'm annoyed, but then I feel the soft mattress beneath me and relax into it. A moment later, I'm asleep.

The sun is high in the sky when I wake up again. I'm still tired from all the dancing last night, but at least I'm not hungover. Mama always said liquor was the devil's juice and full of empty calories too, so I tend to stay away from it.

A sunny Rada appears in front of me. "It's another trial today. Time to get up."

I groan, needing a little more time to wake up before dealing with Rada's good morning cheer. "Why aren't you hungover? I saw you and Sophia break into the top-shelf liquor cabinet together."

"We did break in and then we drank all the most expensive alcohols inside. Sophia said everything else in the place was peasants' swill." Rada lowers her voice conspiratorially, "I couldn't tell the difference."

My stomach rumbles with hunger and I sit up. This time I

notice the long, flowing scarves attached to the ends of our beds.

"Ohhh," I say, climbing out of bed to inspect it closer. "I didn't expect accessories, and whoever managed the color choices is a marvel."

I hold mine, a husky pink, up to my cheeks, watching as Rada fingers hers—hunter green—with a concerned look on her face.

"What's wrong?" I ask. "Want to trade? I don't think it's a strict rule that redheads shouldn't wear pink—"

"These aren't scarves," Rada interrupts me. "And they're not accessories. These are flags, as in *capture the flag*." She knots the green one at her belt, tugging on it to check that it's secure.

"What do you mean?" I ask as I do the same with my own scarf. "And by the way, whether you're calling it a flag or a belt, that's still an accessory."

"It's for the trial," Rada says, frowning when her flag falls away from her belt with another sharp tug. "It has to be the final part of Artemis's trial. It's why we've been working with our horses. Epona helped with its inception."

"If you have insider knowledge, you better spill," I tell her.

"If I had to guess...we're going to melee."

"Where's that?" I ask.

"Melee," Rada repeats, retying her flag to her belt. "It's not a place, it's a battle. An unorganized one. Everyone for themselves." She eyes herself in the mirror, still tightening the knot at her side. "I don't think the gods like that we formed alliances. They're pitting us against each other on purpose."

"Well, I don't want your scarf," I say. "Earth tones have never agreed with me."

"BJ," she says, spinning from the mirror, clearly exasperated as her knot fails her again. "Don't you know how serious this is? Epona has us melee in class sometimes. You have to stay within the parameters of the field. If you leave the battle, you're out. If you lose your scarf—I mean flag—you're out. I wouldn't be surprised if more than one of us is stripped of our power today. A melee is an ugly thing, and I guarantee you *will* take my flag if you get the chance."

"I do understand how serious this is," I tell her. "Has it ever occurred to you that I'm trying to cut the tension? And who the hell taught you how to tie a knot?"

I jerk her flag from her belt and retie it into a double wrap French knot. Rada stares at me then gives an experimental tug.

"Oh, that's not coming off easy, honey," I tell her. "And for your information"—I swiftly arrange my own flag into a Pan Am knot— "I won't take your flag, even if I can."

Rada looks up from her belt, confused. "BJ, that's a terrible strategy. You know that I'll take your flag if given the chance, right?"

"Yup, I do."

"And you do understand that you're not in an alliance with me?"

"No, I'm not," I say, pulling my hair up into a high ponytail. "But there are bonds that go beyond alliances. Like, for instance, we're roommates. We know if the other snores, drools all over their pillow, or farts all night after going overboard at the dining hall ice cream bar."

Rada's cheeks go red. "I'm slightly lactose intolerant, okay?"

"I know, roomie." I pat her on the back as we head out the door. "I know."

———

We meet the others at the archery field. It's been transformed into something more like a football stadium, only ten times the size. The targets are gone, and there's a fine, low hanging mist in a perfect oval surrounding the field. Beyond that, bleachers are set up. Amazons are already filing into place, taking their seats and jostling one another for a better spot.

"Melee, I knew it," Rada says under her breath.

Our horses are waiting for us in a nearby paddock and Whiskey flares his nostrils at me, rolling his eyes like he's asking me what's different about today.

"I don't know, buddy," I say, resting a hand on his flanks. Even though he hates me, there's comfort in knowing I'm not going into this alone.

I reach out to touch the fine, white wall of mist we had to pass through in order to reach our mounts. The mist reaches up to my waist, but dissipates before it touches the ground, leaving my shins and feet visible.

"It's a magical boundary," Zahara says, rubbing her horse's nose. "I wouldn't get all up in it, if I were you."

I pull my fingers back, rubbing the pads together. But nothing has stayed behind. "Seems harmless."

"Harmless enough, until you get disqualified," Sophia says, brushing past us as she leads her mount through the mist and onto the field.

"What's that mean?" I ask Rada, as I swing onto Whiskey's back.

"If you leave the field of battle, you're out," she says. "If you lose your flag—"

"You're out, yeah I get it," I say, urging Whiskey forward. We've reached the point where I only have to run my finger along the outside of his ears to encourage him into a walk, which is a relief, given the amount of horse earwax I've had to dig out from under my fingernails lately.

"Contestants," Epona's voice rings out, and the stands—now full of eager Amazons—fall silent. "If you would move to the center of the field, we will begin."

Malik, Sophia, Zahara, Trevor, Rada, Alaric, and I all move our horses to stand before her. Artemis and Devana stand on either side of Epona, holding bows and arrows. As we gather before them, they circulate among us, giving each of us a bow and a quiver of arrows.

"Are we actually supposed to shoot each other?" I ask.

"Da. Dey are round tip arrows. Dey bruise ya. Dey maybe take out eye. So, no real harm. Get five shots, left-handed strong girl," she tells me. "Maybe think about vat Devana say, ya?"

"I. Am. Right. Handed," I grumble at her.

"You are girl who misses all her shots," she says, moving on to Zahara.

Alaric seeks me out. "Use the arrows to spook the horses, or make them run a certain way. I'll try to help you as much as I can."

I nod. "I'll try not to get in your way." Argh, is that the best I can offer?

Artemis goes on to explain the melee to us. Each of us has a flag at our belts. The goal is to capture each other's flags by any means necessary. If we flee the battlefield, or pass through the magical boundary—which is now active, she informs us—we will be disqualified, our flags stripped from us and delivered to whoever happens to be nearest.

"It's last woman standing," Artemis declares. "Or man, I suppose," she adds, although I can tell by the glance she tosses to Rada that she expects her girl to win.

And, I have to admit, Rada has the advantage. She is by far

the most accomplished rider among us, easily the best shot, and she has experience in a melee.

Artemis, Epona, and Devana take their places in the stands, where Athena is already seated.

I lean into Rada. "How do we know when to start?"

She gives me a wicked grin. There's a bellowing noise, like the blowing of a horn. "Now!" she shouts, and makes a dodge for my flag.

"SHIT!" I scream, which makes Whiskey do exactly that. Luckily he also lurches forward, and Rada's fingers only skim my scarf.

"Ha!" I yell over my shoulder, but barely miss being clocked in the forehead by Sophia, who isn't going for any grace points. She takes a swing at me with her bow, and I barely glide under it as I lean backwards, my skills from the Limber Little Limbo Ladies pageant coming in handy.

It's close, though; her bowstring twangs off my chin, and her horse nips my thigh as he passes. Like a true vampire, she trained him to bite.

The Amazons are screaming in the stands, rooting on Rada, and booing me—thanks, girls—when I manage to stay on Whiskey's back. I flip them double birds and a pageant smile as I pass the bleachers, which most of them gleefully return, although a few are smiling back.

Just in front of me I spot Malik, bent low over his mount's back. He's closing in on Zahara, who is on foot now. Her horse is panicked, dancing in front of her as she tries to calm it. It's not like Zahara not to be able to control her mount, but I don't have time to figure out what's gone wrong for her. Whiskey is in an all-out gallop, and he's cutting the distance between me and Malik, who is going for the easy prey—a distracted Zahara.

My hand is inches from yanking Malik's flag—a bright yellow—from his belt when an arrow whizzes through the air, cutting past me with a high pitched zip. Malik's flag is torn away, the arrow pinning it neatly to the ground, making it easy for Rada to bend down from Manathan and yank it free, whooping up a storm—literally, thunder is breaking all around us—as she claims the first flag of the melee.

The Amazons go wild, and Malik kicks the ground in a fury, his emotions getting the better of him. He accidentally shifts into his cat form and his mount panics, veering sideways and crashing into Sophia's horse. The vampire flies over her mount's head, but is able to recover in midair, hovering for a moment before coming to the ground. But her horse is down, screaming in pain, two legs folded awkwardly, broken.

Whiskey instinctively runs away from the sound of his fellow horse's pain, taking me out of the path of danger just as Trevor swoops in behind Sophia. She's beside her horse, crying, her hands on its muzzle as she tries to give it some comfort. Without hesitation, Trevor yanks her flag—a dark fuchsia—from her belt.

What the hell? Trevor and Sophia have an alliance.

She whirls, equally shocked to find herself betrayed, but ready to fight back. Her fangs erupt and she goes for Trevor's throat, his horse putting distance between them as fast as possible.

But Sophia is a vampire—and she is pissed. She goes after him, and the crowd cheers her on, ready to see Trevor's blood, when the misty boundary forms a tentacle, and neatly slaps her out of the air.

"Disqualified," Athena bellows from the stands. "You have lost your flag and must leave the field of battle."

Spitting with rage, Sophia gets up, her dark gaze following Trevor as he takes a victory lap, waving her flag overhead as he does. Whiskey circles the perimeter and I spot Zahara, still struggling to bring her mount under control. I guide Whiskey over to her, and she instinctively whirls, hand moving to protect her flag.

"What's wrong?" I ask. "What's going on with your horse?"

"I don't know," she shouts back, raising her voice to be heard over the roar of the crowd as Alaric takes a shot at Trevor. It flies wide and into the crowd, one of the Amazons nonchalantly raising her shield to keep from being struck.

"He panicked," Zahara says. "And I can't get him to calm down."

Honestly, I can't say I blame him. Rada's letting her thunder roll, Malik turned into a lion, Sophia flashed her fangs, and one of his buddies just got downgraded from warrior horse to next week's glue.

So yeah, I'd be panicking too.

But Zahara's horse went wild before any of those things happened, and I can feel Whiskey shifting uneasily beneath me. He rears, suddenly, a frenzied whinny erupting as his hooves slash the air.

"Look out!" I scream at Zahara and she dives out of the way, barely avoiding his forelegs just as two hands erupt from the dirt beneath her feet.

"Zahara!" I yell. She turns just in time to see people emerging from the ground. If I thought the guys at the bar last night looked rough, these people are way worse. They look and smell like corpses...

Ohhhh.

Shit.

They're zombies.

As I absorb the horror of this, four more crawl out of holes around the field.

"What the Hades?" Zahara cries, dodging a zombie's grip. I grab her wrist, meaning to swing her onto Whiskey's back behind me, but she twists away, still protecting her flag with her free hand.

"I'm trying to help you!" I shout over my shoulder at her as Whiskey makes a run for it. I grab his ears and turn his head just as he's about to break through the barrier of mist. He veers to the right, and we barely avoid being disqualified.

He slides to a halt, breathing hard, and I survey the field. Zombies are loose everywhere, creating havoc. One is feasting on Sophia's downed horse while she screams and tries to break through the barrier to help it. But the magical mist won't let her through.

Zahara is still horseless, though she's now spread her wings and taken to the air. Using her arrows, Zahara attempts to shoot the zombies below. One of the zombies now sports a back prickled like a porcupine, but it's not slowing him down. I've got a bad feeling that it'll take a direct head shot to bring one of them down for good, and I know Zahara's aim isn't that great. Plus Devana only gave us five arrows. Zahara has already burned through three without doing any real damage.

She descends slightly, her brow furrowed as she takes aim —just as Trevor runs his horse directly underneath her, snagging her low-hanging flag—a dark brown—and tearing it from her belt. Her arrow goes wide and she spins out of control in mid-air, hitting the ground with a hard thump that knocks the breath out of her, one of her wings folded at an awkward angle.

"Zahara!" I yell, just as two of the zombies attack. She tries to shuffle out of the way, but blood stains the side of her mouth, her bad wing dragging behind her.

I don't hesitate. Digging my fingers into Whiskey's ears I send him into a mad gallop straight at one of the zombies, who rolls under his hooves, bones cracking. I grab Zahara's arm and swing her up onto Whiskey's back. Her arms encircle my waist, her head resting against my shoulder.

"Thank you, friend," she barely manages to say, her breath knocked out of her. I pull Whiskey to a stop at the edge of the field, handing the injured Zahara over the misty barrier to a couple of Amazons who climb out of the stands to help.

"What the hell is wrong with you?" I yell at Artemis, who —with Epona and Athena—is on her feet in the stands. "You thought it was cute to throw in zombies as an extra curveball?"

Sophia's horse gives a last, horrible scream, as if to accentuate my point.

"The zombies are not part of my trial," Artemis says loudly.

"Pull down the perimeter. We need to stop this trial!"

Athena turns to the field, raising her hands. But nothing happens. Confused, she shouts. "Someone else has control of it! The mist isn't obeying me!"

Realization rushes through me. No one is coming to help us.

None of the other contestants looks like they're fleeing. Nobody wants to lose. Stubborn entitled jerks. Well, I'm not going to let my friends become zombie bait because they're a bunch of idiots.

It's up to me to save their dumb asses.

23

———

S uddenly I notice Alaric at my side, bashing in a zombie's head. It seems like the zombie was about to take a chomp out of Whiskey's leg.

Okay, so maybe I have to get saved so I can save the others.

Rattled, I fumble with my bow and nearly drop it under Whiskey's dancing feet.

Alaric pulls Whiskey's reins to calms him.

"Brandee," he shouts at me. "Stay close. I will get you to the barrier and you'll be safe."

"Oh no," I tell him. "I'm in this until the end."

"You infuriatingly stubborn girl," he tells me. "You have no business being on a horse for a walk in the park, much less a melee packed with zombies. Leave now before you get yourself killed."

"No," I yell back. "This fool is going to help fight the zombies!" Tugging Whiskey's ear, we gallop away.

A moment later, Alaric and his horse are beside me. "Stay close, you gormless girl. And remember, we're allies."

"I got your back," I tell him.

"Yes, well, don't accidentally put an arrow into it. I haven't Rada's healing powers."

"That was an accident!" I screech at the same time that we hear a shrill scream from Trevor's horse.

A zombie is climbing up its hindquarters. Trying to shake it off, the horse dances crazily on the perimeter. Another zombie has Trevor's horse by the head, mouth gaping wide as it prepares to bite into the soft fuzz of its nose.

"No, not *my* horse, you vile brain-eating tossers!" Trevor swings his bow at them, having apparently spent all his arrows.

There must be something wrong with the front zombie because it is super slow. Even so, Trevor can't fight them both at the same time. With his focus on keeping the one zombie from eating his horse's face off, he forgets about the zombie climbing up the back of his horse. Until it's right on top of him.

"Brother! Help!" he yells, grappling with the back zombie which is now trying to take a chunk out of Trevor's face.

Alaric looks to me, as if asking permission, but before I can even say 'go', he's wheeling his horse around and I'm left in his dust.

I try to follow, but am swarmed by a zombie horde. I have to retreat while trying to watch Alaric. I spot him as he reaches Trevor. He comes charging, an arrow flying from his bow, penetrating an eye socket of the zombie Trevor is struggling with. It goes limp, sliding from the horse's back to be trampled by Alaric's mount as he pulls up next to his brother.

"Are you hurt?" Alaric asks, and from across the field I can see Trevor's crocodile smile.

"I'm fine, Ricky," he says. Then he grabs Alaric by the shoulders and pulls him off his mount. Twisting in his saddle, he tosses Alaric outside of the misty perimeter.

Alaric cries out, but it's too late. His flag—royal blue—unties itself from his waist and sails through the magical mist to tie itself around Trevor's waist.

Well, Mama always did say that family ties can easily hang you.

The zombie holding his mount's head snaps its jaw shut and looks to Trevor…as if for instruction.

"Piss off! Your job is done." He kicks out a leg and the zombie falls to the ground. "Off you go wankers, time to cause more chaos."

Trevor is in on the zombie uprising? What the—

Okay, it's not really that shocking. He is a total liar and a cheat who just stabbed his own brother in the back.

"Traitor!" Rada screams from the far side of the perimeter. She lets loose an arrow at Trevor's head.

Guess I'm not the only one who saw Trevor ordering around those zombies.

Trevor's eyes narrow as Rada's arrow narrowly misses him.

"You're next," he says, pointing to her.

Right then more zombies erupt from the earth, surrounding Rada. One grabs Madathan's tail and he goes into a wild spin. The zombie loses its grip and goes flying, but the arrow Rada was preparing for a zombie goes wide. It sails into the stands, where the Amazons are trying to get past the magical mist barrier and help us.

The barrier has been spelled to not allow anyone to enter or interfere with the trial in any way. Arrows fly from the audience members, but are incinerated to ashes as they pass through the mist. And when the girls begin to use their bodies as battering rams, flames flare up out of the mist, pushing them back.

Flames. Zombies.

I'd bet my Miss All-Midwest Gourd & Pumpkin Princess

sash that Hades is behind this. When Alaric rejected him, he must've run straight back to Trevor.

Rada shouts as Madathan is overwhelmed by more zombies, pulling him down to the ground.

Her scream is like Shauna's. The look on Rada's face is as desperate as Shauna's had been when she glanced back at me. I could see she was terrified as our eyes met for one long moment, and then Shauna was lost in a cloud of motorcycle exhaust.

I'm not letting it happen again. I'm not losing another friend.

I ran that day with Shauna. It didn't even occur to me that there was another option. But that's not me anymore. I will help Rada even if it means I don't make it out of here alive.

I'm rounding on the group of zombies surrounding Rada, when I feel a firm touch on my shoulder. I slap at it, expecting to feel cold, dead zombie fingers, but instead there's a spreading warmth, and a musical voice in my ear.

"Welcome, my daughter," the voice says. "Welcome to the sisterhood of the Amazons."

I'm infused with a sudden strength. Not the power of Zeus, which lies only in my muscles. This is different, deeper, something coming from my core and enveloping my entire body.

I also suddenly realize something else. Devana was right, damn it—I *am* left-handed. I am a left-handed Amazon beauty queen from the Midwest who is not putting up with any more bullshit.

I transfer the bow to my right hand and let three arrows fly in quick succession, all of them hitting their mark. Zombies fall away from Rada as she stands on Madathan's corpse, desperately beating them away. I see the surprise in her face as the tip of an arrow comes jutting through one's nose. Her gaze travels past the zombie and up to me.

Rada's eyes widen, and then, amazingly, she laughs.

As I gallop towards her, Rada lifts her arms, ready for me to pull her up. She swings behind me onto Whiskey's back and we spin together, both bows raised as we turn to face Trevor.

He bears down on us, his eyes are alight with a manic glee. It's a much scarier look for him that his usual charming rogue act.

"Asshole," I say.

"Shit stain," Rada counters as we focus on our target.

"Buttweasel."

Rada snorts. Then her voice dips low and I know a good one is coming.

"Target practice."

We let loose, my arrow tearing his flag—blood red—from his waist, and Rada's taking his left ear off neatly. He falls from his horse, face as red as his flag, blood streaming from the side of his head as I swoop to gather my prize—his flag.

"You bitch!" he screams at me, running for Whiskey in a mad dash, as if he'll attack my horse if that's what it takes to get to me.

At that moment, Athena and Artemis manage to pull the barrier down, although it takes most of their combined magical strength. Their arms fall limply to their sides as Amazons swarm the field, dispatching zombies. Lilliana and another girl intercept Trevor, pinning him to the ground.

"I didn't cheat!" he shouts. "I did nothing against the rules!"

Lilliana pulls a blade from her belt, holding it to his neck with a smile that could get her first place in a toothpaste contest. "You have been knocked out of the contest, little fae. What happens now is between us."

Despite Trevor's absolute dickishness I don't want to see

him gutted on the field. "Let's see what Athena says," I yell down to her.

She looks up at me and to my surprise, gives me a nod of agreement.

I pull Whiskey to a halt in the center of the ring as the last of the zombies fall under the wrath of the Amazons. As I dismount, Rada slides off his back as well, landing in a low crouch at my feet.

"Mother Hippolyta has touched you here today," she says solemnly as she tears the flag from her side. "You are a true sister warrior, Brandee Jean Mason. You saved my life even though we were combatants." Her voice catches a little. "I cede my place in this contest to you."

All around us, the Amazons have come to a halt. The crowd splits, allowing Athena, Artemis, Epona, and Devana to pass through.

"This trial—this entire contest—has been tampered with," Athena says, throwing a dark glance to where Trevor lay, still pinned to the ground. "I cannot in good conscience guarantee that any further trials will be performed with honesty and good sportsmanship. I vote that we declare this melee the final contest, and the winner—Brandee Jean Mason—as the rightful inheritor of Zeus's position as head of the gods."

"No! Absolutely not!" Sophia shouts. "That whole trial was a shit show and it's a fluke that BJ won."

"It was no fluke," Rada steps up. "She was blessed by Hippolyta. She is now a true Amazon."

There's a gasp from the crowd of Amazon warriors, then amazingly, they cheer. For me.

I give them my best pageant humble wave.

"I'm in favor of crowning Brandee Jean Mason," says Artemis.

"This isn't fair," Malik says. Alaric remains silent, and his face is blank so it's impossible to guess what he thinks of all this.

Zahara stands beside Rada, wincing from her damaged wing. "I support Brandee Jean as well."

"You have got to be joking," Sophia yells. "You want to give this piece of white trash the power of a god?"

"There are worse contenders," Zahara says, looking from Sophia to Trevor, and back again.

I feel like I'm taking part in Little Miss Practical Joke again. That was a one-off pageant where someone thought it would be cute to tell the losers they won, and then scream, "April Fools!"

"I support Brandee Jean," adds Epona.

"Myself as vell," agrees Devana, giving me a glance. "Although she vould make gud magician's assistant girl. Zip. Zip."

I thought they all hated me. I was the underdog. The white trash wonder. The faux queen with the plastic pageant crown.

"Do I have the blessing of my fellow gods?" Athena asks, raising her voice to the sky.

Around us arrows fall to the ground, most of them blue with a few red marking the bunch. But the blue heavily outweigh the red. I can guess by the look on Sophia's face that it must mean the gods have voted in my favor.

"Brandee Jean Mason, Amazon sister. It means that you are going to be leader of the gods," Rada says.

"And Miss All-Wisconsin Cheese Wheel winner," I remind her. "And don't you forget it. That one came with a lifetime supply of cheese, so it's gonna be pretty hard for this gig to measure up."

24

There are so many people who want to attend my crowning that the ceremony has to be held on the same field where we just had the melee. It seems like maybe not the greatest place, vibes wise, but I don't want to act like a total prima donna and have them think the whole new Zeus thing is already going to my head.

It's almost disturbing how quickly the ground has been smoothed. The hoofbeats and holes where the zombies dug their way out of the underworld have been filled in. Like it never happened. Although none of the contestants were bitten, there was still a price to pay.

Rada is doing a good job of hiding her pain, but Madathan meant a lot to her. I even feel a tug on my heart for Sophia, who might have lasted longer during the melee if she hadn't tried to comfort her dying mount.

The stage has been moved to the middle of the field with a sea of Amazons and gods in the audience. I'm wearing a shimmering deep purple ball gown. I'd originally opted for black, in honor of the dead horses—and the death of Trevor's dignity—but Rada insisted I wear purple.

"The color of royalty," she said.

Now, Rada, Sophia, Zahara, Malik, Alaric, and Trevor are arranged on the opposite side of the stage, waiting to have their powers stripped and transferred to me. Lilliana and another Amazon stand by Trevor's side, ready to grab him if he tries to bolt. Edie waits by the chair for me to be seated and gain my powers. Catching my eye, she gives me a goofy thumbs up.

For now I'm the only one in the middle of the stage with Athena. I try not to stare too hard at what's in her hands; a delicately crafted golden crown perched on a pillow.

It is, without a doubt, the most beautiful thing I've ever seen.

I hope I'm worthy of it. No, I will prove I'm worthy of it.

Finally, everyone is settled and the ceremony begins.

Athena opens by settling down the crowd, giving a quick recap of the trials, and denouncing Trevor's machinations during the melee, his alliance with Hades, and his general bad sportsmanship throughout the contest.

The Amazons boo him, and some even send arrows toward the stage—too close for comfort, but not hitting him. I wonder if he'll make it off this island alive once the ceremony is over.

Cocky to the end, he smiles and waves, treating each arrow like a compliment.

I notice that while all the other contestants have their mentors beside them, Stranger sits in the audience, his eyes glued to Zahara.

When she's done recounting the trials, Athena turns to me and nods solemnly.

"Brandee Jean Mason, you are worthy of Zeus's powers," she tells me. "You are worthy to be Queen of the gods."

I press my lips together to keep myself from blurting out, "Are you sure?" Saying such a thing would ruin the moment, and probably make Athena rethink putting that crown on my head. And, oh man, I really want to wear that crown.

Staying silent, I tilt my head slightly and she places the crown upon my head. I almost forget that there's no sash or flowers—that's standard, even at the most third-rate contests. You'd think Demeter would have put together some roses, at least. But the crown is perfect and feels as light as air on my head. So I make do, not cradling flowers, but instead waving gracefully as I make my way over to the chair.

Edie gives me a proud mama smile. "I knew you could do it," she tells me.

I sit and cross my ankles like a proper lady and wait for the powers, hoping no one can tell how nervous I am.

Rada—not just my roommate, but truly my friend—is first. She requested to give her powers to me first, like it's an honor. She also dressed for the occasion in an emerald green cocktail dress. Her skin looks glorious, her freckles echoing her vibrant personality.

But there's no smile on her face. Instead, she looks...terrified.

Behind her, Sora follows.

Wait! Sora?? But he's dead!

He died in the maze and his body...oh, shit.

His body disappeared.

Sora has one hand on the back of Rada's neck, her skin already bruising from the pressure. Confusion spreads through the crowd as he guides Rada to the middle of the stage, then forces her to her knees.

"Edie?" I ask, my voice a hoarse whisper. "What's going on?"

Her hand is on my shoulder, her palm damp and wet. "I don't know."

On the other side of the stage, behind the rest of the contestants, I see Athena. She's arguing with someone. The other contestants stare at Rada and Sora when I glance toward them. But Alaric meets my eyes. And he mouths one word. Run.

I stand, ready to do exactly that. But I'm not running away. I'm headed straight for Rada and Sora. I don't know what's going on, but Rada is clearly horrified. If my friend is scared, I'm going to her side—not the other direction.

But I'm not fast enough. Sora pulls out a blade, and slides it across Rada's throat.

A spray of blood arcs across the stage and I slip in it, going down on my hands and knees.

"Rada!" I scream, reaching for her, my palms slick with her blood. A foot lands on my back, pinning me in place. I glance back to see a grinning Hades.

"Next Zeus?" He wags a finger at me. "I don't think so, little girl."

I struggle, but can't get a grip on the slick floor. Desperately, I look around for help. But a fresh wave of zombies has overtaken the stage. My fellow contestants and their mentors have been backed into a corner trying to fight them off.

Overhead, a dragon swoops down, incinerating zombies to ashes. My heart lifts as I recognize Edie. But even in her airborne flamethrower mode, she barely makes a dent in the zombie army. One group turns to smoke, and immediately another and another and another is on its heels.

Apparently the zombies at the melee were just the warm-up. This right here is the real thing.

But at least with Hades on my back, the zombies are keeping away from me.

Digging my fingers into the ground, I drag myself forward, one inch closer to Rada. Close enough to see her eyelids flutter as she tries to heal herself. I watch the wound begin to close, slower than it should. Skin desperately trying to knit together as blood gushes down her beautiful dress and on to the stage.

"Come on, Rada," I say, stretching a hand toward her. "You can do it."

Sora stabs her again, this time in the belly.

I scream, a mixture of fury and despair, while Rada can only softly moan.

Her power struggles to keep up with the wounds, distributing itself as both wounds glow in an attempt to self-heal. But not quickly enough.

Kneeling beside her, Sora widens the wound in her belly, then forces his hand inside of her.

Rada tries to scream, but all that comes is a bubble of bright red froth from the slit in her neck. A bright light appears in her midsection and Sora clamps his fist around it, maneuvering it up and out of her.

"No," I cry, still trying to claw my way forward, even as Hades's foot presses deeper into my back.

He can't do this! Sora doesn't have the ability to take Rada's power! It takes multiple gods to perform the transfer ceremony.

And yet somehow, he is. Sora's arms are shaking but he's managing. He pulls the light from Rada's body, and slips it down his own throat.

Rada falls to the stage when he lets go of her, limp as a rag doll.

The pressure on my back is suddenly gone. I surge forward, half leaping, half crawling until I'm at Rada's side. She gurgles, blood in her mouth as well as gushing from her throat. She reaches up, touches my face, mouths the word sister.

The light goes out of her eyes.

I look up to find Sora towering over me. Hades flanking him.

"Glad you could join us, brother. Things are not the same without you. The gods have greatly missed the company of Zeus. Well, some of us have, anyway."

"Zeus?!" Alaric shouts. He's fighting to get to me, but Trevor is holding him back, a slimy smile on his face. Gods, previously part of the transfer ceremony, have Lilliana and her Amazon sister restrained rendering the girls powerless.

I look up, cradling Rada's dead body. Edie is at my side, her warm hands on my shoulders.

The king of the gods looks down at me through Sora's eyes. A rumble of thunder booms across the stage.

"That's right, kids," Zeus says. "It seems that the news of my death was greatly exaggerated." He looks directly at Edie. "You can't get rid of me quite so easily. I'm here to take back my powers."

Reaching down, he grabs Rada's body, tearing it away from me. Then he flings her over his shoulder, as if she were garbage.

"One down," he says. "Who's next?"

THE END

———

Continue the series with the next book **Battle & Brawl, Mythverse Book 5**!

Want to know about all the latest releases? Sign up for our Newsletter at MarleyLynn.com! When you sign up you'll receive **FREE SHORT STORIES**—all set in the Mythverse!

ALSO BY THE AUTHORS

See the Mythverse through different eyes with the beginning of a whole new series…

GRAVE NEW WORLD: Down & Dirty Supernatural Cleaning Services Book 1

Sometimes you have to play dirty.

I'm Paige Harper and I clean up supernatural messes. But my personal life is something I can't seem to straighten out.

I accidentally married a fae, and even though we've been divorced for years, Jax still manages to land me in hot water. Like, putting my house on the table at a high stakes poker game type of hot.

Now, he's been arrested for murder and the cops want to pin a series of vampire killings on him. I don't know if he did it or not. But I do know he needs to be at that poker game or else my house is gone.

In order to get Jax out, I turn to Nico, a one-eyed werewolf private detective, for help. Nico is a handsome, dangerous, ladies man and I have no intention of falling prey to his charms.

Although, that's easier said than done as the two of us begin crawling through the dirty underbelly of the supernatural world…

It's a good thing I brought my broom.

Grave New World is the first book in an all new paranormal mystery series filled with laughs and romance!

BATTLE & BRAWL SNEAK PEEK

The king of the gods looks down at me through Sora's eyes. A rumble of thunder booms across the stage.

"That's right, kids," Zeus says. "It seems that the news of my death was greatly exaggerated." He looks directly at Edie. "You can't get rid of me quite so easily. I'm here to take back my powers."

Reaching down, he grabs Rada's body, tearing it away from me. Then he hefts her over his shoulder, as if she were garbage.

"One down," he says. "Who's next?"

I stand, shakily, drenched in the blood of my friend. "I won the competition," I say. "I am a Queen, and you are in serious trouble."

I look to Athena to back me up. This is her school. And Rada was her student. An Amazon. Instead she's watching with an expression that can only be described as calculating, while a god with winged ankles—Hermes—whispers urgently in her ear.

No help there, I guess. Great. Having a goddess on your

side is always a positive... especially when you're facing down a god.

This is probably the point where I should quickly backpedal. Tell him I love how he's wearing Sora's face—though maybe a little blush and bronzer could help with the zombie pallor. But I can't play nice when Rada's blood is on my hands.

Instead I simply push my shoulders back, lift my chin, and repeat again, "I am the Amazon Queen."

He scoffs, such an ugly look on such a beautiful face. "Do you think that crown makes you a Queen? You are nothing. You are dirt beneath my feet. You have nothing. I am again alive, and I demand my powers back. Give me that crown now," Zeus orders in the sort of tone that silently adds, *or else I will kill you.*

Seeing as how he just killed my BRF (best roommate forever) by reaching into her midsection and tearing her nearly in two, I don't doubt his follow-through.

Zombie Sora is a real asshole.

Which is sad, because the real living Sora seemed like a pretty good guy. At least from what I could tell before he died.

I didn't know him long. He arrived here at Amazon Academy around the same time as me and eight other teenagers. We'd all been recruited to compete against each other in a series of weird tasks devised by the Greek gods. Last man—or woman, we were evenly matched —standing would become the new Zeus.

They needed a new Zeus because the old one was dead. And apparently the moment he kicked it, the whole world started crumbling to pieces. Literally. Massive earthquakes will do that. Everyone panicked and society melted away faster than the butter carving of my face Mama paid for one year at the Wisconsin State Fair. That was a damn shame, because the sculptor really captured the twinkle in my eye. And doing that with dairy products couldn't have been easy.

'Course the end of civilization was a damn shame too, although the end of the pageant circuit might have been the first thing on my mind, since that's how Mama and I made our bread and butter. Like, literally. They gave us what was left of that sculpture and we plopped it in the freezer. Ate off that thing for like three months.

So, a contest to get things back on track with a new Zeus seemed like a good idea, especially if I had a shot at being the winner. Too bad Mama didn't hang around long enough to see it pan out…she had taken one look at the Dollar Store being looted and said, "Brandee Jean, when people are fighting over Slim Jims, it's time to call it a day."

And she did, although she waited for it to be night, at least. Maybe she thought it'd be easier for me if I found her in dim lighting. Or maybe she just knew that, at her age, she looked best in the rose gold of sunset. She was positioned so that her good side was showing when I found her, so I do think some thought went into it. I popped her into the freezer next to what was left of my butter face and decided to worry about burial at a later date.

That later date hasn't come yet; competing to become the next leader of the gods has had all my attention, right up until two seconds ago when one of the supposedly dead contestants came onto the stage during my crowning and murdered my roommate - which definitely goes against his character. It does, however fit right quin with what I know of Zeus. The god that's supposed to be dead, but apparently— with the assist from his brother Hades—plopped himself into Sora's body.

Which, let's be honest—good call. Sora's body was way too nice to let go to waste. Too bad the personality inside could use an attitude adjustment in the form of a sledgehammer to the head.

"Don't make me repeat myself," Zeus says. "Give me that crown, or more will die." He tosses Rada's body onto the stage floor, apparently done using it as a prop in his strutting parade.

"I heard you," I say, my hands reaching up to the crown. My fingers close around the delicate gold filigree, my thumb rubbing against the huge ruby the size of my fist. A weird rush fills me.

This is straight up old-fashioned Midwestern beauty queen anger kicking in.

Instead of removing the crown, I push it further down. Giving up a crown is just not something I can do. I won this, fair and square.

"You know, this was sized for me and it would get all bent out of shape if you tried to put it on your head. You'd look like the god of the scratch and dent sale, know what I mean?"

Zeus leans toward me and exhales angrily. His breath is so stank my eyes water. Poor Sora. He had such good hygiene. "That ruby on the crown came from the sword used to kill me. It contains my own blood. Ichor."

"Yeah, that is icky," I agree.

"Ichor!" He repeats, angrily, stomping one of Sora's feet. His big toenail splits down the center, and a maggot crawls out. Then his toe immediately heals itself. Anger fills me at the power—and the life—he took from Rada. "It's my blood! And it will never be used against me again!"

With that he grabs the crown, happy to tear my scalp right off along with it, if I don't do as he asks. Before I can even say, "Don't mess up my hair!" he flies backwards, landing on his ass.

I look behind me, wondering who came to my aid. But everyone on the stage is restrained. All the remaining contestants, my mentor, Edie, Alaric (my kind-of-guy-I-might-kiss-again-sometime-maybe and fellow contestant), as well as Lilliana—an Amazon sister and no bull-shitter who is fighting against the zombie who holds her. His forearm is shredded to the bone and he hasn't even blinked, but she's still digging away at him with her nails.

Trevor—a contestant, and Alaric's half brother—is holding Alaric back from helping me. He was part of this whole mess, helping Zeus and Hades to recover the crown.

Artemis and Athena are oddly still, along with all the other gods there to perform the ceremony. Hermes still stands beside Athena, a hand on her arm now. None of them are interfering, only watching intently as the drama plays out onstage. Why aren't they helping? The audience, comprised mostly of Amazons—and all of them armed to the teeth— have been efficiently flanked by an army of the undead streaming down the aisles.

We're pretty evenly matched, number-wise. But if this goes wrong—and it's looking like it will—Amazon blades don't stand a chance against bodies that don't die. I've got to walk this back, and fast.

"What the Hades?" Zeus sits up, clearly rattled by the blow that someone dealt him when he tried to take my crown. "Who hit me?"

Suddenly, I feel it. Mother Hippolyta. The spirit of the Amazons. She entered me during the final contest, like a sort of blessing. She recognized me as a true Amazon, which means I've got to protect my sisters-in-arms.

Or fight and die with them.

And, let's be honest, by the look of the zombies around here, I'm not in a big hurry to rot and die. Especially if that means Hades gets to tell my dead body what to do. I mean...ew.

"Stop!" I cry out, just as Zeus is coming back to his feet.

Hippolyta's strength rolls through my voice, and he obeys as if he were a dog. It only lasts a second, but it's enough. Athena's head snaps in my direction, the voice of Hippolyta spurring her to action. She stomps down on one of Hermes' ankle wings, and it breaks like a baby bird hitting an eighteen-wheeler at sixty-five miles an hour. The god howls in pain as Athena easily sidesteps around him.

"The contest has finished, Father." Athena declares. "We have a new Queen."

Artemis steps beside her. "You cannot come here, kill our Amazons." Her voice actually catches when she looks at Rada. "You died."

"You should have stayed dead!" I add, but no one looks at me.

"My brother, Zeus, stands here before us. Alive. Athena, you called him Father, so clearly you recognize him despite the change in form!" Hades exclaims, his voice bellowing throughout the amphitheater. "It's a dangerous precedent, giving away a god's powers. If Athena lets this mortal girl from Milktown, USA have Zeus' powers, whose powers will she strip next?" Hades addresses this to the gathered gods. A low murmur sweeps through them and a few heads even nod in agreement.

"Absurd," Athena says, but even she doesn't sound as certain.

"I declare this entire contest moot!" Hades says, taking charge. "All in agreement, say aye."

Chapter 1

Cleaning up after a vampire rave sucks.

Pun intended.

My first one, I came armed with a whole truckload of hydrogen peroxide, expecting blood stains everywhere. In my mind, they covered the walls and floors and ceilings. I expected something like what a plasma donation center would look like if it was run by someone hopped up on way too much Mountain Dew.

It turns out, though, that vampires are not messy eaters. You might even say they don't like to waste a single drop of their meal. It's sacred to them the way Ho-Ho's were to my seventh-grade math teacher.

So yeah, it's not the prospect of scrubbing away blood stains that's getting me down as I drive through the warehouse district searching each building for the 6669 the vamps paint on the wall of their chosen party spot. The number's some sort of vampire humor, I think. Or maybe not. They're hard to read and I'm not interested in getting close enough to find out anything about them beyond that they pay in cash.

"Where is this stupid place?" I ask aloud, even though there's no one else in the van with me. Although...my van is kind of sentient. Like a cross between Christine and Herbie, it's both terrifying and adorable.

Vanna was stolen ages ago. Back when she...er, *it*, was just a normal Grand Caravan with stained seats and a dented back fender from some tailgating asshole. I figured that was the last I'd see of it, but a few months back I opened my door and there was Vanna (yes, I named her and yes I hate myself for it). The same...but also totally different.

I would've sent her straight back to the impound lot where she was found if it wasn't for the fact that I was desperate for transportation. The transmission had just died on my previous van and without wheels I had no job. So I used Vanna, figuring I could just pretend she was normal. Just another vehicle.

That didn't last long.

In response to my question, Vanna takes over steering, which is always annoying. But I forgive her as she parks us in front of a building, the 6669 on the wall straight ahead.

From the outside the warehouse looks totally unremarkable. Just another big boxy building. I can't hold back a big sigh as I grasp the handles on the giant sliding door. Putting all my weight into it, I pull the door hard. With a groan it gives way, gliding open and allowing a bright shaft of sunlight to cut through the dark interior.

"Aw fuck," I say as a giant water tank fills my vision. I'm not talking about some little pet store thing; this is Sea World size. I have no idea how I'm gonna drain this thing and scrub it spotless. That's the job, though. I'm supposed to leave only the dust motes and a sparkling clean tank behind when I'm done.

This alone would be a monumental task, but as I walk into the warehouse and closer to the tank and the moving shadows within, I know it's gonna get worse.

And it does.

Sharks. Big ones, too. They glide through the water with silent menace.

Those asshole vamps decided to have an underwater rave and feed on fucking sharks.

I thought the lions were the worst. Before that, I thought the pigs were the worst.

Clearly, I was wrong all those times. Because really, vampires are the worst. Always and forever—they are The. Worst.

I take a minute to swear viciously and creatively, cursing not just vampires but all the paranormal creatures that decided to come out of hiding a decade ago and totally screw up everything. Sometimes I hear people say that it's better to know than to live in ignorance. I disagree. The time when I believed that werewolves, harpies, and faeries were all just stories was a great time. An easier, simpler one too.

I was only in my early twenties when everything changed. My dad's cleaning business was struggling and I'd just graduated with a degree in English that I was quickly realizing was pretty much useless in the real world. Then we had a little apocalypse. Cities disappeared beneath the sea. Crops failed. And all the supes came out to play. Suddenly college degrees didn't mean much. Survival was our entire focus.

I got married to my boyfriend, 'cause it felt like we might all die and I guess I wanted to wear a white dress first? I don't know. It wasn't the greatest decision. I also went into business with Dad. But we revamped it. Pun intended.

Harper Cleaning became Down & Dirty: Supernatural Cleaning Services. Dad said we were kinda like the clean-up crew for the Ghostbusters. "Think about it," he'd say. "Someone had to mop up that marshmallow mess, and I bet they got paid good money. Hazard pay, right?"

He was right. The business thrived. My marriage failed. But overall, life was good.

Until my parents disappeared along with a few hundred thousand other folks.

But that's another story.

Right now, I gotta figure out how to get these sharks outta this tank.

Luckily, we're in the Newark Port district. I understand now why they chose this location. But still, the Bay is a good ten minutes away. Can a shark survive that long out of water?

Pulling out my phone, I start to Google.

Some people might think I'm just a cleaning lady, but in truth, this job requires way more than just a mop and broom.

Yesterday I was choking on feathers cleaning out a frat house that had been full of chicken shifter strippers. Today I'm wrestling sharks. Tomorrow I might be scrubbing harpy droppings off some vocal Humans First protester's roof and lawn.

Down & Dirty is more than just a job. It's a lifestyle.

R ead the whole 7 book series today!

ABOUT THE AUTHORS

DEMITRIA LUNETTA is the author of the YA books THE FADE, BAD BLOOD, and the sci-fi duology, IN THE AFTER and IN THE END. She is also an editor and contributing author for the YA anthology, AMONG THE SHADOWS: 13 STORIES OF DARKNESS & LIGHT. Find her at www.demitrialunetta.com for news on upcoming projects and releases. Or join the newsletter list for DEMITRIA LUNETTA

KATE KARYUS QUINN is an avid reader and menthol chapstick addict with a BFA in theater and an MFA in film and television production. She lives in Buffalo, New York with her husband, three children, and one enormous dog. She has three young adult novels published with HarperTeen: ANOTHER LITTLE PIECE, (DON'T YOU) FORGET ABOUT ME, AND DOWN WITH THE SHINE. She also recently released her first adult novel, THE SHOW MUST GO ON, a romantic comedy. Find out more at www.katekaryusquinn.com and make sure you're receiving newsletters from KATE KARYUS QUINN

MARLEY LYNN is a lost child of the gods, who waits on the shores of Lake Erie for her parents to bring her home. In the meantime, she contents herself with reading, writing, and gardening. Find out more at www.MarleyLynn.com or sign up for MARLEY LYNN'S newsletter.

ACKNOWLEDGMENTS

Thank you to Marin McGinnis for taking care of our copy edits!

And, of course, a big thank you to our families for putting up with us crazy writers.